Anne Giardini is a lawyer, a writer and a mother of three school-age children. She has written numerous articles, stories and essays on wide-ranging topics, and is particularly interested in 'the vexing subjects of family, love, work, and the ingredients of happiness and sorrow'. She was a columnist for the *National Post* for three years. She lives in Vancouver.

D0256026

ANNE GIARDINI

The Sad Truth About Happiness

A Novel

HARPER PERENNIAL

London, New York, Toronto and Sydney

For my mother and father

Harper Perennial
An imprint of HarperCollins*Publishers*
77–85 Fulham Palace Road
Hammersmith
London W6 8JB

www.harperperennial.co.uk

This edition published by Harper Perennial 2006
I

First published in Great Britain by Fourth Estate 2005

ISBN-13 978-0-00-719670-8
ISBN-10 0-00-719670-9

Set in Centaur

Printed and bound in Great Britain by Clays Ltd, St Ives plc

Home is the normal—whatever place you happen to start

from, and can return to without having to answer questions.

It's a metaphor that may seem to fit reduced expectations.

We no longer seek towers that would reach to the heavens;

we've abandoned attempts to prove that we live in a chain of

being whose every link bears witness to the glory of God.

We merely seek assurance that we find ourselves

in a place where we know our way about.

SUSAN NEIMAN,
EVIL IN MODERN THOUGHT

Eaves

In my family, which is middle-class, white, loving, and mildly claustrophobic, I was the child known for contentedness. A perfect middle child, as my mother often referred to me, a buffer between Janet, who is two years older than I and who tortured us all with her sulks and moods and whims and silences, and stormy Lucy, two years my junior. Unlike Janet or Lucy, I could be counted on to share, to give way, to make room, to forgive, to take the broader, longer-term, higher-level view. My parents, both of them also as it happens middle children, had the same equanimous traits, so Janet and Lucy were a daily reminder to them that one does not always get the children one deserves. I have heard them describing having children as a lottery, a game of chance. They do not approve in any way of gambling.

As a very small child, my sister Janet, the oldest of us three girls, refused to eat anything other than dry cereal, cold whole milk (but not on dry cereal), finely chopped tuna, tinned applesauce, and mangos cut in half and sliced crosswise in their skins into the shape of diamonds, with the skins then turned concave, so the smooth fruit took on the appearance of an orange hedgehog. Her excessive fastidiousness with food continues to this day. She has, she sometimes pridefully reminds us, a highly sensitive gag reflex. A fleck of color in the yolk of a boiled egg makes her shudder. Anything left sitting out uncovered for longer than a minute gives her a horror of contagion. Her teeth are set on edge by even the smallest lumps left in cream soups or mashed potatoes or porridge. She turns pale when faced with food that has parsley on, in, near, or under it. Carrots must be cooked to just a precise point of resistant, tender firmness. If they are cooked past this point they feel, to Janet's sensitive tongue, she says, as though they have been lightly coated in a particularly revolting organic slime.

As the youngest daughter, Lucy's parlor trick was to refuse to sleep. Her bedtime tantrums were remarked on by our neighbors, against whose walls and ears her cries of outrage reverberated. She taught herself to read when she was four—both of my sisters are very quick and clever—by leaning over my shoulder, demanding that I speak each word aloud as I deciphered it. Within a few weeks, she no longer had any need of me; she had discovered how to decode the marvelous marks on the pages on her own. From then on my mother left Lucy's bedside light switched on after tucking her in at night. Lucy would read a book—she usually helped herself to whatever I happened to be reading at the time—until midnight, and then switch off her light herself. To all of our amazement, she would be up ready to fight her way through another day by seven the next morning. It was impossible to sort out after that whether her relentless ill temper was due to sleep deprivation or was simply her natural character, since there was never a well-rested Lucy against which to compare our daily, combative version.

I was sometimes allowed to overhear my parents' baffled speculations about the source of the bad dispositions of two of their three children. My parents had provided the same environment for all three of us, the same, unstinting measures of constant love, guidance that was gentle and founded on principles of fairness and reason, wholesome food, sturdy clothing, bright, educational toys, weekly trips to the library, liberal schools, excursions, diversions, and medicines when needed. But still I was rational and levelheaded, and Lucy and Janet were querulous, quarrelsome, and discontented.

Ancestors were hauled out of the attic for scrutiny, their histories examined closely for signs of inheritable ill temper, egotism, or willfulness. My father's grandfather, Hiram O'Sullivan, had been a Book of Revelations-obsessed hellfire-and-brimstone preacher from a particularly acid-soiled, rock-infested, bog-damp patch of Ireland. Hiram moved to Aurora, Ontario, in 1881 to take charge of the white clapboard Church of the Rose of Sharon. But his admonishing sermons, two and three hours long, taxed the patience of the practical farmers of his new community. They had nearer goals than the heavenly gates—another quarter-acre, a new plow, a two-storey brick house—and little time in any case to stray from the straight path. Or it might have been that their enchantment with the larger, better, and new made them resistant to the sulfurous anxieties with which old Hiram sought to bind them to his thrall and that his crabbed ministry was predestined to wither under the boundless skies of the hopeful new world. Ousted by a civil but resolute committee, Hiram returned home to Ireland to await the Day of Judgment—surely imminent!—only to find that the flock that he had abandoned there had irretrievably (and no doubt gladly) scattered to more genial churches. His comely wife (several photographs of her survive as evidence: she had thick fair hair piled soft and deep, wide dark eyes, a conscienceless brow, and a smooth chin that was round and downy and cleft as a peach) proved unexpectedly willful. Amelia refused to return with her dour husband to his stony land. Instead she moved their four children, the oldest nine and the youngest (a girl, Charlotte, who would grow up to become my grandmother) only a year or so old, to a house in the High Park area of Toronto, neatly solving the growing problem of how to pay the rent by putting it about that her husband had been sadly drowned on the way back to Ireland, declaring herself to be a widow, and marrying the elderly landlord in a brief civil ceremony at the old city hall.

It was a match that lasted seventeen years, no doubt longer by a dozen years than Amelia had predicted. But she stuck to her side of the bargain until finally with her own death at fifty-nine did them part. Her putative second husband lived on for another fifteen years, to age one hundred and four, irritatingly attributing his long life not to happiness but to clean living. He had, he told a reporter from the *Toronto Star* on his hundredth birthday—my parents have the yellowed clipping preserved in a photo album—never smoked or touched alcohol, he read the sterner passages of the Bible out loud every night, and every Sunday he took himself to church (then staid Queen Street Presbyterian, now a United Church that offers weekly services for gay and lesbian members). He died friendless, deaf, and blind in a house infested with mice, bats, squirrels, and raccoons, forsaken by his stepchildren and unloved by his step-grandchildren. He was not noticed missing for two months when he was found in the basement on a cold morning in January by the boy who delivered the coal, who noticed that none had been used up since the load before. There is a second clipping, much shorter, with no photo, describing how the old man had one hand clutched round a small lump of coal that he appeared to have stooped to retrieve from under the hod.

People are said to have remarked on the fact that he was as much a father to those four children as if they had been his own, by which they meant that he was as hard on them.

At about the same time that Amelia was marrying her peevish landlord without benefit of divorce from her jeremiacal husband, my mother's grandmother, Begthora, was taking to her narrow plank bed on the family farm in Iceland. She had not yet risen from having given birth to her fifth child and only son, Thorvaldar, when he coughed three times, turned yellow, and died. He was five days old. Begthora took a fever, weakened, then languished on her comfortless bed for nineteen years until she achieved what may have been her goal all along—to join her son wherever it was that he had gone. Begthora became addicted during that time to a blood restorative provided by a local doctor in whom her pale languor must, it has occurred to me, have inspired a sexual charge or disturbance. When the old stone house was torn down in the 1940s and replaced with one of yellow bricks, hundreds of thick glass bottles were discovered in the root cellar, most of them still unshattered, the exact size and shape of rum flasks, and of the same opaque green colour, but with the peeling yellowed labels of the patent medicine. There are no photographs of her. Her husband, a fisherman, sought more active company in a nearby village where a second, half-acknowledged family of four girls was hatched and raised in happiness by their mother. So there was a happy set of girls, and an unhappy set. All four of the unhappy ones made their way to Canada to settle in the snowy fields of Manitoba, near the town the Icelanders named Gimli, which means paradise in Icelandic, and, over time, became less unhappy. The happy girls remained behind.

Despite their forebears, all of my four grandparents were steady and reliable, exemplars of the kind of peaceful, orderly, prudent, self-ruling, tax-paying citizenry simultaneously prized and taken utterly for granted by successive Canadian governments, and my parents were, as I have indicated, models of their kind, so there was nothing to explain my changeable sisters. Lucy and Janet remain, while cherished, an unsolved puzzle to my mild, well-intentioned parents. My disposition, however, has always been satisfactory, seldom commented on, never questioned. I am clearly my parents' child, although of their three children I look least like either of them. Both Janet and Lucy have our father's height and thick, dark, straight hair and my mother's narrow waist and hips. I have my Icelandic ancestors' high brow, light hair that I have always worn long and usually loose, although I tie it back when I am at work, and fair skin covered faintly in freckles that I have always believed make me appear much less serious than I consider myself to be. My shape makes me feel a close kinship to the curves and cambered balance of egg timers, since I have broad hips, and my breasts are a size or two too large. When I stand still, I often rest my hands on my hips, thumbs behind, spread fingers forward. My body is a comfortable one; I inhabit it with the same ease with which I lived under the broad, sheltering eaves of my childhood house.

My parents are both librarians edging these days toward retirement. They met at university in Waterloo, Ontario, in 1964, when they were fellow members of the Young Socialists League, and they are socialists still, although of the most benign sort. Since neither of them has the sort of temperament it takes to change the world, or even to ask it to change, however diffidently, they have compromised by undertaking to at least do no harm. They have been vegetarians for many years. My mother decided one day when I was about twelve that she would no longer allow anything to be cooked or consumed in the house "if it once had a face." Any meat we girls ate after that we bought and barbecued for ourselves on a blackened, stubby-legged charcoal hibachi that my parents kept tucked out of sight in a shed behind the house. We were at our most complicit then, turning the chunks of flesh over the gleaming coals with kitchen forks and consuming them with our fingers in gulps, hunched like Neanderthals on the back steps. The greasy streaks of animal fat made their way onto our clothes when we wiped our hands on our jeans, and into our hair—oily evidence, we thought, of our increasing independence. We would make different choices from those our parents made, and have lives different from theirs in ways we were certain of but could not predict.

My parents' Vancouver house, the one I grew up in and where they still live, was built in 1914 from a kit sold by Eaton's. The advertisement has been preserved, along with the original plans, in a cupboard built high into one wall of the upstairs office. The entire kit cost $4,500, including the lumber, shingles, and nails, even the sink and tiles in the bathroom, all but the wallpaper, paint, and furnishings—although Eaton's sold these too. The original owners left the house to their son, who lived in it single and strange, until he sold it to my parents, who were drawn to its simple, straight lines and open spaces. It has absorbed our natures and lives, and I have sometimes felt that it knows us better, and with more kindness, than we know or think of ourselves.

My mother goes to yoga twice a week, not power yoga, but the traditional kind. She has a certificate in healing touch, and is neither skeptical about nor a believer in its powers, but maintains a balanced interest in the possible benefits of its application to the ill and bewildered. My father belongs to a running group that meets on Sunday mornings. The runners wear unstylish gear and take their bad post-exercise coffee in a dimly lit café named Joe's run by a succession of guys named Jerry on an unfashionable side street. Several times a year they take part in races that raise money for a good cause—cancer, muscular dystrophy, marmots, or refugees. They all sponsor each other, so after each event a flurry of checks is exchanged. Both of my parents do volunteer clerical work at the local Oxfam office on Thursday nights, deftly folding leaflets and stuffing envelopes and affixing labels—skills acquired from decades on the political margins translated perfectly to an organization set up to assist the economically marginalized.

The two of them bicycle each day from their small house near the top of the westernmost rise of West 16th Avenue to the university, where they work, my father in the fine arts library and my mother in the medical sciences library. In order to keep their proletarian credentials untainted, they have taken pains over many years never to be promoted. They have lunch together every day at one or another of the student cafeterias, and they cycle home together in the evenings. They are so equitable-minded that in the morning my mother leads the way and on the homeward trip she follows. Even their gardening is responsible and democratic. On fine evenings, they sit in uncomfortable Adirondack chairs (purchased from a workshop that employs the mentally handicapped) in their backyard, which they have strewn with wildflower seed and planted with native grasses that never need watering. In the springtime, the pollen from the grasses makes them sneeze. In the autumn, their wildflowers, which are little more than brash and brawny weeds, go to seed, catch a ride on the passing breezes, and self-sow throughout the neighborhood. I have no doubt that their neighbors would protest if they could, but I have never known anyone aside from my sisters who could voice more than the faintest reproach when face-to-face with my mild, sincere, gently blinking parents. They live in a haze of determined goodness.

Although I was an easy child, I don't believe that I was any happier than average. I had the usual sorrows and fears, all of which I felt it was important to conceal from my parents, who I believed were counting on me. For example, from the time I was eight, I was acutely afraid of the dark, a mistrust that has never entirely left me. It isn't the darkness that worries me, but what it might contain, the thing or person or beast that might, with a sudden inhalation, a low growl, and a scurry of nails against the floorboards, as the only dreadful, brief forewarning, spring out to seize me, then pull me limb from limb or worse. A fear of the unknown, unseen, unseeable. I do my best to rationalize away the remnants of this fear that still linger, and I am usually successful.

Another worry was my conviction, for at least a couple of years, that my parents would move away while I was at school, neglecting to tell me or leave behind their new address, forgetting, in fact, all about me, although they might, I hoped, at least retain some impression of having had at one time quite a nice little girl, whatever could have become of her? There must have come a time when this fear ebbed, when reason overtook it in size and credibility, but I cannot at this distance of years identify the day the worry had finally lifted and I could walk nonchalantly through the front door after school, confident that the familiar furniture and my sisters and the sitter would be there.

Since I was the ideal against which my two sisters were measured, it is surprising that I was and have remained on good terms with both of them. It would be easy enough for them to dislike me, to blame me in some way for having been the pattern on which my parents frequently sought to focus their attention. But each has usually treated me as her friend, courted me in fact, partly to pre-empt the other, it's true, but mostly because, I think, they are both genuinely fond of me. They have never, however, got on well with each other. Chalk and cheese my mother often calls them, which isn't true now that I think about it. They have more in common with each other than they have ever had with me. They are both subject to urgent, irresistible compulsions to put their own wants ahead of everything else. They are similarly self-indulgent in the transcendent respect they have for their own feelings, and in the ef-fort they devote to ensuring that their needs and desires are ful-filled. Both Lucy and Janet refuse to consider that the whole world might not be as concerned as they are with ensuring that their evanescent moods are understood, their cravings sated, and their spiky passions appeased. Janet, rising on a bright morning after an overnight rainstorm, will call everyone's attention to the exact manner in which the howling of the wind, as if with focused, spe-cific malice, pierced during the night the thin, insufficient fabric of her sleep. Lucy is more subtle; she will spend the morning picking fights, finding fault, relentlessly complaining, until someone (it is never her) figures out what it was that put her in a bad humor. To-gether, they are incendiary, although they do make more of an ef-fort now than they did when we were girls, when they made no effort at all. Then, they were certain that any conflict was entirely the fault of the other, and they nursed grudges for weeks and months, making sure that everyone else was aware of the source and magnitude of their grievances.

We didn't have a television when we were growing up, since my parents identified it early on as a capitalist tool designed to incul-cate bourgeois, consumerist beliefs and behaviors. (Television programming has since proved to be far more trivial than they feared.) My sisters complained, but I never needed one. My sisters provided all the entertainment I needed, and, when they were too much, I could always retreat into books. So long as I was careful not to be scorched in the emotional bonfires Lucy and Janet set everywhere they went, the flames and furor were often thrilling. I was able to manage all those years at home by tolerating their moods and ignoring their more extravagant behaviors and by burrowing through books brought home from the library located a convenient seven blocks north of our house. I learned to let much of what they said and did wash over me, in the same way that when you are caught outside in a cold rain shower you pull your hood closer around your face and keep on trudging, not unconscious or unappreciative of being protected from some of the storm's fury. In somewhat the same way, it seems to me now that for several years I allowed my life to wash over and around me, as if I were carrying the spark or essence of my true self cupped within my hands like a small bird with a minute and shuddering heart, moving slowly to preserve whatever it was that I was trying to keep safe from being jarred or shattered or frightened.

Gate

It was in September, the month the world rouses from summer languor, gives itself a shake, and begins to change its camouflage from green to gold, from stasis to evolution, that I began to take a different approach to life. Eventually, I discovered what I might have understood all along if I had only known where and how to look. How the pieces fit together. How to live more directly. How to create and shape my life, and be a part of it, instead of gazing onto it at an angle like a bystander, like a person skipping rocks onto the flat surface of a pond, like an onlooker watching an experiment in which she cannot take part for fear of influencing the outcome.

We were, my roommate Rebecca and I, thirty-two years old, solvent, housed, gainfully employed, partly out from under the tidal pull of our families, and between boyfriends, in fact beginning to wonder whether having them at all might be a thing of the past. Rebecca is a freelance writer of sorts, and I was in my first year working as a radiation technologist.

Several years ago my two sisters and I each inherited a medium-sized amount of money from a childless great-aunt. Enough for Janet to make the down payment on her house, for Lucy to spend what was to have been a year in Florence learning Italian and studying art, and for me to quit my job as a receptionist at a downtown law firm, after a period of indecision, and go back to school. I was waiting to hear whether I had been accepted into the Ph.D. program in the English department at the university when my friend Luba called to tell me that she had found a lump in her left breast. She described the mass to me on the telephone as hard and resistant under her fingertips and about the size of two lentils, leaving me with a stubborn image of her lump as disk-shaped, sharp-edged, and a malevolent shade of orange-brown. I went along with Luba to her mammogram appointment, and I sat beside her and held her hand while she had a small bit of follow-up surgery. The lentils turned out to be a simple cyst, free-floating, benign, swiftly removed, no more than an alarm, one of life's blind alleys. But I was struck—no, more than that, *moved*—by the brisk efficiency, the manifest *usefulness* of the crisply efficient woman who administered the mammogram. She had sleek, very fine brown hair pulled back and tied in a broad yellow velvet ribbon, and a manner that was calm, serious, accommodating, careful, and discrete. A few weeks later, I withdrew my application at the university and signed up instead for the radiation technology course at the Institute of Technology, acutely conscious that I was swapping a white-blouse future for a blue.

This decision pleased me and my parents, and unsettled my sisters Lucy and Janet and Janet's husband John. John spent hours trying to talk me into sticking with literature. "There are entire lives in there, Maggie," he argued. "One long afternoon with Proust, or Flaubert, even Mallarmé, will allow you to experience infinitely more of the world than a year in any medical clinic." John, who has a degree in modern languages from McGill and an M.B.A. from one of the better eastern universities, runs a bookstore in one of the not-quite-yet gentrified areas of downtown. He has a higher opinion of French writers than anyone I know. I like and admire John, in fact I adore him, and I longed to give in, to lean into his older, doubtless wiser judgment, but I could not be convinced. I could see no reason to change my mind. What I wanted—intensely as it turned out—was to do something manifestly practical.

When I wavered, which I did now and then, I summoned to mind, and this served as a warning, a cautionary tale, the memory of a doctoral candidate who had been a teaching assistant for one of my first-year undergraduate courses. She was large-boned and confident, with an impressively thick and gleaming helmet of close-cropped, uncombed, copper hair. She wore many-colored tunics and flowing scarves flashing with peacock hues, trailing a rumor of creative brilliance in her wake through the narrow corridors of the English department like the plume of a jet stream. But, when I asked her one day for directions to the student union building, she couldn't do it; she couldn't even point me in the general direction. She hadn't a notion either where it was or how I might find out, although its bright red roof could, I quickly learned, be seen from the wide, unwashed windows of the main lecture hall. I didn't want to become like her—all exquisite sensibility but with no common sense, thinly rooted in the world, living life narrowly, brilliantly, but ineffectively and theoretically.

There was a clamoring demand for radiation technicians when I graduated, as there still is. The school's placement officer, an intense, efficient Asian woman with sleek black hair, a wardrobe of red sweaters and short black knitted skirts and tights, and a frequent, shrill laugh that struck me as somewhat out of keeping with her role of directing newly trained students into suitable places of employment, told me about a job at the new mammography clinic that had just opened at St. Matthew's Hospital downtown. I had good marks, and references that were solid and burnished, and was hired immediately. For luck I tied my hair back in a satin ribbon when I went to St. Matthew's for the interview. I always wore it that way at work after that. Smartly tied hair. A brisk, intelligent manner. Competence. Assuredness. A single well-learned skill. You can accomplish a lot, and command respect and a respectable salary with very little more than these.

Two days before graduation, and feeling like an impostor, I took myself to a store on Willow Street that specializes in uniforms for medical professionals. Under the counsel of an officious saleswoman, I acquired two long jackets that resembled lab coats, one pale green and loosely cut, the other plain white and sharply tailored. In a nearby store, one with more indolent staff, I bought two pairs of comfortable shoes, one of which—bone-colored, lumpen, thick-laced, constricting at the toe, spongy at the heel—I wore only once. The other pair, a sort of supple clog made of softest calfskin and dyed the same pink-ivory color as the under slope of my breasts, proved perfect for the hours on my feet and the treks along endless tiled corridors. Never underestimate the importance of good footwear for work that involves a lot of standing and walking.

At about the same time that I started to work at St. Matthew's, I took over an apartment on Beach Avenue from my friend Dana who had decided to move to Quebec to woo, successfully as it turned out, a dry-humored, red-haired civil engineer who taught at the Université de Montreal. Dana and I had been close friends since high school, but we both knew perfectly well that the keenness with which I would feel his loss was tempered by the opportunity to take over his apartment, which was high-ceilinged, airy, and spacious, and which I had always coveted. The rent for Dana's apartment was close to double what I had been paying for my old place on West 12th near Oak, so I put a notice up at the community center on Denman Street, seeking a nonsmoking roommate, no pets. Rebecca was the fifth person I interviewed, and even though she wasn't perfect—I would have preferred someone who had an office to go to every day—she seemed to be a reliable, unobjectionable sort of person. She was the only person I interviewed who turned the meeting into a two-way process, with each of us appraising the other. I liked the respectfully probing questions she set for me as much as her calm, assured answers. Both questions and responses had an expansive subtlety; she conveyed her firm understanding of boundaries as being vitally important but reasonably mutable. Two adults sharing an average-sized apartment must be skilled in social navigation on the smallest scale; each must be able to discern that behavior that was perfectly appropriate yesterday might be entirely out of place the next.

It was the way Rebecca is put together that made me trust her as much as anything she told me. She is sturdy, long-limbed, and muscular under her pale and amply freckled skin, with a face and features that are discernibly larger than usual and generous hands and feet, like a tennis player or Eastern bloc Olympic swimmer. She gave every appearance of being sound, stable, dependable, steadfast. Rebecca was moving out of another apartment a few blocks away on Pacific, where she had been living with a boyfriend who hadn't worked out, and was able to move in on a Saturday morning in the spring, only a few weeks after I had moved into Dana's apartment myself.

"What if she's messy, or needy, or irritating?" Lucy warned me over the telephone, her voice low and urgent. "Where will you go if she gets on your nerves? There's no room for you to stay here. You know how little space I have already."

"What will John and I do if we need to leave the children with you overnight?" Janet wanted to know. She had stopped by Dana's apartment while I was unpacking and she stood in the center of the living room pushing at a pile of foam packing chips with one toe of her shoe. Janet has perfect size 6 feet, one of her several vanities, and wears beautiful soft leather shoes in colors that cannot be easily named—bronze with a hint of purple, pearly gray-black, peach with a golden cast. She picked up several of my just-unpacked possessions one by one as she spoke, turned them over and over in her hands, and then set them down again without looking at them. My hardbound copy of *To the Lighthouse* with its fraying red ribbon marker. A green glass fishing float with a tiny chip that Dana had left behind. A framed photograph of our handsome grandmother Charlotte wearing a high-necked lace evening gown and smiling guilelessly. A rounded, cream-and-blue crackle-glazed vase that had been a gift from my friend Luba and that had always reminded me of a neat, still bird with its head tucked under its wing.

"Have you done a criminal background check on this woman? This is not something on which you should simply trust your instincts. She's a complete stranger to us. You are just too naïve, Maggie. Everyone takes advantage of you."

"It will be good for you," my father said. The pupils of his eyes came into focus on me for an instant, then softened into their usual deep brown worn-velvet pools. "Your mother and I loved living in shared houses back when we were students in Waterloo. There's always someone to talk to. You'll never be lonely."

"It will be nice to have someone to share the chores," said my mother. She reached up and gave my shoulders a quick, encouraging squeeze. "I am sure you picked someone practical and useful. You have always had such good judgment."

"How do you see this working, Maggie?" Rebecca asked. It was just after eight on our first Monday morning together in the apartment. She had already been up for several hours, on the phone and stabbing at the keys of her gently humming computer, and was taking a break. She sat on a stool at the kitchen counter, sipping from a cup of coffee. I had begun to gather together my lunch and umbrella to walk through the rain to St. Matthew's. I liked to get to my desk a few minutes ahead of time to put my papers in order and get ready for my first appointment. I felt careful of Rebecca, and anxious not to do anything that would put her off this odd arrangement, two strangers living together in intimate proximity. I had also identified in myself and was struggling to overcome a slight, sharply unpleasant tang of territoriality about the apartment, a sensation that left a small, metallic taste in my throat and mouth. The apartment still felt as though it belonged to Dana, and to me by extension, since it had come to me by means of our friendship. This bloom of irritation over having allowed a portion of my space to be invaded was disquieting, like the bitter smell of scorched wool or the slight, gritty chaffing of sand in a shoe. My annoyance was unreasonable, I knew, and, since I have always despised unreason, I was certain that I could overcome it.

"What do you mean, *this?*" I answered, searching for my keys underneath the newspaper sections Rebecca had distributed across the counter. She had begun to generate clutter, although so far about the right amount: not so much that I felt overwhelmed; not so little that I might feel impelled to be neater. I couldn't tell yet if she was on her best behavior. It would take me a while to learn that Rebecca is always measured, always precisely and carefully herself.

She lacks the chameleon skill that most women have of being able to change to suit her surroundings. She has no illusions about herself that I have ever noticed; her store of self-knowledge seems limitless. Everything she does is quiet, self-contained, assured, and judicious.

"I mean meals," she said. "Would you like me to make you dinner?" She reached over and began to help me by straightening up the paper. I noticed that she matched section B carefully to the back of section A, and then C behind B. Good.

"Oh, I see." I found my keys under a supermarket flyer and hooked them on one finger. "No. I'll look after myself or pick something up. I usually make something simple. Sometimes I just have a sandwich or a bowl of soup, I'm afraid. I'm not much of a cook." I walked past her on my way to the door, swinging the keys into my purse, my mind already advancing down the hall toward the elevator.

"Well, I am." Rebecca swiveled on her stool to face me. "I like to cook. And since I start early, I usually stop working at three o'clock or so. All of my editors are back east, so it's easier if I start and end my day when they do. Why don't I cook dinner for both of us?"

"Today, you mean?"

"No. Every day. Or, at least, how about four days a week? Mondays to Thursdays. I'd like to. It's no fun cooking just for myself. And I'm not a bad cook. I won't poison you. We can split the groceries if you like. On weekends, we'd be on our own, or any evening we have other plans, of course. Why don't we try it for a week and see?"

"What if we don't like to eat the same things?"

"What don't you like?"

"I can't think of anything. Except salted peanuts. And the obvious things like Cheez Whiz and Spam."

"And I like just about everything except kiwi fruit. They're too fuzzy and mucousy. And canned soup. All that salt. Let's try it, OK? Unless you really don't want to."

"It wouldn't be fair, though. You'd be doing all the work."

"I cook for myself anyway, and it's no more work to do it for two. You can clean up, if you think that would make it fairer. You'll be doing me a favor. I need someone to practice new recipes on."

We agreed that Rebecca would take on the cooking. I did the dishes. We split the food bills. I paid for a cleaner to come in once a week and Rebecca kept things picked up in between. Rebecca could work her way around the apartment with a dust cloth while talking to an editor or interviewing an expert, the telephone tucked between her shoulder and her chin. We were apart most of the day, and in the evenings we had the same level of desire to accommodate each other without either of us having to make any significant changes to how we were already living.

Part of what made things work was Dana's apartment. It was a quarter-floor of an older building, one of the large, square, half-timbered imitation Tudors they built back in the 1940s. The building was elegant, permanent, and plainly superior to the badly aging stuccoed low-rises that had been built all around the neighborhood and painted in Florida colors that faded and streaked in the city's frequent rains, looking like they were slowly melting away, like giant slabs of Neapolitan ice cream left sitting outside on a warm day. Some of these newer buildings were in fact already being consumed by rot, and spent months shrouded in enormous green tarps while mysterious repairs were conducted underneath. When the tarps were finally whisked away, the ice-cream buildings would reappear, like a magician's trick, jaunty and freshly painted.

Dana had lived in our building for years, and over time, as other tenants moved up or moved away, he had worked his way from a basement suite at the back up through each of the floors to one of the two apartments on the top floor with a partial view of the water. There were two bedrooms, a large living room, a dining room with wainscoting and two built-in china cabinets with leaded-glass doors, a kitchen big enough to hold a drop-leaf table and two chairs (a narrow ironing board dropped out of a slender door fitted into the wall), and a boxy storage closet off the hallway that Rebecca converted into an office by installing a desk, shelves, and an overhead light. She found it easier to concentrate there than in her bedroom or the living room, both of which had a view of the bay. Rebecca brought her grandmother's oak dining room set out of storage, and I had bought some very good living room furniture from one of the lawyers at the firm where I used to work when he moved back in with his wife—not that their *entente* lasted very long—so between us we had everything we needed. I got the larger bedroom since I was there first, and Rebecca had the use of the closet for her office. The kitchen was also mainly hers. I went in there to make toast and tea in the morning and sometimes a snack at night.

Rebecca cared about food, how it was prepared, how it looked, its textures and temperatures and flavors. I had never been too interested in what I ate, so long as it wasn't terrible, burnt, overwhelming, or insufficient. Without Rebecca, I was clearly headed for the kind of single woman's diet I live on now—lightly buttered toast, soft-boiled eggs, fruit, overripe from neglect by a day or two, sliced into bowls with plain yogurt, infrequent knuckle-sized servings of flavorless meat, dry toast and bitter coffee on the weekend mornings when the milk and butter run out. Rebecca bought goat cheeses soaked in olive oil, fat sausages of lamb and fennel, thinly sliced Parma ham, and crusty Portuguese buns from an Italian store on Victoria Street. She talked the owner of the grocery store around the corner from our apartment into putting the reddest peppers, the curliest lettuces, and the heaviest, sweetest melons aside for her. She convinced him, through the charm of her gravelly voice, the subtle gestures of her expressive hands, and the intimate incline of her neck, that the two of them alone in all the city truly appreciated the best.

Rebecca had very low expectations of me as her audience. She didn't expect me to be home on time so that she could take something foolishly complicated like a soufflé out of the oven at the exact right moment. She didn't watch my expression carefully as I took the first bite, in order to gauge my reaction. She prepared good food, put it on the table, and then was ready to eat it, talking about other things. I took to work for my lunch whatever was left uneaten from dinner the night before, since Rebecca had a horror of leftovers. "That's so yesterday," she said to me once when she saw me cramming a plastic container with the remains of a dish of scalloped potatoes. She was only half joking. No matter how hard she had labored the day before to prepare the perfect soup or stew or salad, by the next day her interest had transferred to that day's projects.

I drink very seldom now—too dangerous, I think—but Rebecca poured out wine every evening when we sat down to eat. The heavy glasses shone in our hands like incandescent fruit or oversized synthetic jewels, and the wine started our conversation and kept it running along. Rebecca liked to hear about my safe, stable

childhood—the more mundane details filled her with wonder—
and she traded her day's events for mine.

What Rebecca was doing all day, while I was pressing women's
breasts flat and x-raying them to check for the embryonic seeds that
might blossom into tumors, was designing quizzes and questionnaires for periodicals, the kind of tests that are common in
women's magazines: "Is He Right for You?" "Test Your Shopping
Smarts." "Are You Well Read?" "How High Is Your Self-Esteem?"
She did her research on the Internet, and at our local library or the
central branch over on Georgia Street.

Although at a glance her tests looked like the most frivolous
kind of filler, the sort of nonsense that is intended only to pad the
space between makeup advertisements and weightier articles,
Rebecca always treated her subjects seriously. Even for lighter
topics—"Rate Your Sense of Humor" or "Are You Cat-Crazy or
Dog-Devoted?"—she always explained exactly what the test results
represented, and suggested what could or should be done with
them. For example, at the end of a quiz testing fitness awareness,
she would recommend websites and books that promoted health.
For a questionnaire on love affairs, she emphasized the need for
people whose relationships tested as abusive to steel themselves to
bring things to an end, and told them where they could find help if
they couldn't break away on their own. She received fan mail from
readers every day, many of whom told her that one or another of
her quizzes had stirred them to make significant changes in their
lives. Some of them wrote to seek her advice on their own particular situation, and Rebecca always responded, not with further advice but with a list of resources: therapists, specialists, or the better
kind of self-help book. What she enjoyed, she told me, far more
then advising the bewildered, was the mathematical and architec-

tural precision of designing an intelligent, balanced test, one that would expose an unexpected pattern, or bring unexamined truths to the surface.

Rebecca produced roughly one quiz a week, which didn't seem like a lot of work to me at first, since in my job I sometimes saw as many as twenty patients in a day, but over a few months I began to see the challenges of her unusual job. In addition to designing the questions and determining the range of possible answers and the right weighting for all of them, Rebecca had to come up with and pitch the ideas, consult with editors and make any changes they insisted on, and send out invoices and collect payment. All I had to do was turn up at work, carry out a series of more or less routine procedures, prepare my reports, and collect my paycheck every two weeks. I had good benefits—disability, life insurance, and extended health—and eventually I would be able to retire and collect a pension. Rebecca sometimes earned as much as four or five thousand dollars for a single test, but she had to put aside enough money for her taxes and retirement plan, and, as she had told me during our twenty-minute interview, she was saving for the down payment on a house.

Rebecca had her life planned along strictly defined routes and timetables. She wanted to share the Beach Avenue apartment with me for two more years, and then buy a small house in one of the settled neighborhoods east of Main Street. She would then have a child, with a husband if one appeared, or by adoption, from Russia or China or South America. She intended to have her house paid off before she was fifty, and to resist any temptation to ever buy a larger house or move to a different neighborhood. She liked the thought that the first house she bought would be the only one she would ever own, and would be the one she would die in. She wanted her child to grow up in one place. Rebecca had been the fifth child of an army sergeant and a licensed practical nurse, and had lived with her family in a succession of bungalows and town houses. She had gone to nine schools in five provinces and another near the Black Forest in Germany.

September is when the days begin to close in, like a collection of nested gold and orange and red Chinese folded paper boxes, each one a size smaller than the last. The sun has been getting up later and going down earlier since its glory days in June, when, this far north, it rules many more hours than it sleeps. By September, the dawn is sluggish, reluctant, slow-moving and dusk bites impatiently into the end of the day. Rebecca had begun to serve dinner by candlelight. It was too early in the autumn for the firefly glimmer of the candle flame against the approaching twilight, but the candles softened the edges of the evening shadows that reached through the window and crept across the meal laid out on Rebecca's grandmother's table.

"Did you work on your quiz on longevity today?" I asked her over dinner one late September evening.

Rebecca put down her fork and leaned toward me across the table, cradling her glass in her hands. She was always happy to talk about her work.

"Yes, but it's not about longevity exactly. It's actually a test for how long you are going to live, which might be long or short, depending. If you fill it out completely honestly, it will give you the date that you're going to die."

"Do you mean that you can predict to the year or month how long someone is going to live?"

"To the exact day, in fact. I find that accuracy in the result helps inspire faith in the process. People who take this kind of quiz aren't looking for general guidance. They feel—and I've come to understand this—that once they've invested a half-hour into finding a pencil, carefully answering all the questions, and working out their score, they are entitled to a precisely calibrated response. It would have made you doubtful of the discerning powers of your teacher if, after you took an exam in school, you were told that you did all right or pretty well. You needed to know that you had scored 84 out of 100 in order to be sure that your work was thoroughly evaluated. And you wanted to be able to measure yourself against your last result and against the 82 per-cent someone else scored. That's why I have to provide a precise date of death. Of course, the dates are only conjecture until the person dies. But I really do think my test is accurate, give or take, and allowing for outlying cases." She took a sip from her glass, then swirled the remaining wine around and around, starting up a small, glittering vortex. She was clearly excited and pleased by her day's work.

"What about random causes, like crossing the street and get-ting hit by a bus?" I still didn't know Rebecca well enough to judge whether to take her entirely seriously.

"Good question," Rebecca said. She swallowed the last shim-mering drops of her wine and set down the empty glass. Her hands began to sketch through the air in a professorial manner.

"I've tried to draw out any predilection for risky behaviors, like being absentminded or refusing to use condoms or playing haz-ardous sports or taking illegal drugs. My thesis is that the kind of person who does these things is also more likely to forget to pay at-tention to the traffic, or to take a chance dashing across the street or using a dirty needle."

"What if the person taking the quiz is in denial?"

"I probe for careless behaviors by asking how many traffic accidents the person has been involved in, whether they talk on a cell phone while they drive, whether they would accept a pill from a stranger at a party, that kind of thing."

"Where did you come out?" Rebecca always takes her own tests. She ended things with her last boyfriend, a successful stockbroker named Garry, a few days after he earned a highish score on a quiz she designed called "Is He Trouble?"

"I am going to die on February 1, 2050. Of course, it's only a theory until then. Unless I die earlier, in which case at least I'll be spared the embarrassment of knowing I was wrong."

"You're kidding me. No test can be that exact."

Rebecca shrugged, smiling. She rotated her empty wine glass on its circular foot. "This one is."

"What if I took it?"

"Do you really want to know?" Rebecca asked. She had just reached to pick up her fork. She put it down again, reached to refill her glass, and took a slow, deliberative sip. "Not everyone does, you know."

"Yes. No. I don't know. You're not serious. Is this a joke? Is this one going to run on April Fools' Day?"

"It's not meant to be a joke, but you are free to take it seriously or not, just as you like. Come on. We can do you right now before dessert. It won't hurt to leave it for another few minutes in the fridge to make sure it's completely set. Don't worry! You're healthy. You look both ways before crossing and then you check again. From the sound of it you never had a boyfriend who even remotely qualified as real trouble. You return your library books on time. You don't smoke. Your parents are both alive and well. You'll probably live until you're a hundred. I should make you my executor, since you'll likely survive me by twenty years. I smoked all through high school, and tore the filters off too."

Rebecca went to her closet office and came back with her laptop computer, which she placed on the table beside her plate. She opened it, pressed a few keys, and waited until, with a series of chittering noises followed by a gleam and a hum, it flickered into life. I watched as she scrolled through her files and selected the one she wanted. After a few moments more, the screen changed from its provisional shade of deep blue to a glowing, radiant, hard-working opal. Rebecca paused for a few seconds, and then directed seventy-five questions at me in quick succession. "Just say the first thing that enters your mind," she prompted me if I hesitated, her standard reminder whenever I took one of her quizzes.

The last question she asked was, "Are you happy right now?" I hesitated, thinking about love, and how deeply and rawly I longed for its syrup and sting, the steady heat of someone's thighs alongside mine in bed, and then answered, truthfully, recklessly, "Not completely."

Rebecca glanced at me coolly, appraisingly. "I'll put down 'No,'" she said.

Immediately, she began tallying up my scores in a separate program. I started a second glass of wine while I watched her add the numbers together once and then a second time. Her lips pushed forward and she blinked rapidly as she worked.

"Well?" I asked when she had finally stopped pressing keys.

Rebecca was peering into the computer screen as if studied contemplation of the electronic text would disclose an underlying and essential message.

"When's it going to be?" I prompted. "When am I going to shuffle off this mortal coil? What are mortal coils, anyway? They sound rather intestinal, don't they? Or mattressy. How do you shuffle them off?"

Rebecca took a deep draw from her glass of wine. "OK," she announced. She bounced one fingernail against her front teeth. "There's some sort of problem here. I thought I had everything weighted properly, but the test must still have a few bugs in it."

"What? Am I going to live until I'm 110? My savings won't last that long." I stood up, crossed to her side of the table, and craned around her bent neck to see what was written on the screen. Rebecca hunched forward as if she meant to block my gaze, but then she sat back in her chair and crossed her arms on her chest.

"What does 22-12-99 mean? Does that mean December 22? That's two weeks before my birthday. I'm going to get cheated out of my last birthday."

Rebecca nodded thoughtfully. She gazed again at her computer screen, and at the rows of numbers and letters in neat ranks above the number 22-12-99.

"And 99—what century are we talking about? I don't seriously expect to live to 132. Or 232?"

Rebecca still didn't answer.

You can't mean *this* December 22?"

Rebecca leaned forward, stabbed at the keyboard, and then pressed Enter again. She peered into the flickering screen. In the glassy glow, her nose cast a dark triangle of shadow that masked her eyes. I couldn't read her expression.

"I am sure there's something wrong here," she said. "In the

weightings. Or maybe I've made a mistake in the math. We'll have to go through this thing question by question until I figure it out."

"You think I'm going to die in three *months*?" Rebecca didn't answer. I drained off the rest of my glass and felt the wine's cold golden slide all the way down to my stomach.

Pathway

The next day was Saturday. The alarm rang stridently and early, pulling me too soon from an unusually intense, deep, and saturated sleep. At first, in the dim light of early morning, my dresser, desk, and chair looked formless and strangely still, like living creatures that had been moving about moments before and had frozen in the instant before I opened my eyes. It took a moment before it came to me that this sensation of shaggy, indistinct, rushed stillness had arisen in contrast to my abruptly shattered dream, one that seemed to have been packed full of jagged shards of bright, rapidly shifting colors. The furniture, corners, and edges of my room took a few moments to assume their solid daytime shapes.

A snaking eddy of cold air met my feet when I lowered them to the floor. I could hear the dark, wet winds of autumn pushing against my bedroom windows, and felt in the air the pressure and weight of the night's bad weather. I shivered abundantly for an instant, and then put on black hiking shorts, a white T-shirt, my navy blue fleece jacket, thick wool socks, and my old hiking boots. I filled a water bottle, fumbled a Luna bar out of a box in the kitchen, and was downstairs in the lobby a few minutes later when my friend Luba's tomato red Volvo swung into the driveway and pulled to a stop at the building's front door. After a mostly silent twenty-minute drive, we were at the small break in the margin of thick, green forest that marks the start of the rough rock, plank, and split-log path that runs to the peak of Grouse Mountain. We stamped our feet and swung our arms in the damp chill, exchanged a few words of encouragement, took pulls from our water bottles, then started together to climb past the trees that cling to the mountainside.

The trail to the top of the mountain isn't long, less than three kilometers, but it is steep, more like ascending a ladder than hiking. No matter how many times I do this climb, by the time I am halfway up the mountain my legs are burning and the muscles of my chest are struggling to pull enough oxygen into my lungs so that I can keep on going. The point of the ascent is the exercise—the pull on the long muscles of the thighs and the clenching and unknotting of calves and buttocks, the muscles that are never used in the city—rather than the scenery, and finishing, rather than enjoying, the climb. In any case, the dense, sodden limbs and branches of the crowded rain forest seldom thin or part to allow for a view, and rampant, luxuriant shrubs and scrub and ferns and trees threaten from every side to overwhelm the trail. There are few places to step aside from the path and look around to gain a sense of scale or perspective.

The air tastes and smells as green and damp as the forest floor—a loamy, oxygenated taste of peat and standing water and rot, overlaid with ozone. The ground underfoot, where it can be felt through the tree roots, the slippery moss-covered boulders, and the steep, slick wooden steps decomposing in the still, damp air, is moccasin-soft, with the sinking, saturated, cool resilience of sphagnum, spongy with silent history. The rich and abundant appear-

ance of the topsoil is misleading, however. In fact the earth is thin
and acidic, and large sheets of the loosely tethered ground beneath
our feet are always at risk of slipping off the mountainside in a
tumble of rock, dirt, trees, underbrush, trail, and hikers.

The most serious climbers can get to the top of the mountain
in half the time it takes us to complete the ascent. One man who
passed us that morning was carrying an eight-kilogram weight in
each hand. He was breathing hard and steadily, his eyes focused on
some goal far beyond the top of the trail. A woman of forty or so,
thin and taut as a predator, sprinted past our deliberate feet as if
she had negotiated an exemption from the laws of gravity. A somewhat younger man followed her, his thinning hair matted close to
his head in the saturated air. His muddy calves looked as though
they were fashioned from sinew; they made me think of the knotted strips of hide that dogs are given to worry at. Sweat trickled
along channels that ran from his temples to the hinges of his jaw,
and drops fell behind him as he climbed, punctuating each stride.

Every week we see people like these, who wear their bodies like
machinery. Luba and I are manifestly soft, unchallenging, and human in comparison, uncompetitive with each other and with the
hikers who pass us on the climb. We strive to keep up a steady pace,
even on the discouraging third quarter when it seems that no
progress has been made, that the trees will never part, the end of
the path never appear, but we take our time, talking as we go, catch-
ing up on the week just past.

By the time we reached the top of the mountain that morning
we were dripping from effort and from the drifting mist that
threatened to condense at any moment into a frank shower of rain.
We refilled our water bottles with tepid water at a tap in the washroom and then bought coffee at the café. I told Luba about Re-

becca's quiz while we sat with our hands wrapped around our mugs, drawing the heat from the pottery into our bones. One of my calf muscles trembled and jerked under the table, adjusting crankily to the contrast between the hard climb and this sudden, warm respite in the humid restaurant.

"I probably shouldn't bother exercising at all," I said, stirring two measures of sugar into my cup, "since I won't live long enough to reap the benefits. I should lie in bed and eat chocolates and read books instead."

"You've kept it up this long, so you might as well try to die in good shape," Luba answered. Her tongue darted forward to test the temperature of her cup, and then she took a shallow sip of coffee. "You're going to want to look good in your coffin."

"Rebecca and I stayed up until midnight trying to work it out. But we couldn't get the date to change by more than a few days either way. The only answer that made a significant difference was the last one."

"What was the question?"

"The question was 'Are you happy?' "

"What did you say?"

"I said 'Not completely.' I mean, I am happy overall, but I could be happier. 'Yes' would mean I was completely happy, wouldn't it? Is anyone completely happy?"

"What happens if you change your answer to yes?"

"That's the strange thing. If I say yes, then the date I'm supposed to die jumps all the way to 2063. I'll be ninety-six then. Ancient. Certainly past looking good in my coffin, no matter how many times we force ourselves up this mountain."

"How long you're supposed to live depends on whether you are happy right now? How much sense does that make?"

"Not much, I guess. Rebecca couldn't explain it."

"Couldn't or wouldn't? Is this some passive-aggressive thing? Maybe she's trying to get you upset over nothing."

"I don't think so. She's not like that. And I could tell that she was as bothered as I was. Maybe more. She kept saying that her test wasn't designed to have that kind of result."

"Why don't you change your answer to yes? You seem happy to me."

"She said that I have to be completely honest."

"What happens if, by some chance, between now and the end of December, you become happy?"

"I asked her the same thing. But she wasn't sure. She was still working on it when I went to bed. And she was asleep when I went out this morning."

"Look. Rebecca may mean well, but she's not a doctor and she hasn't got a crystal ball. These quizzes are meant to be entertainment, a diversion, something to while away the time at the hairdresser's. This is the kind of thing that sells magazines. That's all. It's a joke, not something you take seriously. You look healthy to me, and you're happy enough. Anyway, like you said, who is perfectly happy? Maybe there's no such thing. In fact, I'm certain perfect happiness doesn't exist. It's an illusion, meant to sell toothpaste and beer and tennis bracelets."

"Are you happy, Luba?"

Before she could answer, two men, one dark, one fair, both dressed from collar to boots in Gore-Tex in vivid primary colors, red, yellow, and blue, and both with the somewhat unkempt and dissolute look of men who were in their mid-forties and between marriages, asked if they could sit at our table with their coffees and their paper plates, which held the café's giant, iced cinnamon buns, as substantial as steaks. The only empty tables were outside in what was now an icy, drenching rain. Luba looked at me, implying that the decision was mine, and that she knew what it would be but was hoping I would display a sterner resolve than usual. I glanced back a message that we could hardly say no in the circumstances, and that, if she wanted them to go, she would have to be the one to tell them. So the two men sat down, and we went along with what they seemed to assume to be the implied arrangement—that in return for agreeing to share our four round feet of laminated tabletop, we would allow them to entertain us. After a few of the gondolas that ferry people up and down the mountain had come and gone, Luba said that she had an appointment to keep, and one of the two men—Mike, the fair-haired one more in need of a shave—asked for her telephone number. She gave him her number at work, and they said how much they had enjoyed meeting us, and Mike, look-ing at Luba, said that it would be great to get together again.

Luba and I caught the next gondola and rode down the moun-tain in a crush of tourists who had been ferried up the mountain on an earlier car. The tourists' brightly colored T-shirts and synthetic jackets reminded me of a flock of exotic birds. The morning was not yet half over. We plunged down through a scrim of rain and clouds that hugged the near hip of the mountain just in time to see the mist over the city begin to dissipate and drift out toward the ocean, so that we fell down and along the mountain slope into an expanding and brightening view of downtown, the inlet, and Lions Gate Bridge.

The city unfolded from the fog like a shiny present tumbling out of plain wrappings. In the filtered light, the bridge looked freshly made, like a child's new toy, and it was ribboned with gleaming streams of rain-glossed traffic. Cars streaked toward and away from the city, their headlights yellow and rich and dim, like old gold, against the gray concrete. Around me, the cameras of the visitors clicked and whirred with sharp ticks and snaps, like the clacking of beaks. The tourists craned and dipped and turned their necks, and their plastic coats rustled like stiff plumage. Their voices were audible, in the manner of people in public places who feel confident that they cannot be understood or that it doesn't matter who overhears since they are unlikely ever to meet the listeners again. They pointed and chattered and seemed to me to be—at least for the short duration of the descent to the parking lot, where their tour bus no doubt awaited warm and rumbling—perfectly, entirely happy.

On the drive home in Luba's steamy car, we talked about her parents, who were in their late sixties, aging badly, and had recently been forced to live apart. Her father's Parkinson's disease had compelled a move to a care facility in Vancouver. Her mother wasn't managing well on her own and had decided to leave the second-storey apartment they had shared for over thirty years above the dry cleaning business that they operated when Luba and her sister Rachel were growing up. Luba's mother was looking for a smaller, more manageable apartment where she could be nearer to her husband. It seemed impossible to house them together, since, although their wants were identical, their levels of need were so different. Luba was at a loss how to help them. There seemed no place they could be together and happy, and there was little Luba could do apart from helping her mother plan the move and drive her to visits with her father.

Rebecca had gone out by the time I got home, so there was no competition for the apartment's only shower. I stripped off my muddy clothes, let them fall in an untidy pile on the bathroom floor, and turned the water on full, as close to scalding as I could bear. I stood for a long time in the surging hot water, waiting for the pressure and heat to drive the chill of the rain and the climb's tight pain from my muscles, and thinking about happiness and unhappiness. Several times during our discussion the night before, Rebecca had pointed out in her completely earnest way that I would add sixty years to my life span if only I were happy instead of unhappy, and, in the mountain coffee shop that morning, Luba had been urging the same solution on me.

"What does happiness mean?" I had asked them both. "It doesn't *mean* anything."

"It's what you think it means," Rebecca had insisted. "Only you can know. No one else. You have to give me the truthful answer to the question for you."

"That's impossible. Happiness is more complicated than that. You're asking for an absolute answer to a question that has no absolutes. It's not like happiness is a switch that can only be set to on or off. Anyway, I am not unhappy. Just not, overall, completely happy."

"So the right answer is the one you gave first. It usually is. If you are really not happy, you can't change your answer simply to get the date you want."

"Then take that question out. It's killing me off before my time."

"It's not the question that's killing you. It's the answer."

I thought of Luba, who had told me more than once that she could never be completely happy again. Would Rebecca's quiz kill her off as well?

The heat and pounding water worried at thoughts and emotions that seemed to have been lurking just beneath the surface of

my skin, waiting to be awakened. The water fell on my skin like liquid sandpaper. It battered and abraded my body, which felt soft
and vulnerable under the water's sting, exposed, like a snail extracted from its tough protective shell. The spray felt invasive, like
needles intent on piercing my skin, or a scraping tool worrying at
old paint. A storm surged and roared in my ears. Steam churned
and massed in gray clouds. The closed shower stall felt clammy and
close, and I struggled to catch my breath. Hot, damp air filled my
throat and blurred my vision. My chest felt tight, my throat raw. At
the point that I thought that I could bear it no longer and reached
to turn off the taps, I felt the pounding water tease a hollow, cold
sensation from somewhere deep inside me, from the marrow inside
my bones perhaps, or some hidden spot in my smooth, twisting
viscera.

I felt an icy slide, like the long, sick shock you suffer when you
cut your finger deeply or blurt out words that should not even have
been thought and cannot now be taken back. A shuddering chill
rose in a wintry slither to the surface of my burning skin, like an ice
snake, like the dank, blind, grubbing, invading roots of bindweed
burrowing upward through stony soil or some specter in a horror
movie slipping free from the grave. I shuddered as I felt something
mocking and lonely and cold tear away from me. For the smallest
moment, my perspective abruptly shifted. I felt for that instant as
though I were hovering at the top of the shower looking down into
the narrow steamy stall. I saw myself: small, wet, burning cold in
the swirling heat, hair slicked back, my skin mottled and rough.
Crystals of sharp, stinging salt burned in my eyes. I ran my hands
over my breasts and thighs and torso. My skin felt hot, tight, almost electric. After several minutes longer, I could feel a few heated
tears escape. They were lost immediately in the swirling steam, and

trickled away in the streaming water. My tears brought no sense of release or relief. Their flight felt like the lightest, coldest touch of a departing lover.

I felt then as if I had plunged into a place in the world that I hadn't known existed. A place of utter abandonment, of loss, insignificance, failure, sorrow. My body felt as though it was opening up in the steam and intensifying heat like a hard-edged shell being prised apart. I raised my hands to my face and felt the coursing water strike my fingertips and stream along the sharp bones at the back of my hands. The water fell to the drain after tracing a retreating caress around the islands and crevasses of my shivering body. I felt solitary, absurd, hollow, hopeless—swept by a longing for something that I could not name or picture. It felt like the deepest, most intense thirst I had ever known.

Front Steps

I had spent all of my life worrying about the happiness of one or the other of my two sisters, Janet and Lucy. This felt to me like a responsibility if not a vocation, although one more or less willingly assumed. It had always been, in any event, one of the few absolutely clear purposes in my life. The crises my sisters experienced or created were more numerous and significant than mine, and I felt an obligation to do what I could to preserve and restore their so readily lost equilibrium.

That fall I was most concerned about Lucy, who was pregnant with the baby who would turn out to be Philip, and who had just become engaged to Ryan. For the first time I could think of, my sister Janet was sailing smoothly along under a kind of mantle of serenity. Janet had been married for five years to John, and they had Claudia and Thomas, the twins, who were four, and sweet, fat Marie, who had been born that spring. Janet had given up her part-time job at John's bookstore a few weeks before Marie's birth and now spent her days ferrying the children in her white Volvo between home and the park or to the swimming pool where the twins were enrolled in Aquatot lessons. She kept placid baby Marie in a pouch on her stomach whenever Marie wasn't asleep or riding in her car seat. Janet had always been fast-moving and tense, and quick with her immutable decisions. Since she could first talk she had had a staccato way with words—sharp, pointed, relentless, critical. But now she seemed to be consciously absorbing some portion of Marie's calm. She had a slower walk these days in her perfect shoes, her camber altered by the weight and bounce of the baby suspended below her throat, and her gaze was newly moderated by some subtle, hidden shifting of the uncompromising elements of her anxious nature.

Lucy had recently returned to the city after several years away. She had been living in Rome, in a tiny apartment on the fifth floor of an ancient building on Via dei Pettinari in the labyrinthine crux of the old city, not far from the square where Giordano Bruno had been burned as a heretic four hundred years ago and where his statue still stands as a warning to others.

Lucy had first gone to Florence for a year, to study art history, but had immediately become involved with Corrado, an artist she met there, and dropped out of her courses and moved with him to Rome. I knew only a few things about Corrado. As evidenced by the photos Lucy sent us—they showed Lucy dressed in a filmy skirt and low-cut blouse clinging to his back on an immense motorcycle—he was intensely, extravagantly beautiful. He worked in oil paints slathered thickly onto his canvases with putty knives and trowels. He then slashed the canvases with razor blades and mended them roughly with heavy, waxed sailor's thread pushed through the canvases with a sailor's palm. Lucy had one of his paintings, and I found it savage and disturbing. Another thing I knew about Corrado was the way he pronounced my sister's name. She echoed his voice for me on the telephone. "Lu-chi-ah! Ah, ti voglio bene, Lu-chi-ah!"

Soon after the move to Rome, however, the *bello* Corrado took up with one of his models, a long-limbed young man from

Palermo with skin, Lucy reported, the color of burnt oatmeal and a dark head of fat, oiled curls. Corrado ended things with Lucy quite abruptly and cruelly. She bought a ticket home, but the day before she meant to leave, a friend she had moved in with temporarily, a freelance journalist, suggested that she apply for a position that had come open at the Roman bureau of an American television station. Gleaming with the brittle brilliance of the newly jilted, she dazzled the three men who interviewed her, and was hired immediately.

Lucy's job in Rome was to organize details for the journalists, their tickets, money, and documents and telephone and e-mail connections, before they went on assignments. At the end of the first month of her new job, as she drove her moped back to the office after an errand at the bank, Lucy was mugged by a skinny, nervy man, who, the police told her later, had been waiting in a lane outside the bank watching for her or someone like her, alone and with lots of money. He sprang on her as she kicked the motorbike off its stand and started forward, slashing out at her with an X-acto knife. She had two thousand U.S. dollars in cash concealed under her leather jacket in a zippered pouch slung on a webbed strap around her waist. The man was nervous, or perhaps haste marred his aim. The slick blade of his knife sliced through her jacket and the waistband of her jeans and only shallowly into the soft flesh of her waist. Lucy felt her rich, dark blood begin to ooze out of the wound before she felt any pain. She shrieked, threw a weak punch at her attacker's face, and then kicked out at him hard with one booted foot. The man fell to the ground; Lucy's lucky kick had caught him directly in his groin. He curled into a ball, loudly lamenting, and was captured instantly by four passing Italian youths, who joyfully threw themselves onto him and held him fast, one each to a limb, while a nearby shopkeeper who had been pulled from his store by the clamor dialed the police on a cell phone belonging to one of the four heroes. Several police officers arrived within a short while and took the man away, the X-acto knife encased in a plastic bag for evidence.

Lucy was left with a superficial gash below her lowest rib, a sprained thumb, a yellow-and-purple eye, and a bruised shoulder, but her stash of money and her pride were intact. Her colleagues at the bureau had an impromptu party for her when she got back to the office after a detour to the hospital to be bandaged and stitched in the company of two gallant *carabinieri*. (It is safer, she told me, not to stay in an Italian hospital for any length of time, but to get in and out as fast as possible.) Plastic cups of wine were served, and someone's commandeered lunch of provalone sandwiches cut into thin strips. Cups of bitter espresso, rattling on their saucers, were fetched on a tray from the *caffè* down the street, and a few of the pastries left over from a meeting earlier in the day were cut into quarters and arranged on the lid of a cardboard box, with sparklers stuck in them in a festive blaze of fervent, fleeting glory.

Lucy told Janet and me about her adventure that evening on the telephone, taking pains not to minimize the drama and danger, although she had the sense not to tell our parents. The part of the story I liked best didn't take place until a few days later. When Lucy next parked her moped near the bank on another run for funds, a proprietor of one of the businesses on the stretch of road where the attack had taken place caught sight of her, and he came out with all of his neighbors to inspect her bandage and her fading bruises. They stood in an animated group at the curbside and recounted their versions of the assault, including gestured reenactments, and they all praised Lucy's spirit and valor in fending off the attacker. One of the shopkeepers, a butcher, waved his cleaver about to demonstrate to the others what he would have done to the mugger if his store had been nearer to the attack, and if he had not been quite so occupied with selecting a morsel of veal for a particularly demanding customer, although a woman who managed a housewares store next door to his shop whispered to Lucy that the butcher was in fact milder than a mouse and could barely bring himself to carve the carcasses that came to his store with the life already drained out of them.

Lucy's apartment in Rome was so small that the shower was a corner of the blue-tiled kitchen, with a clear plastic curtain hung above it and a drain in the floor. The toilet was in an alcove concealed by a louvered screen.

Lucy picked up Italian like that, and acquired the hand gestures too, that steeple shape she makes, joining her fingertips at the top like a tent, and moving her hands back and forth at the wrist to show disbelief or frustration. She learned that in Rome from Gian Luigi, her next boyfriend, or whatever he was. And that rotating motion with her right hand, flicking upward, thumb arching outward, as a kind of dismissive insult—she got that from Gian Luigi too. He is a very impatient man.

Lucy loved Rome. She loved her job, which took her to all the troubled spots in Europe and Africa, the places where things were happening or were about to happen. She loved Gian Luigi, who was hairy and large and completely equal to her rages. But, this being Lucy, there were problems. The main ones were, first, Gian Luigi was married, and, second, shortly after she got back to Rome from a visit to Vancouver, Lucy discovered that she was pregnant.

Lucy had come home for two weeks at the end of March. She sent me an e-mail to say that she was coming to see Janet's new baby, but I was certain that she was coming home to try to give herself some distance and time to think things over. It had only begun to become clear to her, she told me one evening when we went for a walk after an early dinner, that Gian Luigi might never ever actually leave his wife. We were walking the steep blocks from Janet and John's house downhill toward the beach. In Vancouver, by late March the spring season grows daily more rooted and vigorous, and the sun is already able to hold off the nighttime hours until eight o'clock, so we walked under a chilly and weakly shining sun.

Under our feet, the sidewalk was narrow and uneven, the concrete slabs pushed up, shifted, and displaced by spreading tree roots—mountain ash, cherry, copper beech, and plum—and the few short-lived freezes of the winter. The small painted houses and brick corner stores that we passed had been built on a snug, human scale; they were one and a half stories high and no wider than a few stout paces. They seemed to lean forward intimately as we proceeded, eager to eavesdrop on the discussions of passersby.

Lucy was wearing black high-heeled shoes that pitched her forward, and a finely knit black sweater. She walked with her arms crossed over her chest and her head bent. The lazy early-evening breeze was starting to pick up its pace, and the temperature was dropping steadily. The air was already colder by a degree or two than it had been when we had left the house a half-hour earlier. The sky gleamed soft blue on our left, toward the west, shading to a darker hue, almost purple, over the roofs of the more densely spaced buildings to the east. The sun, pink-streaked where a haze brushed across it, was fattening and turning blush red as it approached the horizon. The sun's rays were being pulled down toward the water, lower and lower. They looked solid, physical, like brilliant metallic threads strung along a loom under the mackerel evening clouds. The dove- and pearl- and abalone-colored clouds gave the sunlight an opalescent sheen, and the slanted, lustrous strands of light caught paint and grass and concrete and fabric at an odd, flat angle, brightening the colors of the houses and the vivid jackets and shopping bags of the people we passed; their faces gleamed yellow-gold in the oblique light like the gilded faces of saints in medieval paintings.

"Gian Luigi doesn't get it. He acts as if he doesn't understand when I tell him what I need. He just can't believe there will ever be any need to change anything," Lucy was telling me. I glanced toward her and saw shards of tears standing brilliant as diamonds in the inside corners of her eyes. She would have been furious if I had said or done anything to suggest I was aware of them. I turned my gaze instead toward the approaching beach and ocean.

"He's completely content for all of us to stay as we are," Lucy went on. Her voice was uneven, her words cautious, as if she were still working out what she thought as she spoke.

"He seems to believe that there's absolutely nothing wrong with staying with his wife and continuing to have me at his beck and call. All his friends do it, he says. And they all think it is some sort of point of honor to stay with their wives, however cowlike and boring and fat and stupid and useless they've become. They think that staying somehow means they haven't done anything wrong, even though they all have someone to fuck on the side. Gian Luigi says that he and his wife and both their families would lose too much face if he were to leave her. She could never marry again. She has got fat, apparently, as big as a house, and she's emotionally dependent on him. And divorce would ruin his career—her father got him his place with the bank. Then there are the three children. The oldest isn't twelve yet and the youngest still wets his bed. He made it clear a few weeks ago that he's in no position to leave. He'd lose everything. Wife, children, family, job, *la bella* fucking *figura*, all of it."

"Is that what you want him to do?" I asked her. "Leave his wife and children?"

"Most of the time, yes."

"But not all the time?"

"I don't want to feel like I was responsible for breaking up his marriage."

"Wouldn't that be his decision?"

"No, it would be mine. He's made it clear that if he left, *if*, it would only be to make me happy."

"Would that make you happy?"

"Yes. I'm tired of getting slices of his time, as if he was a damn pizza. I deserve more. I want a wedding. I want to have a man full-time, a husband. I want to have a child of my own."

"Does he want to have another child?"

"He says he does. That's one of the things that you'd love about him, Maggie. He adores children. In fact—can you believe it?—I found out last month, by accident, he'd left some papers lying around, that he and his wife are still trying to have a fourth. He even admitted that they'd been to see a fertility specialist in Milano, for god's sake. He's such an asshole, Maggie. I'm so fucked up about him."

Lucy ran into Ryan the next day when she was standing on a downtown corner waiting to meet a friend for lunch. She'd known him forever, since they were teenagers and had gone for several summers to the same music camp on Galliano Island. Lucy was a more than adequate flute player, although in the end her talent didn't carry her very far compared to other players who actually practiced. Lucy was wearing her red lipstick, an intense and glistening shade, almost purple, her skinny Italian jeans, a white linen blouse ironed to within an inch of its life, and her high black leather boots. Her fine black sweater was draped around her narrow shoulders.

She saw Ryan through her enormous sunglasses. He was guiding a group of students across the street toward the lobby of an office building. The students were carrying musical instruments in battered cases that were stencilled with the name of their high school. Ryan was dressed like a student too, in baggy jeans, a black T-shirt with a picture of the rock group Marilyn Manson on it, and a red cloth jacket with a broken zipper. Some of the students had broken away from the main group and were crowding around a hot dog stand on the opposite corner. Photocopied pages of sheet music had escaped from their grasp and were dancing along the sidewalk and rushing out into the street, where they were being swept along under the wheels of passing cars.

Lucy helped to round up the papers and students, and then bought sandwiches in a café and sat on a folding chair to watch while the students performed a free jazz concert. Afterward, Lucy went for coffee with Ryan. He had become a professor at the university, teaching in the music department, and he played bass clarinet in the city symphony. He was in charge of the school band only for this one concert, to help out a friend who taught at his old high school who had caught the flu. Ryan and Lucy agreed to meet for dinner that night, and they were together all the time after that until the day came for Lucy to go back to Rome. Ryan drove her to the airport. I have no idea what was said. A few days after Lucy left, Ryan called me to ask for her address in Rome. Lucy had left her sunglasses behind, he said, and he wanted to mail them to her. I could read nothing in his voice.

One morning, a few weeks later, when Lucy was back in Rome, the cappuccino that was thrust across the counter toward her at the narrow bar across the street from her fifth-floor apartment made her stomach clench. Bile filled her mouth, sharp, metallic and sour. Her period should have started, but it had not.

"At first I was pleased," she told me in August after she had moved back to Vancouver to stay. "You know how I suffer, for three weeks out of four at least. I thought things might have slowed down because of the heat, or because I was so busy, or because I had lost a few pounds. You know how easily I lose weight. I have a far better metabolism than you or Janet. Finally, I went into a *farmacia* to buy a pregnancy test. Of course they weren't out on the shelves, like they would be here. That would be too convenient for the customers. They haven't figured out customer service there. Everything has to be this big dramatic transaction, drawn out and awkward and filled with many layers of meaning and possibilities for misunderstanding. So that meant that I had to join the long line of people waiting to talk to the pharmacist. I was concentrating on trying not to throw up—I still thought that I probably just had flu—so it wasn't until I got to the counter that I realized that, although I knew the word for test—*una prova*—I couldn't think of the word for pregnant or pregnancy. I didn't have the strength to go and look it up and then come back again, so I leaned across the counter and said, as quietly as I could, '*Vorrei una prova per . . .*,' which means 'I want a test for . . .,' and then I mimed with my hands having a big belly. 'Ah,' the woman behind the counter cried out, and she smiled and held her hands out in front of her as if she had a bulging stomach. '*La gravidanza!*' Everybody behind me in the line laughed and smiled too, and, after I had my test in a paper bag and had paid, they all wished me *buona fortuna*. One of the women told me that she hoped I would have '*un maschio*'—a boy. That's what it's like there. Life is more of a spectacle. It's such a backwater here. This isn't even a proper city, when you look at it. It's more like an overgrown small town."

"Did you ever consider not having the baby?" I asked her.

"No. Not even once. It feels planted inside me, like a tree. And I am happy to be having it. Thrilled. With or without Ryan."

When Lucy told Ryan on the telephone from Rome that she was pregnant, he asked if she would come back and marry him, and she agreed. She couldn't imagine how she could manage otherwise, how the baby could live with her in her apartment—in truth it was no more than two rooms, including the kitchen-slash-bathroom— how she would work, who would take care of it. And she didn't even want to think about what the effect of the news would be on Gian Luigi. So Lucy told Gian Luigi that she was moving back to Canada without mentioning the baby. He was, she said, very upset, and came as close as he had ever done to suggesting a permanent relationship. He would buy her an apartment in Trastevere, he said, and he promised to spend every second weekend there with her, if only she would wait for him until his children were out of their teens. Lucy calculated what this meant. Since his youngest child was four, what Gian Luigi was asking meant at least a sixteen-year wait. Instead, she gave notice at work, re-sublet her sublet, left the job and city and people she loved, and moved into Janet and John's basement for the few months before the wedding, which was set for December 30. Philip was due to be born on December 31.

It seemed to me to be a very bad sign that Lucy hadn't taken any steps to plan the wedding, aside from a single meeting with a priest at Our Lady of Sorrows, the church that Ryan's parents attended, and where he had gone as a child. Our parents, of course, had taken great pains to ensure that we were raised in absolutely no religion at all. I was in my midteens before I realized that pictures of Madonna and Child referred to a specific mother and a specific child, rather than to motherhood in general. It seemed to me possible that Lucy had set the wedding so far in the future because she wanted to allow enough time for Ryan to change his mind. Lucy didn't make any effort to conceal from anyone, Ryan included, that she was still in love with Gian Luigi, and was marrying Ryan only because it was the sensible, practical thing to do. She implied with every sigh and roll of her eyes that her decision to marry Ryan was evidence of her moral superiority and advanced state of maturity, which should inspire admiration in her family and friends.

Given the inescapable fact of Lucy's pregnancy, Ryan's family priest agreed to marry them even though Lucy wasn't Catholic. "There is still hope for the child, so we must overlook the failings of the parents," was how Lucy reported the interview, acting out his pursed lips, his reproving manner, his hands judiciously knitted over the mound of his stomach. The priest encouraged Ryan and Lucy to move the date forward, in light of the circumstances, but Lucy refused.

She wasn't working. Nothing, she insisted, could match the excitement and thrill of her last, lost job. She was living on her savings, which were substantial, although she had been badly paid—it seems that Gian Luigi had met most of her expenses in Rome—and helping with the twins while Janet spent time with the new baby. She and Janet continued to bicker in a half-spirited way, although now that Janet was so strangely calm all the time, she didn't take or set the bait as often as she used to. Even Lucy didn't seem to have the energy for their old all-out battles. She spent more and more time in the hammock on Janet's porch, reading paperback bestsellers, drinking iced tea, and stroking her expanding stomach.

I would have worried less if Lucy and Ryan had been living together, because that would have given them a chance to find out whether they were what I, no doubt quaintly, thought of as compatible. I would have been reassured even to see them spending more time together. But Ryan was devoting all his spare hours to working on the house they would be moving into immediately after the wedding. They did not plan to have a honeymoon. We'll do something later maybe, Lucy had said vaguely when I asked her one evening what they were thinking. She was reading a fat, blue book called *Divine Secrets of the Ya-Ya Sisterhood*, and she seemed annoyed by my questions. She kept her thumb stuck in the place where she had been interrupted while I waited to see if she would pick up the conversation. She exhaled deeply and dragged her fingers through her hair. "I can't be bothered about all that right now," she murmured. I allowed myself a small responsive sigh and left her alone.

The house they would be moving into was Ryan's, a small, white, one-and-a-half-storey Cape Cod near Trimble Park, several blocks north and west of my parents' house on West 16th Avenue. Ryan had bought it soon after he graduated from university, when the smaller, more rundown houses in that area were still affordable, using as a down payment the money he had earned traveling with a blues band between terms. The band broke up, amicably, in Portland at the end of August before the start of his fourth year, when two of the members decided to hitch up with another band that was headed south to New Orleans, as backup to a women's group that would later achieve a small but not insignificant measure of fame as the Brawling Broads.

Ryan lived in the Trimble house in the provisional, haphazard manner of a bachelor. He had attended to only the most necessary upkeep until wife and child were suddenly imminent. Now he was working hastily to repair the negligence of many years, his and the owners' before him, sanding and scraping paint, patching plaster walls, removing and replacing crumbling insulation. The paint was saturated with lead, and the insulation was friable and laden with dust, ancient cobwebs, and mouse droppings. Ryan and Lucy decided that it would be safer for the baby if she stayed away from the house until the work was done. They were together the few evenings Ryan wasn't working on the house, or performing with the orchestra, or teaching night classes, but all they seemed to do on those rare nights was watch TV on the small set in the corner of Lucy's bedroom in Janet and John's basement.

Lucy had become someone I hardly recognized—inactive and passive. I was afraid that her decision to marry Ryan might be a mistake that could only be undone with great difficulty and pain, that she would be unable to resist blaming Ryan later, and maybe the baby, for taking her from her old life in Rome and replacing it with one that was predictable, conventional, and perhaps loveless. I felt certain, though, that Ryan would not change his mind about marrying Lucy. He adored her. He smiled whenever anyone mentioned the baby, a smile that smoothed his brow, crinkled the corners of his brown eyes, and dug deep brackets in his freckled cheeks.

There is a kind of very nice man who tends to marry short-tempered or self-absorbed, even neurotic, women, maybe because such women provide their lives with some critical measure of conflict and friction, or because this sort of man realizes that he has enough virtue for two. Or it may be that the cheerful expansiveness of such a man makes him unable to believe that the selfishness manifested by the woman he loves is either inherent or incurable. Ryan is this kind of good-souled man, which is why, it seemed to me, he was prepared to put up with Lucy's gloomy inertia.

Janet's husband, John, is another example. John is one of the most sociable people I know. He adores the dynamic, looping intricacies of a good conversation. He dives into talk like a swimmer, leaning in toward the others in an irresistibly attentive and energetic way. He never falls prey to the common male vices of feeling impelled to do most of the talking, or to ensure that his views prevail. John has an astonishing ability to remain his convivial, deft, concentrated self even while working a room. When he throws a party or book launch at his store, he bounces around on his small feet (he is a very large man), managing to spend an equitable amount of time with everyone without appearing rushed or unctuous or superficial or overly adroit. John owns one of the few remaining independent bookstores in the city, and it thrives, not in a major way but consistently. His store is called Niche Books, and the name describes both the small, specialized markets he serves and the interior of the store, which is painted in browns and golds and wine colors, and has wooden cabinets and shelves, most of which John built himself, many nooks and alcoves, and window seats with red-and-black-checked cushion covers. Janet worked there full-time before the twins arrived. She worked part-time after that, and quit altogether when Marie was born. She was also, I finally learned, taking a single, eight-sided yellow Pacicalm every morning and she now appeared to be happier than anyone I knew or have ever known—a change that I found not entirely settling.

"My moods were chemical, Maggie," she told me one day when Marie was four months old. I was visiting her on a Saturday afternoon. The twins were playing around our feet and Marie was sleeping in my arms.

"I felt things slip sideways after I was pregnant with the twins," Janet continued. "I couldn't bear it. I felt as though a gaping black hole was opening up in front of me. But it wasn't until after I had Marie that I knew something was seriously wrong with me. I became more and more convinced that it would be better for the children and for John if I wasn't around anymore. I began to be obsessed with the idea that I had to find a way to disappear, to take myself out of their lives, for their sakes. I found myself scouting out single mothers at the park and at the community center to see if there was anyone who might be a good replacement for me if I could just devise a way to introduce her into our lives before I left. But John realized that something was wrong. He caught me crying in our bedroom and in the kitchen—the stupidest places—and he noticed that I was losing weight. I wasn't eating; I was living on coffee and nerves. He suspected that something was wrong with me physically, and he insisted that I go to see our doctor. I didn't intend to tell her anything, but I had been through a bad day when she saw me. I was at the lowest point ever. I think I weighed less than a hundred pounds. I was a wraith. My hands were shaking, for god's sake. She asked me a few questions. Had I been sleeping? Eating? Thinking about harming myself? It spilled out. All of it. I couldn't have managed much longer. I was coping on the surface, but underneath I was miserable, terrified, sick with anxiety. I didn't feel like a good mother or a good wife or even a good person. Taking care of myself didn't seem to be worth the effort. Some days I couldn't even lift my arm to comb my hair. The doctor said that this depression, or whatever it is, has probably been affecting me all of my life, at least since my early teens. These things are hormonal.

The changes of having children make it far worse for some women. But now I'm fixed. It was that simple. One pill a day, every morning. It's marvelous. I wasn't meant to be unhappy. My chemistry was a little out of whack, that's all."

I have never been in the habit of worrying about myself. I was pleased with my new job at St. Matthew's, which I had discovered I was good at. It was a sea change from being a receptionist, which I had stuck to—amazingly, looking back—for eight years. I had held the job summers when I was going to university and I went back when they needed someone in a hurry right after I graduated. Then somehow I had stayed on for years. The firm had a hard time keeping receptionists. All of the women—I have never met a male receptionist—who had been in the position before me had either married one of the lawyers or clients and quit, or taken the first opportunity that came their way to move "up" into secretarial work, and so the firm was willing—eager—to overpay me.

I was bored from the first day. Remembering people's names, taking coats, and bringing cups of coffee—that strong, cindery law-firm coffee—taking messages, listening with half an ear to the couriers chatter about their drug trips, parties, near-misses in traffic, bruised shins and hearts, and puny paychecks. But, whenever I looked at other jobs, like editing, or even, one time, a position as a trainee insurance underwriter, I found that they either required long hours, or paid terribly, or both. I was able to stand it for so long because I spent most of the time in a kind of trance. I could read novels when things were quiet, which was a good deal of the time, so I spent those years working my way through the nineteenth- and twentieth-century women writers—novelists, poets, essayists, everything. For some reason, mostly men had been taught when I did my English degree. I got an entire second education. I read

Mary Shelley, the Brontës, Virginia Woolf, Margaret Drabble, Margaret Atwood, Alice Munro, Doris Lessing, Joyce Carol Oates, Edna O'Brien, Nadine Gordimer, Jane Smiley, Amy Clampitt, Carol Shields, Barbara Kingsolver, A.S. Byatt, Annie Proulx, Muriel Spark. I was a dreamy, inattentive receptionist, running on automatic, making the appropriate sounds and acting out the expected role. The better part of my mind was always somewhere else entirely.

Aunt Rae's money when it came—twenty-five thousand dollars each for me and my sisters—was large and unexpected enough to pull my head out of my books, an odd and sudden sensation, like a champagne cork jumping clear of the bottle—I could almost hear the pop. I knew it was time to make a change. I ordered brochures from a half-dozen universities and spent several weeks at my desk reading them between hanging coats and connecting calls. I actually got as far as sending in the forms to apply for admission to the graduate English program. That was when Luba found a lump in her breast, and I made the switch to radiation technology. I had the prerequisites, and the course seemed doable and more obviously practical than a higher degree in the arts.

One of the requirements for the students in the program was to have a mammogram ourselves. I was one of the few who did not find it painful. The job of the technician is to arrange the breast and as much of the surrounding tissue as possible on a metal plate. Another plate is screwed down on top of the first, with the tissue pressed out as evenly as possible in between. Then a low-level x-ray beam is sent through the tissue to produce a picture in the form of a flat-film negative. The negative creates a two-dimensional representation of the breast—its lobes, ducts, blood vessels, and soft or fibrous tissues. Soft tissue, such as fat, shows up on the film as gray.

Lobes, fibrous areas, ducts, and tumors, if they are present, show up as whiter areas, crystals of snow in a field of gray granite.

I had never had a mammogram before. Most women don't start having them until they are about forty, depending on their risk factors. One of the other students, a young Chinese-Canadian woman, with a sensitive round face and delicate hands, switched immediately afterward to the pharmacology program. She could not, she said, imagine inflicting such a humiliating, tormenting procedure on anyone. But to me the procedure felt like being stretched and pulled, no worse than that.

Everyone's response to pain is different. There is no way to be sure that any two people feel pain in the same way. So much depends on our idiosyncrasies, how finely attuned our nerve endings are, how tightly or loosely our pain receptors are wired in to our brain and spine and fears. Our responses are entwined with our history and emotions, and are unmeasurable in any case. Even if we did all experience the same stimulus in the same way, there would be no way of knowing it. It is impossible to tease out the physical from the complex overlay of our motivations, anxieties, and tolerances. Pain has a limited and far from perfect vocabulary. I read once about an African language that must have arisen in a country with a great deal of experience with suffering. This language had a word for a malaise as specific as a painful pinching in the armpit. English is much less precise. Not much useful is conveyed by the words "sharp," "searing," "throbbing," or "dull."

Quite a lot of pain arises out of simple fear. I sometimes reassure the more nervous patients who come in for routine screening by reminding them that, although a mammogram can be uncomfortable and frightening, they are far more likely than not to receive a notice in the mail a few weeks later saying that nothing unusual was found. What I don't say, but believe, is that even women who are going to receive very bad news are better off knowing and planning for the worst.

I have also learned that no two sets of breasts are identical. Although of course they mostly follow the same basic template, they come in an expansive range. I have been surprised by how often breasts remind me, oddly, but perhaps appropriately, of food. They can be as lumpy as potatoes, as firm as mangos, as soft as butter, as fine and consistent as white flour, as withered as windfall apples, as dimpled as cottage cheese, as stiff as meringues, as round and dusky as plums, as flat as naan bread, as pliable as dough, as golden as lemons, as dusky as late fall grapes sprinkled with frost and yeast. They come in all colors and sizes. Some breasts are enormous. I remember one woman who raised her sweatshirt and nursed her newborn son for a few minutes to settle him before we started on her mammogram. He was exceedingly small, a preemie perhaps, and as red as a crab. He sprawled out like a minute red spider clinging to the vast expanse of her yellow, pillowy breast. Some women have a scant thimble of breast tissue, or a saucer, teacup, or baseball cap full. Some have breasts with skin so transparent the veins show through, like a roadmap from the heart to the surface. There is an endless array of nipples: red, orange, peach, brown, black, blue, yellow, cream, nipples smooth as a kindergartner's knees, nipples surrounded by tendrils of short, fine hair or ringed in dark fur, nipples the size of dollar coins or larger, nipples as small as a thumbprint, nipples pointed in every direction: forward, downward, upward, sideways, even crossed like lazy eyes. Some women have inverted nipples, which always remind me of seersucker. I have seen several pierced nipples, which I find unsettling—an odd and counterintu-

itive impulse, to poke holes in ourselves. One of the other technicians had a woman come in who had three breasts, two in the normal places and a third, much smaller, below the others. In one of my
textbooks there was a picture of a man with twin rows of rudimentary nipples on his torso, like the buttons on a double-breasted suit.
And, of course, many women have been left with only one breast.

Most women are relatively matter-of-fact about having a mammogram, especially once it becomes routine. But some of them have
an intense and complicated relationship with their breasts. They are
shy about them, or humble beyond all reason. They worry that their
breasts are too small, too large, uneven, lopsided, stretched out, too
low, too high, too far apart, a strange shape, or tipped with the
wrong sort of nipples. A few women actually apologize to me before opening their gown, their hands hovering in the air, shielding
their breasts from impending scrutiny. A lot of fuss over sweat
glands, which is what breasts are, essentially. Enlarged, specialized
sweat glands. Breasts have become loaded with meaning, far more
than they can bear. We are fascinated by them; we interpret them
like a text, men and women both, in much the same way that we
read faces, for signs of sexual availability, modesty, or confidence,
and we label them: beautiful, sexy, maternal, comfortable, thrilling.
A woman's breasts provide balance and ballast. They ornament her,
attract a mate, enhance her sex life, and feed her children.

And they can kill her, which is the reason the women come one
by one with their breasts two by two into the clinic where I work.
The machine that I operate provides a shower of low-level x-rays,
invisible rays of energy that travel though the breast and leave a
record on the film of any dense, irregular areas. Trouble spots show
up as small white specks gathered together like a distant constella-
tion in the breast's gray expanse.

I take infinite care. It is important to me to get it right the first time, to avoid having to call a patient back in. I check and check again to make certain I have produced an accurate picture, one that the radiologist will be able to read readily. Whenever I see any sign of thickening, hardening, or other transformation, my breath catches at the back of my throat and I experience an instant, sympathetic ache inside my ribs. These whiter areas—they look like starbursts in a night sky—will cause the radiologist to frown into the shadowy film, striving to read their meaning, interpret their message. The radiologist may start to consider, even run through the words that may become necessary. How to tell a woman—it is almost always a woman—that her life might just have changed from an orderly unfolding, opening and spreading like the unfurling of a perfectly made origami bird, to something crabbed and closed, clenched tight against the dreadful draining of hope?

It has recently occurred to me, in part because of my somewhat unusual circumstances, that hope is a fundamental part of the human condition, a characteristic inherent in our species. In school as a young girl, I was taught that we are tool users and that we have opposable thumbs—these were the traits that set us apart from the other animals. It has become clear to me that this is not sufficient to define what makes us human, and I have come to think that hope may be the missing and defining element of our natures. Because we have the ability to contemplate the future and compare it to the images our imaginations conjure, and because of our stubborn un-uprootable expectation that the machinery of providence will continue to function, we have hope.

It seems to me not entirely impossible that we might be found to have somewhere in our chests or brains, or in one of the twists of our damp, shiny bowels, an as yet undiscovered gland whose role it is to produce faith in life's outcomes—a rich, oily substance that suffuses our cells and subsumes fear. Although hope often defies common sense, paradoxically, the ability to sustain hope in the face of affliction and tragedy, the ability to place a fundamental level of trust in the world and its offerings seems to be the very hallmark of mental health. Something to love, something to do, something to hope for. Someone, I can't remember who, once said these are the essentials of happiness.

Hope cares nothing, I have noticed, for facts. It is unrealistic, impractical, frivolous, unserious, idealistic, a kind of magician's trick. After it has been folded, spindled, and mutilated, sliced, diced, and scorched, it bursts forth fresh and whole and beautiful, like the spring's first green shoots or a baby's first lusty, longing cries.

A man beside me on my flight back from Italy that time I went to visit Lucy crossed himself hurriedly as the plane took off, in hopes, no doubt, of coming down again safely. I felt the same hope, and it must have sprung from the same place and need, although I kept my hands neatly folded in my lap. My hands have no practice in invoking the gods to provide me with favorable outcomes.

Some of the people I see are very sick, sick beyond the power of words to describe, but few are truly lost to absolute despair. Although they may have spent thousands of hours feeling sorrow, anger, helplessness, and fear, hope seldom seems to leave them entirely. If there are hours when only the most ghostly memory or shadow of hope remains, in time it rushes back like the surging salty tide, sweeping, brave, doughty, optimistic, ridiculous, grand. People from whom hope has retreated—I see them sometimes in the waiting room at the hospital: the husband sitting in one of the orange plastic chairs clenching and unclenching his large, empty, powerless hands; a patient's sixteen-year-old daughter with a pierced, pouting, blood-dark lower lip, and with thick and sullen eyebrows drawn low over flat, anxious eyes; the preoccupied mother in her late fifties whose vibrant daughter is my patient, who reads to her three small, edgy grandchildren as she waits—these people look as untethered as a kite whose string has snapped, as abandoned as a failed farm left unprotected from the scouring wind. Hope has departed abruptly, without notice, and without any promise of ever coming back.

"Never allow your patients to lose hope, even when they are obviously dying," one of my instructors taught us. He reminded us in the next breath not to encourage people who are sick or dying to place their scant store of hope in false treatments or impossible cures or miracles, and instead urged us to remember to encourage hope for other, perhaps attainable, goals. To have time to spend with the people we love. To have the strength to attend to things undone. To have the ability to forgive, and to set aside all bitterness. Not to suffer unduly. Not to die alone.

Mostly, of course, what my patients hope for is life itself. An elderly neighbor of my parents died early last February. In the sweet, soft days of early March, I was surprised to see crocuses sprout all over her front yard, their bright heads bowed as if in prayer to the pagan gods of spring. They were scattered throughout the grass in small haphazard knots and random clusters, rather than tucked away neatly in the flowerbeds or marshaled into straight rows. At first I imagined that my parents' neighbor had planted the bulbs last fall as a kind of joke or cheerful welcome to passersby in the spring since she must have known that she could not possibly expect to be there herself to greet them. It was only recently that it occurred to me that she must have planted them for herself, hoping against all hope to be there to see them on that cold, bright, sunny morning when the first pastel shoots rose up in the grass, as vibrant and brave as flags after a terrible storm.

I have always thought of myself as a lucky person, raised in good fortune, with little need of the consolations of hope. I was lucky to have loving and steady parents. I have always had close friends. I made my way through university with good grades and had even had it suggested by several of my instructors that I might profitably stay on to do graduate work. (One professor was impressed by my paper on the perpetration of myths of masculinity in Mordecai Richler's novels, and talked me into submitting it to a critical journal where it was printed in a thicket of others of its ilk—self-conscious, clever bordering on arch, wider in ambition than in scope.) I had my new job, a wonderful apartment, a genial roommate, books, interests, all the ingredients of happiness. Maybe, it occurred to me to ask myself, I was happy but didn't know enough of sorrow to be certain.

Threshold

$\mathcal{I}$ *do* of course know something of sorrow. Luba's younger sister, Rachel, was my best friend from the day we first met on the sidewalk halfway between her family's apartment above a string of stores on Dunbar and my childhood house on West 16th Avenue. That was a year before we started school together—same class, same day. Rachel died at age fifteen from leukemia when she and I were in grade 10 and Luba, who is older by a year and a half, was in grade 11. During the last few months that Rachel was alive, Luba and I spent increasing amounts of time together, first at the cancer clinic and then at the hospice where Rachel was cared for at the end. We went to school less and less often until, by the middle of May, we weren't going at all. Luba's parents were past caring about her schoolwork, and my parents were committed to letting their daughters make their own important decisions, so no one interfered with our constant attendance on Rachel.

The principal of our high school, Ms. Sydney McArthur, telephoned my parents and Luba's at home toward the end of June, a few days after Rachel died. She passed on her condolences and instructed them to ensure that Luba and I came to her office together the next day at noon. We went unwillingly, full of fury at each other, shocked at the loss of beautiful Rachel, and resentful at be-

ing recalled like children to a school that we both felt we had out-
grown. We sat brimming with our grievances in the hard wooden
chairs in front of Ms. McArthur's desk.

Ms. McArthur was a woman of normal height, but she managed always to impart an impression of great stature and authority. Her spine was permanently riveted upright, and the set of her
head called to mind the antique concepts of carriage, deport-
ment and bearing. She was able to transmit highly detailed, unmistakable messages by elevating a single arched eyebrow or
increasing the depth of indentation of the two lines that ran between her mouth and nose. She fixed her dark eyes on us as we
slumped in our chairs, and sat still, silently regarding us for a full
minute. I began to feel uncertain, conscious that I was not as in
command of the feelings surging inside me as I had thought. I
shifted in my chair and straightened my shoulders. Luba, whose
arms were folded to her chest, held fast to her set expression and
position.

When Ms. McArthur finally spoke, she told us that she had
conferred with one of the physicians at the hospice, a close friend
of hers, and that they had worked together to prepare a project for
the two of us to complete in lieu of our final exams, which we had,
unfortunately, missed along with several weeks of classes. If we
passed it, and if we fulfilled certain other conditions, she would be
willing to consider exercising the discretion invested in her by the
school board to allow us to move up into the next grade. The project, she told us, would test what ability we had to pay attention,
and would measure the extent to which we were able to absorb and
learn from the world, and put what we had learned to practical use.
Part one of the task that had been set for us, a kind of exam, was to
be taken then and there, in her office. She would be back in two

hours, and we were free to confer on our answers. Ms. McArthur handed us a single sheet of typed questions that it appeared we were meant to share, then turned and left the room.

Luba and I, who had privately resigned ourselves to summer school, turned with reluctance and some curiosity to the task we had been set. The questions were peculiar but designed to be relevant to our recent experience. We were asked, given certain stated assumptions, to calculate drug dosages and blood counts. We were to detail the respective roles of doctors and nurses, and to name and describe the tasks of other medical workers. We were to list and describe in detail the stages of sickness and death that we had observed, to illustrate at least four different approaches to pain relief, and to suggest no fewer than ten ways of coping with grief. Finally, on a large sheet of blank paper, we were to sketch our original design for a hospice, with each room and its function and equipment neatly labeled.

We were too surprised and cowed by Ms. McArthur's peremptory tone to protest. We worked together wretchedly, grudgingly, each of us willing the two hours to be over so that we could escape. After Ms. McArthur had collected our responses, however, she told us that she had conferred with our parents and had secured their consent to the rest of the assignment that she had devised for us. Luba and I were to work together to organize a memorial ceremony at the school for Rachel, write Rachel's obituary for the school yearbook, and work as volunteers for the summer at the children's hospital. That is how Luba and I ended up running an art and crafts program for children who came to the hospital, either as patients or as visitors, both that summer and the next. This gave us more time than we needed to work things out between us.

In the last weeks of Rachel's life, we had become jealous of

Rachel's waning attention and energy and, increasingly, sneakily competitive in our efforts to entertain and distract her. We tried to hide our conflicts and disagreements from Rachel, but I am certain now that we can't have fooled her for an instant. How awful it must have been for her to see her only sister and her best friend squabbling over her, like pilgrims over sacred relics, fighting to be most of use, most essential, most dedicated, most appreciated, most loved. Despite our efforts to ease her pain, I wonder whether in the end we only made it worse.

Rachel hated all the ugliness of dying. The loss of her long, dark, curling hair and her thick eyebrows. The yellowish tinge that her skin took on starting around her eyes and spreading all the way to her long toes. For a while, steroids puffed her face out into a parody, a Cabbage Patch doll of a face. When she gave those up, her bones rose relentlessly to the surface of her skin as if they couldn't wait for her to die. She had been a beautiful girl. After April 28, her fifteenth birthday, she refused to comb her thinning hair or even look in the mirror anymore. She stopped insisting on her favorite T-shirts and sweaters and succumbed to the blue hospice gowns. She refused to totter around the corridors with us, or let us curl up on the bed with her to watch *St. Elsewhere*, her favorite television program. She wouldn't have the television on at all. She didn't laugh or smile or talk to us. She glared furiously at the nurses and doctors and her visitors. Only her mother could soften her, sitting by her bedside stroking cream into the scaling skin of her feet and hands and legs.

The day that Rachel died, she had a panic attack. Luba, who was with her when she began to shake and gasp for breath, ran to the nursing station and demanded that they increase her dosage of morphine. The nurses were, however, slow to agree to give her more of the drug until enough time had passed for the most recent dose to take effect. I arrived while all this was going on, ran into Rachel's room, and saw right away that Rachel was frightened—and who could blame her?

I grabbed Luba's arm to get her attention. "She doesn't need any more drugs," I told her. "It's not the pain. She's terrified. Can't you see? She's frightened of what's going to happen."

"Don't be stupid," Luba hissed at me, shaking away my hand. "You have no idea what she's feeling. I'm her sister, not you. The pain is killing her. She can't stand it any more. She needs something to help her rest."

We started to argue. In a moment we were shouting at each other, and we continued to shout while the hospice staff gathered. They simply stood there without intervening. They had undoubtedly seen it before: friends and family trying to control the illness by controlling the details. Luba and I wound up spending that afternoon loathing each other still, but sitting on either side of Rachel, each of us holding one of her hands, trying to talk over her head about normal, everyday things—school, friends, hair, television programs, music. Although Luba kept up her part of the conversation, huge tears, thick and slow as raw honey gathered on her lower lashes until they were heavy enough to fall, then dropped onto Rachel's blanket, where they ran together and created an ugly dark patch on the light blue fabric. I was obdurately proud of my resolution not to cry in front of Rachel. I told myself that it would be selfish to let Rachel see me grieve, that it would lead her to imagine that I was not still hoping for her to recover. I bit my tongue and the insides of my cheeks hard—more than once I tasted blood—but I didn't allow myself even a single tear.

In the evening, about an hour after her parents had arrived at the hospital from the dry-cleaning business they ran together, the nurses adjusted Rachel's intravenous line and she fell into a drugged and anxious sleep that she never woke up from. That's what I remember of Rachel, although I wish I didn't—the bitter argument over her wasting, passive body. She was so thin by then, stick bones thinly covered by dry, peeling skin, with deep bruises, red and yellow, all over her long arms and legs. When I drew near her from my chair beside the wall, I could detect a change in her breath. For weeks, her breath had smelled like mildew and damp earth. Now, it smelled sharp, medicinal, bitter, like frozen poisonous berries.

I sat with Rachel's family and listened to her struggle her way through an increasingly irregular sequence of shuddering breaths. They sounded as if they contained long, complicated messages, like Morse code. She dragged gasps of air into her lungs by force, by will, and held on to them for longer and longer stretches, until, finally, close to midnight, she stopped trying. We kept the lights on in her room, and sat quietly, the four of us, for a long time after her rough, raw breathing fell into a silence that went on and on and on. I didn't experience what I had been told I might feel, a sense of release, of relief. Instead, I went cold with fear for Rachel, who was going into darkness forever. A chill rattled through me. My jaw clenched, my muscles tightened, and I shook and ached all over, in my joints, in my skin, in my nails and hair and core. The loss of Rachel seemed bottomless and pitiless and utterly without meaning, without any possibility of redemption or significance.

A very young, dark-skinned doctor came into the room. He wore a white scrub coat and glossy black loafers, and he held a clipboard and chart loosely, like a prop, in his hand. He looked Arab or Iranian. He glided to the bed in his soft polished shoes, imperturbable, unhurried. He pressed his long, fine fingers against the chalky skin of Rachel's neck and then placed the palms of his

hands together and stood beside her with his head bowed, not pray-
ing, but respectful, allowing the silence to gather and thicken. I
wanted to rise and lean into him. His shoulder looked in that moment like the one place in the world where I most longed to rest my
head. But I remained sitting straight in my chair beside the wall,
balancing my heavy, buzzing skull on my stiff neck, a spectator to
the frozen, timeless tableau of doctor, family, and surrendered
child.

In addition to this, my greatest loss, I have had my heart seriously shattered twice. Once, at age twenty-one, by my boyfriend for
three of my university years, Chris Andrew Tolnoy, who I met in a
first-year biology lab. Chris wrote me a letter during the summer
holidays between our third and fourth years to tell me that he had
fallen in love with an Austrian girl named Kirsten, whom he had
met while traveling in Greece.

Chris grew up in Montreal speaking Hungarian at home,
French in the streets, and English at school. He was studying modern languages in university: Russian, Italian, Spanish, Greek and
Hebrew. He had already learned French and Latin in high school.
Chris achieved everything he set out to do. He bicycled across the
Rockies to a job in Calgary and back again the summer after high
school. A year later, his leg was badly broken when another com-
petitor in a mountain bike race crashed into him, and he used the
weeks that he was laid up to teach himself to play a fourth-hand violin by listening to tapes of Cape Breton fiddlers. Whenever my
car, an '82 Toyota that had cost me $700, broke down, which it did
frequently, he would find the parts at a junk dealer and make the repairs himself. He left me with the illusion that men are capable of
doing everything.

A few years ago, when I was twenty-eight, Geoffrey Morrison, whom I had agreed to marry (despite what I came to see afterward were serious doubts), asked for his mother's ring back two months after our engagement, saying that he wanted to take it to a jeweler to have it cleaned. The next day, without any word to me about the matter, he moved to Ottawa where he had accepted a job as executive assistant to a Conservative member of Parliament, and he refused to take my calls or reply to the letters and e-mails I sent. After a month of sobbing on my bed, I bought two dozen long-stemmed red roses, left them on newspaper out in the sun on the balcony until the petals were tea-brown and the leaves bitter black, then wrapped them up carefully in white tissue paper and had them delivered to him at work. I longed to do worse, to telephone the press or his party with some truths I knew about Geoffrey. That he had admitted to me that he had smoked dope all through high school, and, by grade 12, was dealing it too. That he once confused two similar names and thus voted by mistake for the Communist Party candidate for city mayor. That his fear of acquiring a pot belly caused him to turn sideways, inhale deeply, and conduct a full-body inspection whenever he passed a full-length mirror. But, so far, my only other act of vengeance has been to take delight in the fact that his M.P. has been a dud, a solid underachiever.

I think now that I decided to marry Geoffrey, who I never trusted enough really to love, because he was tall, blond, imperious, and self-assured. He looked like a spy or a concert pianist, especially when he wore a black turtleneck, which he did often. I understood that he had enough force of personality to keep a marriage together through sickness and health and the rest of it, even if my commitment or feelings were to vacillate. He had fine, golden hair all over his body, and the thick thighs and forearms of a rower. When we made love, he liked me to resist him. He would seize my wrists and hold my hands above my head and push against and into me until my entire body felt abraded and possessed. His kisses were weak and superficial, though, almost sisterly. I sometimes think now that this should have tipped me off to the flaws in his character.

Since Geoffrey, I had gone out with different men and had been in two tentative relationships, each lasting a few months, but nothing had taken root, and this nothingness was beginning to make me feel like an emotional shadow person, incapable perhaps of forming new serious attachments, my heart as purposeless and absurd as a red balloon slowly releasing its helium the day after a party. One evening in the middle of September, my sister Janet noticed that I had tears in my eyes after I had been tumbling on the carpet with her four-year-old twins, Thomas and Claudia.

"What's the matter, Maggie? They can't have hurt you, can they?" She gazed at me with the kind of concern that she had only begun to demonstrate since she had started taking her little pills.

"No. No. It's nothing." My next words spilled out before I could stop them. "It's just that no one ever touches me any more."

When I left Janet's house a short while later, she pressed a small plastic bag into my hands, the kind that zips up with a sliding plastic fastener. "Just in case," she said conspiratorially. I opened the bag a few days later when I rediscovered it at the bottom of my purse. Inside, wrapped in a tissue, were three octagonal, unnaturally bright yellow pills with the letter P stamped on them. Janet had given me a gift from her small precious store of Pacicalm, which I knew her cautious physician doled out to her as if they were as addictive as heroin, which in a way they were, of course.

You might think that there would be a lot of physical contact in my work. But the bulky equipment and the solemn implications of being tested for a fatal illness diffuse what might otherwise be a very intimate encounter. Many women scarcely register me as another human instead of a medical device or perhaps a cyborg in a white lab coat. And I am very respectful of my patients' dignity and privacy. I am careful to drape the areas I am not directly examining with sheets and gowns, and I wear latex gloves when I arrange the breasts on the plates. I maintain eye contact with those who appear to want it, although many don't seem to. I strive for a point of perfect balance between being caring and attentive on the one hand and keeping the procedures professional and impersonal on the other. A few of the women are up-to-date on the latest research and ask intelligent questions, most of which I am required by our rules to leave to the referring physician to answer. Some patients want to talk about nothing in particular—the weather, traffic, recent pieces of news. At least once every day, sometimes more often, a woman breaks into tears. After a few days or weeks of waiting for her appointment, she is convinced that she knows already what might be revealed.

Not so long ago, even as late as when I was a child, serious illnesses were not freely spoken of. Cancer in particular operated as furtively in society as it does in the body, under the surface. I have always thought that this was courtesy run amuck, misplaced, exaggerated manners, but it might just as likely have been fear and a healthy sense of respect for an implacable enemy, especially when remedies were fewer and more insidious. I wonder what people felt then at a diagnosis of cancer? Not shame, I think, but something close to it, an appalled, shocked silence over how strictly we are at the mercy of messy, ungovernable biology after all, despite our claim to lives of thoughtfulness and order.

These days, cancer is acknowledged, although its terror has not ebbed. It seems to be everywhere. I saw over the course of a few weeks a patient who wrote sonnets about her cancer on scraps of paper that she kept crammed into her purse. She would pull them out and read them, or open her notebook and start a new one.

"Sonnets turn somewhere in the middle," she told me, when I asked about her poems. "From the specific to the general; from the facts to the ideas or theory behind the facts. It's the same kind of turn, don't you think, that cancer can take, when the cells either retreat or prevail. Your life can shrink or expand, just like that, between one day and the next."

My patients with cancer are foreigners sojourning in the uncharted territory of ill health and forced to acquire its ungainly, unsought vocabulary, in the same way that when we travel to a strange country we must learn the necessary local words of daily life. Cancer's vocabulary comprises what strike me as the most austere, sere words our language contains. Ducts. Nodes. Blood counts. Biopsy. Surgery. Chemotherapy. Radiotherapy. Metastasis. This is the language that connects the patients I see to their doctors, nurses, and physiotherapists, and to other people who are living or dying with cancer. Cancer makes us expert in the many ways that our fascinating, underappreciated, beautiful, unreliable bodies can go awry.

I provide the kind of comfort we are permitted to provide. That is, I cannot say the words every woman longs to hear: "Everything will be all right." Because everything may not be all right. Seeing me may be an early stage of getting used to a new state of things being not at all all right. I have seen how people at a loss look to anyone around them for clues about how they should act, how they should carry on, manage, until they can work out how to be. I can't, am not permitted to offer reassurance, so what I do is carry myself in a carefully calibrated way, in the manner of someone who is coping well and bravely despite a personal sorrow, almost as an example of what might be possible. This requires a cautious, measured response to people and their concerns. But, when I look at the films that develop in the clever machines I operate, and see that there may well be cancer, and when the woman is young, with perhaps a child or two playing in the waiting room, or if she has already lost one breast, or if she is old or alone or without resources, then I long to bring my forehead down to hers, to press our brows together, like a promise, like a mother, and whisper to her, "Oh, how I wish I could lift this from you."

Front Door

The nights after I took Rebecca's quiz, I slept badly. I felt unsettled, as if the clockwork of my body had unwound or subtly slipped out of gear. Something I had taken for granted seemed to have been shaken loose or shattered.

On Friday night, I stayed up late with Rebecca, worrying over the questionnaire. On Saturday morning I got up early to climb Grouse Mountain with Luba. Saturday evening, I became caught up in a book of short stories by Frederick Busch and didn't put it down until I had finished the last story, well after one o'clock. After I turned off my light, my thoughts began to wander without purpose in the gray, yawning space that expanded like foam between my closed eyes and my brain. It took a long time, well over an hour, before I fell into a kind of busy half-sleep, too turbulent and disturbed to be restful. Chaotic fragments of dreams, colorful and shifting like the glass fragments in a kaleidoscope, resolved after a while into a vision of Rome, where I had gone once to visit Lucy and had become deliciously lost in the labyrinthine streets of the historical central city.

I walked in my dream in streets that became narrower and narrower, until the walls of the buildings were no more than a shoulder-width apart. I pushed through a narrow opening between two red walls that gave way as I pressed against them, like flesh, and found myself in a cavernous library. I wandered along miles of echoing shelves, in search of someone to direct me through the thickets of books to something I could not name but wanted urgently. When I was upon it, whatever it was, the library dissolved into a series of damp, echoing rooms like the changing rooms at the swimming pool I used to go to. All night long I roamed these humid, tiled rooms, which expanded into a never-ending sequence of corridors. I moved from room to room, fully dressed, ankle-deep in warm, chlorinated water. The dream was so vivid that when I woke up, I was amazed to find my feet dry and hot under the blankets.

On Monday morning, one of the other technicians stopped me as I passed by in the staff cafeteria. I was carrying a cup of coffee back to my office before my first appointment.

"You look a bit pale, Maggie," he said. "Are you feeling all right?"

"Yes, I'm fine. I've had a few late nights. But I have a relatively quiet week ahead, so I'll be able to catch up. I'm OK, really."

Later in the day, one of the radiologists paused after reviewing a report with me. He scrutinized my face. "You look different today. More relaxed. You must be getting used to the pace around here. Relentless, isn't it?"

"Oh, no. I like it here. Sorry, if I seem slow. I just need a good night's sleep."

When I had seen my final patient and written up the last set of notes, I made my way through the glass doors at the front of the hospital and out onto Burrard. The day had been unseasonably warm and close. Stray clouds cluttered the skies. They hung heavy and low, compressing the air and straining light and energy from the sun. I felt weighed down by humidity and fatigue. I had eaten a slice of toast at the apartment that morning, but I had drunk far too many cups of coffee during the day and I couldn't remember what I had had to eat for lunch. There had been a few crises and no time for breaks.

I turned right instead of left after reaching the bottom of the steps at the front of the hospital, electing the longer route home. I was hoping to catch the fresh winds that often sweep into downtown from off the water a few blocks to the north. The area of Vancouver between the hospital and the apartment is densely inhabited, but the streets are straight and wide and clean, the sidewalks broad, the traffic orderly, and the pedestrians few, so the overall effect is of a city that is overbuilt and underpeopled. Vancouver is frequently sluiced clean by rain, and although its crisp edges are often masked in fog and the gray gloom that collects under the thick clouds, there is nothing to suggest secrets or intrigue or introspection. This is a plain, frank city, displaying no more complexity or difficulty than a well-oiled simple engine. Most of the people I walked past looked like me: fit, employed, purposeful, and, if not acutely conscious of their good fortune, at least aware that things could be very much worse.

A church occupies much of the first block north of the hospital. On a whim, I broke my stride halfway along this block, and turned up the wide, worn stone stairs leading up to the church. Its massive doors were closed. I had a moment of certainty that they would be locked, but one of them yielded to a strong pull. I went through and stepped inside. The interior of the stone building was cooler and dimmer than I had expected and it took a moment for my eyes to adjust. There was an odd smell, unthreatening but strange, like the awkward embrace of an almost stranger, an elderly uncle, perhaps, who smells of mothballs and stale aftershave and breath freshener. The church had a musty odor made up of old carpet, wet stone, damp wool, ancient dust, and elderly hymn books. The calm, cool semidarkness was a strong contrast to the hectic activity of the hospital and the warm air outside. For a moment I felt the floor pitch underneath my feet, while patches of color, dark and light, swam in front of my eyes. I wiped my palms against my hips and then brought my hands close together at a spot just beneath my breasts. I blinked twice to clear my gaze, stepped forward, and began to look around.

I had been in places of worship rarely—for weddings, baptisms, a few funerals, and as a tourist in Italy when I went to visit Lucy. Our parents had purposefully raised my sisters and me in no religion at all, and none of us had ever taken the least interest in it. I had a vague sense that I was allowed—perhaps even expected—to look around and take note of the church's architectural elements, which were listed and described in brochures stacked on a table near the door that I had come through. But I felt that my rights as a nonbeliever were subject to strict if unwritten limits—that I had, for example, no right to sit in a pew or reach for a moment of peace or transcendence or oneness with God, or whatever it is that churchgoers strive for.

I began at what the brochure called the narthex, and walked slowly up the long aisle on the east side of the church, then across the front of the church near the altar, and back down the west aisle. I looked most closely at the windows, through which the sunlight strained, filtered and brilliantly colored, and the ceiling, which the booklet informed me was barrel-vaulted, and was the largest of its kind west of Winnipeg.

I stopped in front of the last stained glass window and tipped my head back to take it in. It was constructed in pinks and gold, yellow and reds, and it showed a seated woman with a pale yellow face. She was wearing a blue robe over her pink dress. The hood of the robe obscured her hair, but not her expression, which was one of refusal. She held one yellow hand up, palm forward. She seemed to be trying to ward off a broken stream of light that streamed in a pattern of streaks and dashes, like a kind of code, from the pulsing red heart of a dove that was flying toward the woman through a mullioned window made of gold and yellow panes that appeared at the top left-hand corner of the window—a window in a window.

The broken line of white light went straight through the woman's raised hand and entered her right ear, which could just be seen under a fold of her blue hood. The dove was trailing pale blue and gold ribbons and he thrust his scarlet heart before him like a badge pinned to his ash-colored breast. The woman's other hand held a lily, tall, white, yellow, and green. A weighty book lay open on her blue-and-pink lap. Behind her was another window, through which could be seen a stone wall encircling a garden. An iron gate set into the stone wall was closed shut. The woman's minute, slippered feet peeked out from under her blue gown; they glowed red, like jewels lit from within.

"Beautiful, isn't it?" I was startled by a voice quite close behind me.

I turned and made out a shadowy figure dressed in black and patterned over with shifting green spots, afterimages of the red panels in the window.

"I'm sorry. I didn't mean to startle you. I noticed your interest in that particular window. It's always been my favorite." The speaker was a man, deep-voiced and tall; his words spilled down from above my head.

"It's Mary, isn't it? She looks terrified."

"Well, wouldn't you be? She can't have been more than fourteen years old. And she's just been told she's going to have God's baby. What a responsibility."

"You get the idea that she would rather go on reading her book, that she didn't welcome being interrupted."

"Do you see how cleverly the picture is put together? How her face glows in the light that appears to be coming through the small window at the top? The guys who did this knew what they were doing. They were a pair of brothers, fresh from Italy, not ten words of English or a dollar between them when they arrived. Salvatore and Aurelio Gualtieri. They did a few of the windows over in St. James Cathedral too. They were Catholic, of course, but they went wherever the work was. They even did a Masonic lodge over on East Hastings. Good thing too. Most of their work in Italy was destroyed in World War II. Virtually all that is left from a lifetime of work is here in this city."

"Are they famous?"

"No, not at all. They were my great-uncles. Their father and his father and who knows how many of their fathers before that were members of a glass guild back in Italy. Not that there were many Italian stained glassworkers. The big centers were in Belgium, France, and England. The brothers had to go all the way to Brussels to get their training. But they brought what they learned back to Italy, and traveled from church to church. A lot of repair work. Some original work. They carried on doing what they knew after they arrived in Canada. The windows weren't enough to pay their way, of course. This isn't Europe. There aren't cathedrals on every street corner, and there were no shattered windows from the war to repair. So they worked full-time over at the hospital, one in the kitchen, the other as a janitor."

The man fell silent and we stood looking at the window. I could see now that it contained hundreds of pieces of glass, some as small as my thumb. An enormous amount of work.

"I'd better get going," I said. "I just stopped in on my way shopping." I took care not to mention that I worked at the hospital or that I was within walking distance of home. "Thank you for telling me about the window. Your uncles did a wonderful job."

"Go see their Annunciation at St. James, if you haven't already. You might like Mary's expression there better."

I smiled and nodded. I could just make out the white streak of the smile he gave me in return, and the dark thicket of his hair, as I brushed past him—he didn't step aside—and made my way out of the church. I had a glancing impression of a very tall man, handsome in an old-fashioned way, like the father in a 1960s sitcom, square-jawed, good and reliable, earnestly straightforward. Not the kind of man likely to lie in wait for stray women in a downtown church in the late afternoon. I wondered about him as I walked home, until it occurred to me that of course he must be the priest or minister or deacon—I wasn't certain of the nomenclature of the clergy. He had seemed too articulate to be the church custodian, although that was possible too, of course. I had been rude, it occurred to me, not to ask. But if he had been a minister, I might have been expected to call him by his proper title when I left. Brother? Father? Reverend? Sir?

My eyes adjusted slowly to the fading light as I walked home. For a block or two, when I blinked, images from the window were projected against the backs of my eyelids. Mary's long, sallow, dismayed face. Her tiny, tidy slippers. The sharp silvery beak of the soaring bird.

I had seen other Annunciations in art history books, and I remembered the story, although I couldn't remember having seen one

with a bird in it before. I remembered seeing angel messengers in
other depictions of the Annunciation, beautiful, upright young
creatures, neither man nor woman, with pageboy hair, and elaborate, furled wings, usually with one arm outstretched to reassure
and greet the frightened girl. God's angel—Gabriel?—has come to
earth to announce to a very young Mary—Miriam—that she has
been chosen to bear God's son. Mary is horrified at first, but then
yields. The locked garden represented her virginity. The white lily
stands for her purity. I half-remembered reading somewhere that
some theological group of men whose job it was to consider such
things had decided that Mary got pregnant through her ear, liter-
ally by means of the word of God. But I had forgotten the meaning
of the book she held, if I had ever known it. I would like to have
known if she ever had the chance to finish it.

Entryway

Later that week, Luba received a telephone call from Mike, one of the two men who had shared our table at the mountaintop café. They agreed to meet after work on Friday, and Mike suggested she bring me along, since his friend might very likely come along too. I agreed to go, more as a favor to Luba than out of any interest in Mike's friend, whose name both Luba and I had forgotten. Stan? Al? Cal? Frank? His name didn't matter, since he failed to show up, which left me sitting awkwardly with Mike and Luba as they talked.

Mike was in insurance, he told Luba, although he had a degree in anthropology. What he wanted to do was save up enough money to retire at fifty-five, a goal he was well on his way to fulfilling, thanks to tech stocks—which he was into heavily and he could recommend a few if we were interested—and return to a small island north of Samoa, where he had done fieldwork as an undergraduate, to live with "his" tribe, a small band who maintained a subsistence existence fishing and foraging for edible roots in the jungle.

"I have always felt in sync with their ways," he said, taking a large swallow from his second Granville Island Lager.

"Their ways," Luba repeated.

"Exactly. They are a happy, carefree people. They are not attached to possessions, but to the earth, which they share in common. They enjoy each day. Their food. Their families. Of course, they don't experience the same level of attachment that we do. Life is too precarious for that. They accept death as we would a common cold. Cycle of life. Rhythm of Mother Earth. That kind of thing. Should we order the nachos?"

"How do you know they're happy?" I couldn't resist interjecting.

"Oh, they are constantly singing, smiling, dancing, even at funerals. Especially at funerals. I was back a couple of years ago with my wife. My *ex*-wife. Terrible woman. Only out for one thing, money. A real piece of work, I tell you. They perform for tourists now. The tours, which I helped to organize, have had a wonderful effect. The opposite of what you might expect. Reenacting the old ways has preserved their way of life just as it was."

"Just as it was?" Luba echoed.

"Exactly. Only more so. They have resurrected some of the old songs and dances. Well, their interpretation of the old dances. They weren't recorded back then, unfortunately. I was supposed to be working on that when I was with them, but I ended up spending more time with the men learning about their hunting techniques. Male bonding kind of thing. Very profound. They used to hunt a large marsupial there, the kaba kaba. But it has, unfortunately, been hunted into extinction. I killed one myself in 1994. One of the last, in fact. And the language has been mostly lost, so they sing in English. It comes across well, actually. And they have different costumes these days. The old ones were too drab to appeal to the tourists. They're more Polynesian now. And they do the lei thing, putting garlands of flowers around tourists' necks. We bring them in from Hong Kong. Plastic, but you can't tell from a distance. Tourists love that shit, eat it up."

"And you see yourself going to live there among them?" I asked.

"Well, not exactly among them. I'm too old to go without my creature comforts. Not that I'm old, I'm forty-five, still a spring chicken. But there's a resort not far from there, no more than a couple of hours by jeep. Kind of a Club Med kind of thing, but more exclusive. You can get a condo there, right on the links. I've already bought one through a company I've incorporated in Barbados. This company—I own a large chunk of it—runs tours to the old tribe. Sort of a New Age ecotourist kind of thing. People are looking for this kind of integrated, holistic experience. It's very healing to be around so much joy. Redemptive, even. There are condo time-shares available, in case you girls are ever interested. Here's my card."

"Maybe I should book a trip," I commented, unable to keep a dry edge out of my voice. "It's been suggested to me recently that I need to up the happiness quotient in my life."

"Exactly!" Mike enthused. "We all do. Happiness is what we all need. Now. Today. The pursuit of happiness was good enough for our ancestors. They had, after all, low expectations. If they lived to fifty, they were doing good. Times have changed. We want more. We work hard—we deserve more! What people expect these days is happiness without the pursuit of. Off the shelf, so to speak. Ready-made."

"Prefab happiness," Luba suggested.

"Like a suit off the rack," I added.

"Great! Yes, exactly. You girls do get it. Any man who can deliver up happiness to order, like a pizza, that man will be richer than Gates. You should think about the time-share thing. A good investment, look at it that way."

"Sorry. Sorry. Sorry. Sorry. Sorry," Luba said to me as soon as we left the bar. We had explained to Mike that no, we couldn't join him for dinner, that we had a previous engagement. "A dinner party. A women-only thing," Luba had told him. "You know how it is." Mike was jovial in our rejection, and had elected to stay at the bar by himself. "You never know," he said, winking broadly at us and looking pointedly at a nearby table at which four twenty-something women were sitting. "Life is full of surprises."

"It's not your fault," I told her. "His parents, on the other hand. They have some explaining to do."

Hall

$\mathcal{I}$ *went through* another week of sleeping no more than five or six hours a night. I would go to bed at a reasonable hour, between ten and eleven o'clock, and read for a few minutes until my thoughts began to loosen and flicker and the type on the pages began to slip out of focus. Slowly, carefully, I would set aside my book and reach to turn off the light. No matter how much care I took not to jar loose the first seeds of sleep, with their tentative random shoots, darkness catalyzed my mind into life and the space behind my closed eyelids would begin to seethe and ferment with scraps of ideas and unfocused images.

The busy, crawling sensation reminded me of the time when I was very small, perhaps five or six, and I told my doubting mother that I could hear busy, buzzing noises inside the fireplace in the living room. She laughed and said that what I was hearing was my own breath and blood rushing inside my head and echoing in the empty chimney when I placed my ear next to the fireplace—the same noise, she explained, that you hear when you hold a glass or shell up to your ear. (I remember my passing shock at learning in this chance way that the noise inside a shell was not the sea at all, as grown-ups always pretended, and as I had more than half-believed.) But I was insistent. I tried to explain that it sounded to me like hundreds of long-clawed restless rats were living in our chimney, where they scurried and bustled without cease.

After a day or two, my mother finally gave in to my pestering and agreed to come and listen. She followed me to the fireplace, went down on one knee, and bent to listen. The exaggerated curve of her body and the smile on her face as she tipped her head were proof that she was only humoring me. (Children are experts at reading body language, since their understanding of the spoken word is still imperfect.) I saw her pose and the cant of her head change when she too heard the noise. She frowned, and then went to the phone and called in an exterminator, who came that afternoon and injected a smoky chemical into the flue. Afterward he extracted in pieces a large papery structure, a wasp's nest. A good thing we hadn't lit a fire, he told my mother, or we would have set fire to the chimney, and possibly the roof besides.

For days afterward, displaced wasps swarmed dazed around the outside of our house until they found another home in a neighbor's hedge at the end of the block. He was badly stung two weeks later when his hedge clippers sliced into their new nest. For months afterward, I felt keenly my mother's guilt, and mine, for having failed to let him know that our wasps had taken up residence there. Our culpability felt to me to be exactly equal—I hadn't known that hedges were clipped, and my mother hadn't known that our evicted wasps had moved into the neighbor's hedge.

I felt that I needed a similar extraction from my active nighttime head. It felt like the year I was in grade 1, when I came home from school each day with my head stocked with new information of all kinds, information that I felt I had to tamp down firmly in the hours before I went to bed so that it would adhere and still leave room for the next delivery at nine o'clock the next day. The busy, overfull sensation of something new inside my head, something startling or intriguing or mysterious or wonderful, the effervescence of fact and information percolating, catalyzing a brew of thoughts and ideas. Now, all night, whether I was awake or asleep or on the slippery riverbanks of the in-between, my brain seethed with thoughts and scenes, teased by the blunt root ends of emotions and caressed by the soft, tendril fronds of half-remembered sensations.

After many nights, I began to recognize recurrent images that came to me in my short dreams. The steamy labyrinth of tiled rooms. A shop I would stumble on that had racks and racks laden with clothes in brilliant colors and flamboyant styles, all of them my size, all of them to be tried on. A trap door under Rebecca's desk that led to secret passages and new rooms in the apartment, rooms that I had never been aware of. Watching a young man drive past me on a moped, with gilded plaster winged infants, *putti*, tucked under his arms, head forward, the wings and body and feet behind the crook of his arms. This last was something I had actually seen, on Via dei Pettinari in Rome, two blocks from Lucy's apartment. The man was dressed in the white, soiled coverall of a manual laborer; he was undoubtedly working on the restoration of a nearby church or *palazzo*. In my dreams, though, the man on the moped wore a brown robe like a monk and had his face obscured by a dark hood, and the *putti* were squirming and kicking like babies.

During the day, my tiredness became increasingly familiar, like a long, white, finely knit, all-enveloping, and constricting gown that had been sewn around me. When I moved, I felt as if I were awash in something heavier and more resistant than air, sweeter and more liquid and viscous than water. I stopped going to the swimming pool for my daily swims, since the warm water and aqueous motion seemed redundant; I was swimming all day long. Sometimes my hands and feet tingled and buzzed.

I thought, too, that I might be becoming more forgetful. Once or twice, I forgot to bring my lunch to work. The dry cleaner had to call and leave a message to remind me about my gray suit, which I had left to be cleaned in September. I felt slower, languid, a little distracted, but lack of sleep had few other noticeably adverse effects on my customary reliable good health. In the mirror each morning, my face looked little different from usual—round, full, watchful. Perhaps a little paler, that was all. My skin remained smooth and clear. Notwithstanding the steady withdrawal of sleep, I felt increasingly calm and peaceful, as if I had taken one or two of Janet's pills, which were still, as it happens, tucked away in their clear zippered bag at the bottom of my purse. I was certain that I would never need to take them, and I would have returned them to Janet, except that I didn't want her to think that her gift had not been appreciated. She had meant it kindly, and I couldn't bear to reject one of her rare sympathetic gestures.

I started waking earlier every day; at six, then five-thirty, and then a few minutes sooner every morning, until I was regularly entirely awake at four o'clock and unable to go back to sleep. One morning I got up, put on old jeans and a sweatshirt, and removed every speck of dust from the apartment except for the room where Rebecca slept. With a damp cloth, I polished the furniture with broad sweeps. Then I tied the cloth around the bristles of the broom and swept underneath my bed, teasing out the substantial, almost corporeal accumulations of hair and dust that had gathered in the previously undisturbed darkness. Clearly the efforts of the cleaner who came weekly didn't extend to hidden places. Some of the feathery bundles were so large that I thought I might hear them bleat in protest at being brought to the light of day. I cleaned a film of sooty dust from the slatted air vent covers in my bedroom and in the living room and scrubbed the floor under the oven and re-frigerator—other places in which the cleaner had not taken any interest. I even removed the back cover from the hard drive of my computer and squirted a jet from a can of compressed air (difluo-roethane, according to the label) into the fan housing. Several short blasts dislodged a thick, feltlike coating of dust from the blades of a tiny fan. When I put away dust cloths, brooms, and rags, I had a clear sense that I had accomplished something meaningful, on however small a scale. I half-remembered a sentiment from a poem I had studied in university, although I could not recall the lines exactly.

We are discarded oddments of creation.
Minute in size and span against the skies.
But take our measure from what we despise.
And thus assure ourselves of God's affection.

Our fates lie in the stars, not in the ground.
And we are great, complex, and nobly bound.

My sense of achievement, even elation, shriveled, however, when I looked at my bedside clock and saw that I had used up little more than an hour. Obviously I couldn't pursue dust every morning unless I became obsessive. I began to switch on my bed-side light as soon as I woke up—an old pink-and-white milk glass lamp from my childhood, although I had replaced the pink ruffled shade with a plain one made of heavy linen—and read from one of the books I kept in a basket beside my bed. After a time, a couple of hours or more, the light would begin to seep in through the blinds, thinly at first, as if the slatted blinds were straining and reducing it, then more strongly—gray or pink or golden, depending on the impending weather.

I read Nabokov's memoir, *Speak, Memory*, early one morning and came across a description of his hatred for the simple act of falling into sleep, his statement that "the wrench of parting with consciousness is unspeakably repulsive." I wondered then whether something similar to this aversion to the loss of awareness was what made my clever younger sister Lucy so reluctant to sleep as a child, and whether it had some relationship to the small but intense stab of panic that I felt when I startled awake each day.

One dim October morning, I reached into the bookshelf for my old copy of *The Bell Jar*, and found the passage in which Sylvia Plath wrote of a girl who is moving toward madness and who ceases to sleep entirely.

I hadn't slept for twenty-one nights.

I thought the most beautiful thing in the world must be shadow, the million moving shapes and cul-de-sacs of shadow. There was shadow in bureau drawers and closets and suitcases, and shadow under houses and trees and stones, and shadow at the back of people's eyes and smiles, and shadow, miles and miles and miles of it, on the night side of the earth.

I felt reassured by this, since it suggested that my sleeplessness might not after all mean that I was losing my mind. Instead of shadow, sleeping less was making me more keenly aware of the light. I felt conscious of it all the time, from every angle, in all its shades and durations, when and how it arrived and its exact gradations as it slipped away. In the late autumn this far north, the light falls aslant during the day and drains rapidly, like a cup overturned, as evening approaches. The days shed minutes and hours on their forced march toward the end of December, like a cylinder leaking at both ends. The day's light is left distilled, weak, watered down as if to make it last through the winter, tinged an unnamable color somewhere between hope and despair, composed of equal parts gray, salmon, and beige.

One day, a young girl stretched her hand out to me as I walked past her on my way to work. I had seen her often. She was regularly sprawled on this particular city corner and she seemed sometimes even to sleep there. I had on occasion placed a small amount of money into the plastic tub she kept on the sidewalk beside her folded legs, but she had never acknowledged me before. Usually she sat on her folded sleeping bag staring intently at the pavement, as though it were a television or computer screen, the source of the answers to whatever questions vexed her. She was about sixteen or seventeen, and very thin. She had thick, tangled red hair, like matted fleece or wet felt, more like the fur on an untended animal than hair on the head of someone's daughter. Her face was long and narrow, with a heavy jaw and forehead, and her skin was mottled red over yellow, under a layer of gray dirt. She always wore the same thick black wool sweater, which was faded and pilled and stained, and heavy leather boots, cracked at the instep; one dirty toe with a blackened, ragged nail could be seen through one of the broken boots.

I reached into my coat pocket and dropped a few coins into her outstretched fingers. The girl closed her hand around my gift, but she didn't look up. Then, as I turned to walk away, she glanced into my face, quickly, then down again. I heard her mumble something as I stepped away. "Excuse me?" I asked. I stopped and turned toward her, at the same time sorting out the syllables that she had spoken into words. "You are a very spiritual person," was what she had said. She had a low, husky voice with a ragged edge to it, which grated, but not unpleasantly, like a pumice stone.

"Thank you," I said, surprised, wondering if this was a new imprecatory gimmick, like the little handwritten "Tipping Is Good Karma" signs I had seen taped to bowls beside the cash register at coffee shops. "You are a spiritual person," she repeated, and her enigmatic words overlapped with mine.

"Thanks," I said again. I hesitated for a moment. Perhaps she would explain herself. But the girl was again looking fixedly at the pavement. A snarled hank of her dirty hair had fallen over her eyes. She said nothing further, so I turned and continued on my way to work.

I was, in my view, about the least spiritual person I knew. I had no religion and, despite my recent digression into the church beside the hospital where I worked, no religious or mystical impulses. I knew myself to be practical, sensible, reliable, a realist, with no longing for the ineffable, and little patience for the kind of questions that have no absolute answers. I couldn't remember ever having seriously considered whether I had such a thing as a spirit or a soul. In fact, I was not sure what it was that people meant when they talked about these things. I had accepted that there are people commonly acknowledged to be spiritual without ever having considered what it was that made them that way. The Dalai Lama, Mother Teresa, missionaries in South America, red-hatted bishops, nuns gliding leglessly in enveloping black habits. The kind of people who wore their faces folded neatly into an expression of kindness, who moved and spoke with a kind of purposeful peacefulness, a determined serenity. Surely such a manner of interacting with the vast, disappointing world was proof they had mastered their vices, sloughed off the sins of envy, greed, lust, willfulness, and the rest, and risen to a simpler, higher, purer level of existence.

I knew that I was not such a person. In fact I couldn't think of anyone I knew very well who I thought of as spiritual, aside from Luba, perhaps, who still occasionally went to services with her parents, and who had once described to me her idea of the soul as "the faintest fingerprint of God." I had, on the other hand, known a few people who seemed to me to have something in their character or makeup that was larger than common, who had a greater capacity to love or be loved, or an expanded aptitude for happiness or for engendering happiness in others, the ability to make others around them feel valued, enlarged, beloved. One of my professors in university, Jean Ferguson, had this attribute—her classes were always oversubscribed—as had, to some degree, a former boyfriend of mine named Chris Tolnoy. A girl in junior high school, Samantha Livingston, had it too, and never lacked for friends as a result. I wondered, not for the first time, whether any of them had been aware that they had this power, or whether it was the kind of fragile skill, like the ability to suspend disbelief or to fall asleep at night, that could only be maintained if one didn't think about it very hard or at all. I wondered too whether this gift was something that could be learned or taught or acquired by force of will or accident.

There was a doctor at the hospital, a long, gangling man who looked like a country and western singer or someone who repaired farm equipment. Whoever he was near—patients, nurses, other doctors, orderlies, visitors—wanted something from him, some scrap of his attention, a touch, a smile, even simply to be in the same room with him. He appeared to be both conscious of and conscientious about what people expected of him, and it had occurred to me more than once that he was very brave to have become a doctor, a profession in which expectations are already very high and in which there are very few limits on what people might ask of you.

The appeal of a secretary at the law firm where I used to work was more obvious. She was a remarkably beautiful woman, with smooth dark skin that looked plumped out from the inside, black hair that she wore loose in long curls, like dark spilling water, and wide, shadowy eyes that always made me think of ancient portraits of Egyptian nobility. She had the abundance of a rain forest. I had sometimes tried to imagine what it would have been like to be her at twelve, or thirteen, when her body first began to take on the shape of a violin and move with a new pendular heft, her hair thickened into vinelike tendrils, her lips filled out into red petals, and her eyes became as dark and glossy as fresh black figs. I didn't have to imagine the effect she had on men, because she trailed manifestations of lust and adoration wherever she went in the office—longing glances, approaches both furtive and overt, and declarations of love made to the walls or ceilings. She was serenely unaffected by any of this. She had a boyfriend who was studying refrigeration technology at night school, and was of average appearance—facts I had learned from my vantage point at the reception desk. Her devotion to this ordinary boy somehow rendered her immune to the approaches of others. She was completely level-headed, unaltered by what her body might have put her through.

This made her all the more desirable to the men who tried to catch her attention, I think. They may have thought that she had somewhere a mechanism, a toggle, that they could somehow switch on if they could only discover the trick, or that there might be some enticement or persuasion that could open her eyes to other possibilities and make her, perhaps, someone else entirely.

Living Room

"*Nothing wrong* with you at all," my doctor concluded at the end of what seemed to me to be a perfunctory, even cursory five-minute examination the following week. "All of your tests are well within the normal range. There's certainly no neurological impairment that I can see. The only change from your last checkup is that you've lost about five pounds, which is probably healthy. You're still within the right weight for your height and build. To be on the safe side, we'll send you down to the lab for some extra blood work. If we find anything unusual, I'll let you know."

"But I am still not sleeping," I said, conscious of a slight shrill edge in my complaint, which I strove to dampen. I was reluctant to leave without some kind of diagnosis, if not a cure, but did not want to appear too anxious and risk being diagnosed with hypochondria or neurosis or with some other manifestation of exaggerated self-importance or lack of self-regard.

"Maybe you just need less sleep than the rest of us. It's common to need less sleep as we age."

"I'm only thirty-two!"

"These things vary widely."

"What about the tingling in my feet and hands? I can't focus. I feel heavy all the time. I'm more forgetful."

"Are you anxious? Depressed? Have your eating habits changed?"

"No. Just the sleeping."

"Well, this next set of blood tests will rule out anything serious. And I don't see any of the symptoms of multiple sclerosis, for example. We'll keep an eye on you. But my present diagnosis is that you are a healthy woman who is able to get by on less sleep. Enjoy it. Take a night class."

"Maybe not a night class," Rebecca suggested over dinner that evening. "But there are those public lectures out at the university every Saturday night. They are good, usually. Why don't we go to the one this weekend?"

"What's it about?"

"It would spoil it if we knew in advance. The thing is to go on a Saturday night without knowing, with the faith that, whatever it is, it will be interesting."

"Faith."

"Yes, faith. Weren't you listening? You have that dreamy look again."

"It's the not sleeping."

"My cousin's going as well."

"Going where?"

"To the lecture next Saturday. He suggested I come along."

"He won't mind if I go as well?"

"No, in fact I've been meaning to have you meet him."

"Is that what this is about, having me meet your cousin?"

"No. Although come to think of it, you might like him."

"Oh, Rebecca. Don't do this to me."

"I'm not doing anything. And you'll like him. He's a sweetie."

On Saturday morning, Luba and I saw Mike and his friend Al/Brad/Stan as soon as we walked into the café at the top of Grouse Mountain.

"Oh, no," I groaned into Luba's ear.

"Let me handle this," said Luba firmly, stepping forward to the table where the two men were sitting.

"Hi, Mike," she said, putting her hand on his shoulder. "And . . . I'm so sorry, I've forgotten your name."

"Angus. Angus Singer."

"Well, good to see you again. Bye!" said Luba, tugging me toward a table that was still empty on the other side of the room.

"See," she said. "It is better to face up to that which you fear. Evasion only works in the short term. Direct confrontation lasts forever."

"Excuse me." Angus had trailed us to our table.

"It's Maggie, isn't it?" Angus continued. He reached out a hand toward me.

"Yes. Maggie Selgrin. We met the other week." I took his hand and shook it, ensuring that there was no responsive pressure in my grasp.

"I remember. And I understand that Mike got together with both of you since then. He's an old friend, you understand. He's been having a hard time since his wife left him. I know he's a bit of a jerk. I try not to hold it too much against him. We've known each other since we were in grade school."

"Admirable loyalty," said Luba, sipping from her cup of coffee.

"Well, the point is, I thought maybe you, Maggie, might want to come on the climb with me some time. Maybe next week?"

"I can't, but thanks for asking. I always come with Luba."

"I won't be here next week, remember?" Luba reminded me, af-ter Angus had retreated to his table. "I'm going to the broadcasting conference in Halifax. Why not go with him? He's kind of cute. What harm can it do? It's a public place. So long as he dumps Mike, of course."

"Luba! I just won't come next week. Or I'll find someone else to go with."

"You can't necessarily judge people by who their friends are. I stuck with you through the Geoffrey days, remember?"

On his way out of the café with Mike, who smiled at us cheer-fully, rubbed his hands together, and emitted a broad wink, Angus stopped by our table again and handed me his card.

"In case you change your mind," he said. He switched on a smile that creased his face appealingly. A trick, I thought, that he could not be entirely unconscious of.

The lecture that night was called "Dreaming Technology" and was delivered by a visiting scholar from the National University of Singapore.

"Is it possible," Dr. Tse asked an attentive audience of about two hundred, "to consistently design machines that will operate better, more reliably, more faithfully, if you will? I put it to you that the answer is yes, and that the means to do this is not only to make machines that are smarter, faster, more responsive, or even more ex-actly manufactured or calibrated, although these are all important. My topic tonight is dreaming technology, and my dream is one of a world in which our technology is contented if it operates well, joyful if it exceeds your expectations. Can you imagine a machine that wants, with every fiber of its circuitry, to make you, its owner and operator, happy? Close your eyes. Go on, just try it. Can you picture such a world? Think of owning a refrigerator that wants nothing more than to supply your family with wholesome, chilled foods to eat. A car that experiences a measurable ping of electronic pleasure if it gets you home by the shortest route, safely and on time. A cheerful printer that spits out each sharp, bright printed page with glee. A calculator that loves to . . . but perhaps we are now taking things too far. We are talking about happiness in the microchip brain and the nervelike interconnections of a machine, the ability to be glad. Love is perhaps a leap—a quantum leap—beyond mere happiness. Love requires a heart, and I don't think we'll see a machine with a feeling heart in our lifetime. Perhaps our children or grandchildren will have such machines in their world."

"What did you think?" Rebecca's cousin Leo asked me as the three of us were walking back to his car, which we had left in a student parking lot remote from the auditorium. Three days' heavy rain had, miraculously, come to an end during the evening. The clouds were dispersing, and a crescent moon gleamed now and then, slim and hazy, almost coyly, as if through a veil, in the deep, black sky. The pavement was dark and wet, and every now and then the moon's demure image trembled underfoot.

"I liked the part about the potential to conscript medical devices that truly want to help to find a cure for AIDS and cancer," I answered slowly. "But even though his hypothesis seemed sound when he was going through it step by step, it's impossible when you add it all together. It comes across as wishful thinking to me, more fiction than science. Almost as if, simply by wanting something so much, we can make it happen."

"And if you can make a machine that feels happy doing good,

how do you know that you won't end up with a machine that is just as happy doing bad? Remember Hal, in the movie *2001?*" said Rebecca.

"I think Hal was the good guy. Wasn't the point of the movie that the humans were bad?" Leo asked.

"I'm sorry that they ran out of time before I had a chance to ask my question," said Rebecca. "I wanted to contradict his point about not being able to envision a machine with a heart. They made the first mechanical heart back in the 1970s, didn't they? A mechanical heart is a machine that's all heart."

"If love were merely a matter of having a heart, wouldn't we all be lovable?" I asked.

"I have no doubt that we all are," said Rebecca.

Leo smiled at me over the top of Rebecca's head, a smile that floated in the air just above the part in the middle of her hair.

Leo was about thirty, a year or two younger than Rebecca and I. He worked at a small law firm downtown and had come directly from work to pick us up, so he was still wearing his suit and a belted trench coat, both of which sat on him very badly, as if he bought his clothes with his eyes shut, didn't own an iron, and got dressed in the dark. He had sloping shoulders, short legs, a long torso, and a head that was too large for his body and topped with raggedly cut, reddish-blond hair. It seemed to me just possible that he cut his hair himself. He was only a little taller than Rebecca. Leo struck me as the kind of astute man who had taken stock of himself in the mirror one day early on and had sensibly decided to develop his intellectual abilities and a warm personality instead of expending energy on his appearance. He reminded me of a medium-sized golden-furred mammal, a marmot perhaps, with a round body, a rudimentary neck, and an absurd but likable face. I didn't like to think about what he might look like without his rumpled clothes on, although it was impossible to keep from contemplating that he might be round and golden and furry all over. Naked, he might be comfortable and cozy, like a stuffed animal, but far from romantically appealing. Rebecca told me that he had broken up with his girlfriend, an aerobics instructor, a few months earlier.

"What kind of man dates an aerobics teacher?" I asked her.

"Aren't you being a little judgmental?"

"Come on, Rebecca. Smart women don't teach calisthenics for a living."

"I don't think they call it that anymore. And I never met her, so I can't defend her. But Leo's an intelligent man and I refuse to believe that he was dating a bimbo. Anyway, they broke up. Maybe she was a mistake he had to make on the way to finding his heart's desire."

"Here's the car," Leo said. "Why don't we stop for a glass of wine or a beer before I drop you back at your place?"

When Leo was walking us to our apartment door an hour and a half later, he craned over Rebecca's head again and said, addressing only me, "Would you like to go to the lecture next Saturday?"

"That would be wonderful," answered Rebecca.

"And you, too, of course," Leo emended.

"I was accepting on Maggie's behalf," answered Rebecca. "Of course she'll come. If she has a conflicting engagement, I'll make sure she breaks it."

"I am perfectly happy to accept for myself," I said, the polite thing to say, the right thing, although I was already certain that Leo was the kind of man I would like for a friend, nothing more. It was impossible to imagine kissing him without a shudder of aversion that was so small, so intense, that there was something revoltingly agreeable about the sensation.

Dining Room

"*Lucy*, don't you think it's time to talk about what we're going to do about this wedding?"

Rebecca and I had invited Lucy over to the apartment for Sunday dinner and a video.

"No. It's not. What video did you pick?"

"*Four Weddings and a Funeral.*"

"Very funny, Rebecca."

"*The Runaway Bride.*"

"Maggie! I'm not running away, am I?"

"But, Lucy. It's time to get serious. What are you going to do?"

"Let's watch the video and we'll talk about it some other time, OK?"

"Bad news, Lucy," said Rebecca. She rose to her feet and began to clear away the plates. "There isn't any video and I'm going out. Not quite sure what's up. Something about planning your wedding. Janet should be here any minute. In fact, there's the door. That's probably her now. I'll let her in."

"Janet! What the hell are you doing here? Maggie, I'm going to kill you."

"You'll have to kill Janet as well. And Rebecca, too, while you're at it."

"You promised to keep me out of it. Hi, Janet. They're expecting you, I think. I'm off. I should be back by eleven-thirty or so, Maggie. Have fun."

"Lucy, look, I brought some pictures of...."

"I have no idea why you might possibly think that you have any right to be involved in this. What the hell do you know about weddings anyway? You and John eloped, for god's sake."

"Yeah, but you and Ryan decided to have a wedding, remember? Priest. Church. Mass, too, for all I know."

"No. No mass."

"What are you going to wear?"

"Mum said I could have her old dress."

"Her old *wedding* dress?"

"Of course, her wedding dress. What other dress of hers would I ever be caught dead in?'

"Where the hell is it? We used to play dress-up in it when we were girls, remember? Up in the box room?"

"Mum gave away the dress-up stuff years ago. I'm sure the wedding dress went with it."

"Probably gone to orphans in Africa."

"She kept it. It's at the house somewhere. Hung up. Or in a trunk."

"Full of moth holes, probably. And in tatters. We were pretty rough on it. Have you even looked at it?"

"No, I haven't seen it. I haven't looked. She mentioned it one day, that's all."

"It will have to be let out if we can even find it. A lot."

"How can it possibly fit you, Lucy? Think! You'll be nine months pregnant by then. You aren't being practical."

"Eight and a half months. I can get the dress altered. And I am being practical. I'm marrying Ryan, remember?"

"Lucy, this isn't the nineteenth century. Everyone likes Ryan. He's great. But no one's making you marry him. No one even expects you to. You have choices."

"No, I don't. I burned my choices when I told Gian Luigi to *vaffanculo* and quit my job."

"They'd have you back. They loved you."

"Work or Gian Luigi?"

"Gian Luigi's in the past now, Lucy. You don't need him. And you don't have to marry Ryan, that's for sure. You should do what you want to do."

"I want to marry Ryan. I've made my decision."

"You don't seem happy about it."

"At this point, it's not about happiness, it's about doing the right thing."

"I've always thought that doing the right thing would make you happy."

"That's because you're naïve, idealistic, and romantic, Maggie."

"Leave Maggie alone. She hasn't done anything wrong. You're the dumb idiot who went and got herself pregnant."

"Who's so dumb? Thomas and Claudia were pretty damn premature—seven months after your quickie Caribbean wedding. Who did you think you were fooling? Only anyone who can't count. Maggie's the only smart one in this family. So far she's escaped the Selgrin daughters' fate of having to marry whoever gets her knocked up."

"That's because Maggie won't let anyone get close enough to her to give her anything more intimate than a handshake. It was nearly eight months. The twins were premature. Lots of twins are. They were in incubators for three days before. . . ."

"If you guys want a wedding, plan one for Maggie. Leave me out of it."

"Lucy, we just . . ."

"Just piss off, that's all I'm asking you to do. Piss off. How hard is that? If you can't cope, why don't you take one of your little pink pills."

"They're not pink. And don't you dare go barging out of here. Maggie and I have gone to a lot of trouble to—Shit. Wouldn't you know it?"

"Janet, if you could just sit down for a minute, we could—Janet!"

"I'm going after her. She'll listen to me."

"Why? She never has before."

"Don't wait up."

"Damn."

I sat and waited to see if any of them would return, resisting a sudden craving to let my head fall forward on the table and to grind my forehead into the crumbs. After a few long minutes, I sighed and gave up. I finished clearing the table and loaded the dishwasher, dropping the dishes in heavily. I poured in too much soap, slammed the door shut, and switched the machine on, although it wasn't full. The hum as the water warmed, and then the sloshing and whirring as the engine set to work were comforting. White noise.

As I passed by the telephone on my way out of the small kitchen, I noticed the business card I had dropped on the counter along with my empty water bottle the day before.

ANGUS SINGER

Executive Director

THE TANTON FOUNDATION

It was still early. I reached for the telephone and dialed.

"This is Maggie Selgrin," I said when Angus picked up the phone. "We've met a couple of times up at the coffee shop at Grouse Mountain."

"Of course. It's good to hear from you, Maggie."

"I'm planning to go up again next week, and Luba, my friend, is going to be away at a conference. Are you still interested in going up with me?"

"Yes, I'd love to. In fact, that would be great. Shall I pick you up?"

"We could meet in the parking lot at the base of the trail. How's seven-thirty?"

"Sounds perfect. I'll see you there then. I hope you'll have time for a coffee once we get to the top. I'll be on my own. No Mike, I promise."

"That would be fine. I hope I won't slow you down too much. I never time myself against the clock. Too depressing."

"We'll take it at any pace you like. I'm glad you called."

I set down the receiver and heard in the same instant the low click as the soap dispenser in the dishwasher sprung open, releasing the blue-green granules of powdered soap into the surging water.

Study

Angus had recently turned forty and emerged from a marriage that had lasted eighteen years—"Seventeen of them very good," he said. Angus turned out to be unlike Mike in all of the important ways. He frequently stopped talking long enough for me to get entire sentences in, in fact showed every sign of being interested in what I had to say. After the climb, which I managed with Angus's encouragement to complete without stopping, we sat over coffee for the rest of the morning, and then soup and sandwiches until midafternoon. We talked about our work—Angus was the director of a private charitable foundation—our families, places we had been or wanted to go, goals, ideas, the kinds of things people talk about when they are getting to know each other with the possible object of the future exchange of emotional warmth, physical contact, and commitments of various natures and durations. We talked of matters that would have been of no interest to anyone else, but seemed anything but trivial to us as we sat at that small table over cups and plates, surrounded by the music of clattering dishes, rattling cutlery, and the noise and laughter of strangers. I liked him.

I had gone through many phases in my romantic life, so many that I no longer thought of myself as a romantic, notwithstanding

Lucy's view of me, but as practical about the kinds of feelings that are usually, in a dissembling way, said to reside in the heart instead of the mind.

When I was a teenager, I was under the sway of what I think of now as an orienteering metaphor of love, adapted from my days as a Girl Guide, when we would be taken in groups into the woods or fields, given a sheet of directions, and required to locate and record various coordinates with the ultimate goal of finding the single spot that had been designated the object of the quest. The instructions were given by reference to points on the compass, to degrees west, north, east, and south, and to meters and arm's breadths and paces. Even slight errors in interpreting the directions, especially those made early on, became exaggerated with each turn, so that you could easily end up a long way from the appointed goal, entirely disoriented, uncertain of where and how you went so terribly wrong. I was never very good at this exercise, so I learned to rely on cues that we were supposed to ignore, such as footprints left behind by the organizers or the more obvious landmarks—the largest Douglas fir or greenest patch of salal—that I thought were likely to have been used as reference points. In this manner, fudging a little, but seldom obviously, I often ended not far from the goal, but seldom squarely on it either.

At sixteen I was seized with a concern that my path in life might run askew in this same way, that I might make one minor miscalculation, the smallest, most innocent misstep, with the result that I and my one true love might be walking in parallel tracks, keeping pace step-by-step but a block apart or just across the street. Our paths could never converge and we would never meet, even though the distance between us was no greater than a puff of breath, a hand-span, the thickness of our skin.

This notion passed and was replaced, for a stretch of time, by a certainty that chemistry was the key, that I would know when I had met the person I was destined to love most because my blood and bones and senses would be moved by the synchronous beat of our swelling hearts and the complete and perfect perfume concocted by the intermingling of our sweet, unique, magnetic pheromones. The electrons of our bodies would throb to the same jazzy tempo, like syncopated drumbeats. Our bodies would search out and seize on each other's unique, unmistakable scent, like a bee captivated by the sweet lure of lavender. Each of us would suddenly and inexorably become ensnared by the other, engulfed in a fog of promiscuous hormones rising like steam from the surface of our skin toward the ready and willing receptors of The Other.

After that, I came to believe that love was simply the name we give to the practical problem of finding a mate who will be the most suitable partner, selected from a range of people having not terribly different qualifications, bearing in mind availability, age, education, background, references, appearance, health, wealth, stability, sexual orientation, some level of reciprocated interest, and reproductive ability. It was at about this time that a woman I knew but not well—fortyish, single, in the bitter throes of a nasty breakup—said to me, leaning across a friend's dinner table and highlighting her words with an extended index finger, that she would never, ever date again for love. "Show me the portfolio," she said. "If he's got a house, some money, maybe a child or two from his first marriage to prove that he's not gay and he's not shooting duds, that's enough for me."

Now I wasn't sure what I believed, but I thought that love might just possibly have more to do with the mind than with fate or chemistry or an idiosyncratic list of minimum expectations. The hard part would be to avoid being distracted by the more obvious and elemental charms of a possible candidate—physical attraction, the way someone fills out his jeans or T-shirt, his honey-and-yeast odor, the resemblance of his voice to gravel trickled onto a wooden board, his taste in wine or movies or music, the way his eyes crinkle along the sides when he smiles, like bird tracks in the sand, the luscious, grainy texture of his skin—while drilling down to his essence. How he views the world. The shape and trajectory of his life. The measure of his essential goodness. Whether he is happy.

I got home from having spent the greater part of the day with Angus with barely enough time to shower and dress. I regretted having made a commitment to go to the lecture that evening with Leo. I was exhausted and craving a simple supper followed by about twelve hours in bed. But since there was no acceptable way to put Leo off, I met him as scheduled at the appointed time. We went for dinner at a Greek restaurant on West 10th, and then drove together to the university. The lecture that night was entitled "Portrayals of Women in the Classics," and was given, as it happened, by the professor who had taught me "Introduction to the Canon" when I was in my first year of university—a course that I had found about as abrasive, overstuffed, outdated, and slippery as an old-fashioned horsehair couch. Dr. Blossom had since achieved fame—or infamy, depending on your point of view—after publishing a book, *Elegy for the Dead White Male.*

The lecture struck me as the most condescending kind of sop thrown to the "fair sex" (a term he actually used at least a half-dozen times). Dr. Blossom had mined his beloved classics for energetic or bright or courageous or otherwise admirable women whom he trotted forth in the course of his talk as proof that women were, "contrary to popular opinion" (a phrase he also used, and each time he spoke it, the nostrils of his large pink nose pinched together momentarily, then flared grandly), fairly, no, even *nobly* treated in the great literature of the past. Only a few of the women he referred to, such as Fanny in *Mansfield Park*, and Elizabeth in *Pride and Prejudice*, could in my view be credited with having any sort of sound, independent mind. The rest were secondary to the plot or lacked a moral scheme, or demonstrated a deficit of principled logic, or suffered from a fundamental lack of intelligence, such as being hopelessly romantic or whimsically, if charmingly, inconsistent in reason or in passion.

We stopped for coffee on the way home and I tried to bring Leo up to date on the controversy.

"The central question is this: Were the classics virtually all written by men because genius is a country exclusively populated by men, or have works by women been excluded because our common understanding of what makes a classic comprises only what men write?"

"Sounds like one of those chicken-and-egg arguments. Can it ever be resolved one way or the other?"

"Some people think that the only solution is to scrap the old list altogether and start over from scratch. Others argue that only minor tweaking is needed. Most of us fall somewhere in the middle, but tending more to one side or the other."

"It's the same in law, you know," Leo told me. He leaned across the table and fingered my cup, which was not yet empty, in a way that I found alarmingly intimate. I sat back in my chair and crossed my arms.

"It's only in our lifetime that we've begun to recognize that there have been many serious, systemic biases against women, such as the rules about custody and the division of property. There's

been the same kind of controversy that you've described in literature over how to identify the legal biases and reverse them without
tipping the balance too far in the other direction. It doesn't take
much for us live white guys to feel threatened, you know, and we are
getting nervous about all the encroachments on our turf. All your
Professor Blossom is trying to do is help us guys, dead and alive,
protect our franchise."

My doctor's receptionist called me that week to schedule a
follow-up visit. I was still sleeping only a few hours a night and was
looking forward to any insights that he might have on my condition. But he remained completely unconcerned about how much or
little I might be sleeping.

"There's nothing wrong with you at all, Maggie," he told me.
"You are completely healthy. The tests all came back completely
normal. But I have to say that I wasn't 100 percent happy with that
mole on your neck. I think overall we should have it come off. It's
a simple procedure, but to reduce the risk of leaving a scar I have
decided to refer you to a plastic surgeon. She should be able to look
after it right in her office. You'll be in and out in half an hour. And
it's virtually painless."

A few days later, I was waiting in Dr. Crewe's office on Oak
Street near West Broadway for my one o'clock appointment. A man
in a white coat approached me, holding out his hand.

"Good afternoon. I'm Dr. Charles Addenbrook. I am so sorry
that you've been kept waiting. Won't you please come in? My office
is here, first door on the right."

"Dr. Addenbrook? There may be a mistake. I believe that I was
referred to a Dr. Crewe. Dr. Laura Crewe."

"Dr. Crewe is my partner. She called a short while ago to let the
office know that she's running late at emergency. There was a rotten

car accident this morning coming over Second Narrows Bridge, and she has a few teenagers' faces to sew back together. They mind so at that age how they come out. Of course, few of us outgrow that. She asked whether I could squeeze you in. You're fortunate; I finished the last patient in record time. If you would sit up on the table here, we'll have a quick look. This is it here, I see. Any changes in size? Shape? Itching? Bleeding? Right. Well. I think your family physician is right. This should come off just to be on the safe side. It won't take more than a few minutes. Hold on, that's my phone. Please excuse me for one moment. Hello? Already? Yes. Yes. Yes. No. No. Of course not. Not at all. She's all yours."

"I've good news for you. Dr. Crewe is just on her way in. She'll be able to see you after all. She asked if you would wait for her in her office. This is it, the second door on the left. She'll do a fine job, not to worry. I'll leave my notes here for her if you could let her know where they are. Right here on the desk. You will remember?"

I was out of Dr. Crewe's office within another half-hour and was asked to sit in the reception area for ten minutes so that she could make sure that what she referred to as "a minor amount of bleeding, no more than expected," had stopped completely before I would be given permission to leave. While I was waiting, Dr. Addenbrook walked by. He stopped in front of me and went down on one knee.

"You don't mind if I have a quick look?" He raised one corner of the bandage on my neck and peered closely. "Yes. Nice work. A little redness. I'll tell Dr. Crewe that I checked on you. You're free to go." He rose to his feet.

I stood as well. "You make it sound as if I'm getting sprung from jail."

"No, prisons have a better choice in reading material. Or so I'm told."

"Yes, I see from one of your magazines that Princess Diana is dating some guy named Dodi."

"Well, we do like to keep our patients up to date." He hesitated. "Look," he continued. "Since you're not technically my patient, I wonder whether you might be free for a late lunch. I was on my way and I haven't got the knack of eating alone. Or do you have to get back to work? Or home to your family?"

"I don't have to get back to work. I booked the afternoon off. And there's no family. I would be happy to join you."

We walked to Pensieri, a small Italian restaurant on West Broadway near Willow, where the owner obviously knew Dr. Addenbrook—he asked me to call him Charles—from many past visits. Within a minute of our being seated at one of the tables, a waiter set before us bowls of ear-shaped pasta in garlic-scented chicken broth, crisp rolls, and a salad made of endive and escarole that the waiter dressed at the table in olive oil the color of moss, coarse salt, and wine vinegar. While we ate, Charles told me how he had come to elect plastic surgery as his specialty.

"I worked, by chance, with Dr. Schiffmann, a highly successful plastic surgeon in Toronto when I was an intern. He was supremely confident—one might say egotistical—but he was very, very able. He made a large and positive difference in the lives of his patients. Particularly facial surgery. Think of it, going through life with a disfigured face, whether from birth or as a result of an accident. The face is what we present to the world. It's what people see and interpret first, before anything else. If you've a horrific face, you are fairly guaranteed to have a horrific life, unless you are very, very lucky. You've obviously never had to worry. You have the face of a Madonna."

"Oh, no," I protested. I raised my hands to my cheeks, which felt cooler than I expected, and fuller. My new, smooth, sleepless face. It felt under my hands like a still bowl of milk or a golden round of cheese.

"Schiffmann once actually said to me, 'I fix the mistakes that God makes.'" Charles imitated the grave, self-important tone of an older man. "In anyone else, you would think that unbearable hubris. But he is in fact amazingly good. He takes on work that other doctors have tried and failed at, or won't even consider. I have more modest aims myself. I help God along. No more than that. I'm an assistant, an apprentice."

"Do you have far to go?" Charles asked when we finished our meal and he had paid the bill, waving my money away. "I'll run you back if you like. I have a new toy, a convertible, which I love to have an opportunity to take for a spin. My next appointment isn't until four. If you're not in a rush, we can drive along the water and I'll show you my boat. Another one of my hobbies. I have several, as I hope you'll find out."

Family Room

I was now seeing three men, none of whom I had known for more than a few weeks. Angus Singer. Leo Crane. And now Charles Addenbrook, whom Rebecca liked to refer to as "God's little helper"—I had made the mistake of describing to her the conversation I had with Charles at our first lunch.

Leo put in long hours at the law firm, where he worked as an associate advancing aboriginal land claims. We met for dinner or went for a lecture or to a play on Saturday nights. Once or twice, on a Sunday morning, when the weather cooperated, we went for walks along the seawall.

Angus spent time with his two teenaged boys on the weekends, but we got together once or twice during the week to go to a movie or a play. We also hiked together early Saturday mornings while his sons slept in. Luba had abandoned our Grouse hikes. She was in the thick of a new relationship and she preferred to linger in bed on Saturday mornings with her new love.

In addition to his plastic surgery practice, Charles worked a couple of shifts each week at the emergency department of St. Matthew's. He would drop into my office at the end of the work-day and take me down to the marina where he kept his sailboat, *Neptune III*. We would go for a short sail in the inlet—the sun set after a scant hour and it was too cold to stay out any longer—then, after we had tied up again in the slip, Charles would bring out cheese and bread and salads and wine from a small fridge in the scaled-down galley. We would eat inside the cabin, under the soft light of a gas lamp that swayed above our heads. The lamp cast shadows that bounced on the cabin walls as the waves sloshed gently against the boat, loosely tied on its mooring.

The boat was only one of Charles's many passions. Another was houses—he owned six altogether.

On our third time out together he took me on a tour of the one he lived in, in West Vancouver, an echoing glass-and-concrete structure on Marine Drive, strung along a cliff overlooking the inlet, all right angles, alternating textures, rough and smooth, and stark shades of deep shadow and brilliant light. The view from his living room window took my breath away, but the house did not have any sense of home about it. The rooms were echoing, nearly empty—some had only a single piece of furniture in them. There was a sloping leather Eames chair and four giant speakers in the living room, and the bedroom had only a bed: Everything else—closets, dressers, lamps, reading materials—was concealed behind sliding panels of birds-eye maple. Even the bathtub was angular and uninviting, with no curves to rest against. "I never use it anyway," Charles explained.

Charles's other houses were all rented out. They were older, more modest, scattered in different Vancouver neighborhoods. One day he took me to a small three-bedroom house on Barcklay Street in North Vancouver that he had recently bought.

"The house I live in is a machine for living, in the same way that this splendid car is a machine for getting around," he said as we drove over the bridge toward North Vancouver. "That's what Le

Corbusier says a house should be, rather than a labyrinth of furniture. These old houses attract clutter—engender it, in fact. All those nooks and crannies and mantels and cupboards just cry out to be filled with junk. Windowsills, mantels, wainscoting, baseboards, lintels—they get dirty, kicked, scuffed. They collect dust and fingerprints. And they're unnecessary anyway in a properly built house. Le Corbusier thought we should have only necessities, the carefully selected equipment for life. Everything in a house should be useful, and demanding of us, or else we fall into dullness and lethargy."

I had not found Charles's austere, hard-edged house appealing. It had too much of the architect about it, with few concessions made to the reasonable requirements of any family that might live there. There were many clever, self-conscious angles, but no comfortable cubbyholes or niches. There were not very many closets and few cupboards. What could be more basic to human need than a peg on which to hang one's clothes at the end of the day, and a board, rough or smooth, on which to perch one's plate and bowl and spoon and cup? The overlarge windows sacrificed privacy and comfort—for what? For the wonderful views, that glittered brilliantly, sharply, and enticingly out of reach. Only the eye can enjoy a view, I thought, staring out through one of the living room's great expanses of thick glass. A view is at the wrong distance for the other senses—too far away to be caressed, too remote for its sounds or scent or taste to give pleasure. A scrim, a simulacrum, a mural or large canvas could provide as much.

The house that Charles considered his home unsettled me; the scale of the different rooms seemed all wrong. The rooms intended for intimacy or privacy—the bathrooms and bedrooms—were vast, and the areas where people tend in most houses to congregate—the entryway, the kitchen—had been diminished, practically erased. And where was the hearth, the center, the focus point where the inhabitants were invited—compelled—to come together and be at ease?

I went with Leo to a lecture at the university at which a Brazilian architect spoke about the origins of the house. The first homes, he said, were likely no more than a sheltered spot at which a fire could be started and kept alight with some reliability. An unsafe, uncertain place still, but possibly the only refuge of early people from weather, wild animals, and enemies. Society was formed around a fire. The people who were allowed to draw near the embers were by definition "us." Those outside the fire's range were "other." The most intimate acts of these dwellers in caves and rough structures of branches, stones, and mud would have been performed near the fire. The hearth became, in this way, associated with a mother's lap, with sexual embrace, with food, and worship and safety. The fire became the symbol of all our yearnings, the hearth that would hasten the traveler's returning pace, the familiar warmth that we seek still when we enter a house.

The small North Vancouver house that Charles took me to see sat in the middle of its narrow, deep lot on Barcklay Street. It was intended to serve the same function as Charles's cantilevered concrete box—to provide a home, a place of shelter and safety—but in many ways it existed in opposition to, in defiance of, the sprawling Marine Drive house. The cramped rooms of the Barcklay Street house were intended for domestic clutter and familial repose and regard. The house had the same deep eaves and generous sills as my childhood home, and Charles confirmed that it had been built about the same time, around 1915, he thought. We kept bumping into each other in its many bottlenecks—the hallway on the main floor, the narrow steps up to the second, smaller storey, the tiny room between the kitchen and the back door, where, as if to prove Charles and Le Corbusier correct, old bottles and newspapers and rubbish had accumulated in unsteady drifts and piles.

The previous owner, a widow, had died in hospital some months before after a long illness, and Charles had bought the house as it was, untidy and shabbily furnished. The widow's only child, a son who worked in an insurance company's head office in Toronto, had been anxious to avoid a trip back to the coast. The more personal effects—what an odd phrase, I thought, when Charles explained the arrangements to me, a Le Corbusier phrase— had been sorted out and sold. The upright piano, a dining room table, and four matching chairs had been packed and shipped to the faraway son by professional movers. Most of the furniture, the dishes, and the bedding remained behind and had been sold with the house.

The place had been unlived-in for almost a year. The windows and floors were gritty and every surface was coated in dust. I felt an intense desire to look for soft rags, buckets, and cleaning fluids, for vinegar if nothing stronger was available, and start to restore a respectful gleam to the little house. It could never sparkle, it had gone past that point, but there was, I was certain, a patina under the dirt, a luster of loving use, familiarity, and casual wear. But Charles would not hear of it. He pressed his fingers against my lips. A team of workers had been hired to clean and repair the house, he told me. He promised, however, that he would bring me back one day to see it in its spruced-up state, before it was rented out.

On the drive back to the city we talked about the passionate love that houses inspired. Many of my friends were on the hunt for a house to replace the apartments and condos and unsatisfactory arrangements of their twenties. Those few that had managed to pull together a down payment and take out a mortgage seemed as enamored of their real estate as they were of their firstborn children. Like Ryan, they scraped and sanded, repainted, repaired, and renovated. The kind of effort, I sometimes thought, that had been expended on spiritual or personal improvement in simpler times, was now diligently applied to kitchens and basements, as if property values were a manifestation of, or even a replacement for, personal values.

Charles denied any particular affection for any of his houses, even his own. He insisted that he had bought them because they had been bargains in one way or another at the time, and that he kept them for their income and against the practical certainty that they would rise in value, as a hedge against inflation. He insisted that emotion had no part in his decisions.

"They are good investments, that's all," he said. "Not something to get sentimental about."

"But you continue to collect them. You take excessively good care of them. You lay them up like treasure," I pointed out. I told him what the Brazilian lecturer had said on Saturday night at the university, that houses are an extension of our bodies. "I think he was quoting the great Le Corbusier, too," I couldn't resist adding.

We fell silent for a few blocks.

"There may be something to what you say," he said, at last, as we pulled up in front of my building. "There is a clipping in one of my files—a quote from a Spanish writer, Vicente Verdú. What he said was that houses exist between reality and desire, between body and dream, between what is possible and what remains to be longed for." Charles reached for my hand in the darkness and squeezed it. "Something like you," I thought I heard him say, but another car roared past and overlaid his words with senseless noise.

I was still not sleeping. I would fall asleep at midnight or shortly afterward, then start fully awake at four or five. I thought that it might help me to sleep if I got more exercise, so I began to get out of bed as soon as I woke up and go jogging through the downtown streets. There were always enough people about that I felt safe. Other joggers raised their hands in an odd salute of solidarity as they passed by. There were early risers on the sidewalks in quest of coffee. In the parks I saw practitioners of tai chi swooping and ducking like cranes. Night workers drove along the roads, returning home, and morning workers started up their engines as they set out for the day. I liked to watch the city shake itself awake each morning from its short, dark night's sleep. I saw lumbering tanklike street cleaners sluicing down the gritty streets, men pitching fat stacks of newspapers and magazines from idling flatbed trucks onto the sidewalks in front of news agents and placing sheaves of fresh papers into news boxes. There were vans and trucks of all sizes delivering bread, soft drinks, fruits, vegetables, and flowers to corner stores and hotels.

These morning runs reminded me of a book I had owned as a child, one that was brightly illustrated and with few words. It was called something like *The City at Dawn* and showed the busy, industrious, law-abiding people of a large generic city preparing the streets and stores and businesses against the awakening of the sleeping children of the city, like unacknowledged but eminently contented stagehands preparing for the arrival of the chorus line.

I took different routes every day. One morning, I had just turned around to begin my run back toward home when I noticed a dozen or so people arriving alone or in pairs for a morning service at St. James Cathedral. I slowed when I came up to where they were clustered.

"Would anyone mind if I came in dressed like this?" I directed my question to a woman who was rushing up the front stairs of the church. She looked about fifty, and was suitably dressed for a church service in a red pleated skirt, a gray wool coat, and flat black pumps.

"You wouldn't be the first," she answered cheerfully, holding the door open for me. "We get one or two runners like yourself most days. People like to stay fit these days. I never saw the point in it myself, as you can probably tell." She laid one hand lightly on her rounded waist. "Come on in. The service is short, only a half-hour, and there's coffee afterward if you have time to stay."

Despite the obvious sincerity of the invitation, I felt self-conscious in my running shoes, jogging pants, and old T-shirt that was on its second day without a wash. I sat in the back of the church for the service, which was even shorter than advertised, only about twenty minutes. I resisted the scent of coffee drifting up from somewhere downstairs, and remained behind in the church after the others had left, relieved that no one had pressed me to join them. I walked around the perimeter to inspect the windows. On the right-hand side, halfway along the wall, was the window the man in black had mentioned, the other Annunciation.

He was right. This window showed a very different Mary. Her ivory hands lay in her sky-blue lap, palms curled upward, and she was bathed in a glowing light that shone from a bird flying from the upper left-hand corner of the window. This bird was larger, more fanciful, and less dovelike than in the other church. He had brilliantly colored trailing tail feathers, like a bird of paradise. Mary's face, which wore an expression of utter peace and acceptance, even joy, glowed in the shaft of light that emanated from the breast of the soaring bird, like the moon reflecting the light of the sun. I was pleased to see, barely visible under her pink dress, the toes of two tiny perfect red slippers, making her a cousin to the Mary in the window of the other church.

I studied her face more carefully. Although she looked calm and accepting, her expression was intelligent, determined. Her eyes were wide open, not demurely closed, and her jaw and chin were set at an uncompromising angle. She looked beautiful, strong, resolved. I liked her immensely more than the apprehensive Mary I had seen in the first Annunciation. I glanced behind me, half expecting to see a tall man in black with whom I could share my thoughts, but of course he wasn't there.

I went home, showered and changed quickly. Since I was running too late to have breakfast at home, on my way to work I stopped at a new coffee shop that had recently opened up on a corner close to the hospital. There was a line but it was moving quickly, and I was still hopeful that I would make it to work with a few minutes to spare so that I could organize my work area.

A woman of about my own age was behind the counter showing a young man—a boy, really—how to make the drinks. He had the bad skin and poor posture of late adolescence. His massive yawns threatened to tear apart his face while he struggled to focus his blurry attention on her instructions.

"These cups are for dairy, and these are for nondairy drinks. Got that?"

"Uh-huh."

"So, if someone orders a soy milk latte, which cups would you use."

"Um, I'm not sure."

"Listen. These cups are for dairy. These are for nondairy. Now, which ones would you use for soy milk?"

"Can you just tell me one thing?"

"Sure, what?"

"What does 'dairy' mean?"

"You're kidding, right?"

"No. Like, I've heard it before. I just never knew what it meant."

"Hang on. Don't go anywhere."

The woman looked up at me, although there were several people in front of me in the queue.

"Can I help you?"

"Oh, I can wait. Those people are ahead of me."

"That's OK. I'm just about to open a new till here and you can start the new line."

I asked her for a small coffee and an apple muffin.

"Here they are," the woman said, presenting them to me across the counter with a small ceremonial gesture, her palms upward, outstretched. "They're on the house. I'm sorry you had to wait. Training." She grimaced backward toward the teenager who had knitted his fingers together and was beginning to crack his sizable red knuckles methodically.

I wondered, as I walked the rest of the way to work, how it was that I seemed to have become the kind of woman who has three men contending for her time, who is invited to jump queues, to whom compliments are given and favors extended. I glanced at my reflection in the blurry, chipped mirror in the washroom down the corridor from my office. The mirror returned my steady gaze. I looked composed and oddly filled, spilling over with something—secrets or knowledge or certainty, perhaps, although I could not imagine they were. I lifted my hand and touched the cold, flat face in the mirror. The expression didn't change. I dropped my hand, put on my white coat, and walked down the corridor to greet my first patient.

I began to stop at St. James a morning or two every week, timing my runs for the start of the services. I found that the regular, repetitive rhythms of the prayers and songs served as a replacement for sleep, and the color and sound and sensations of the old ceremonies were not unlike the richer kind of dream. I had no sensation of the presence of God, and I didn't join in the prayers or the singing. I would sit quietly in one of the pews at the back and observe the individual elements that came together in what I supposed was meant by the word worship. A bringing together of like-minded, peaceful people. Melody. Entreaties. Contemplation. Hope. When I walked outside afterward, I felt an odd mix of competing sensations—empty and full, calm and excited, not unlike drinking a cup of hot, strong, bitter coffee right after a glass of icy-cold, sweet wine.

Pantry

Rebecca had refused to let me retake her quiz. She overhauled it extensively and then sent it in directly to the magazine that had commissioned it. It was a week overdue by the time she was done, and she almost never even came close to missing a deadline. She was now working on a test on workplace safety commissioned by a magazine called *Canadian HR Manager*. Aside from consulting my doctor, who continued to assure me that I was among the healthiest of his patients, my only other precaution was to go to a lawyer recommended by Leo. I asked her to prepare a simple will for me in which I left everything I owned—which wasn't much, a few possessions, my savings, a tiny pension, my books—to my nieces and nephews. I decided too, in an admittedly superstitious way, to take comfort in the fact that the fortune that Rebecca's test had laid out for me was subject to influence; it foretold a direction from which it was within my power to deviate, rather than a firmly fixed destiny.

One evening toward the end of November, Rebecca went back to her desk to work after dinner and I walked in the rain to the church. I had seen an announcement posted for Evensong service that night. The choir was there when I arrived, thirty or so strong, easily outnumbering the dozen people in the pews. A woman in the choir caught my attention when she sang a solo soprano passage,

and I rested my gaze on her face for the rest of the song, which was
sweet and medieval-sounding, likely a Christmas carol of some sort.

Salve virgo virginum
Salve sancta parens
Concepisti dominum
Virgo labe carrens
Salve virgo virginum
Salve sancta parens

I felt a sensation like the click of a switch in the instant before
a room is flooded with light. When the anthem ended, I was surprised to find it difficult to shift my gaze away from the woman's
face. I was transfixed. I felt an overwhelming sense, like an undula-
tion or a wave, of great peace. I felt like someone whose eyes have
come to rest on the front steps of her home at the end of a long
and difficult journey.

The woman in the choir had a broad, oval face, with very
smooth white skin, high cheekbones, a round mouth with full lips,
and an odd band of white flesh under her chin. This extra roll beneath her jaw made her face look as if she had been prepared by a
particularly unstinting baker. The woman's hair was fine and black;
it dipped down in the center of her forehead, then fanned backward
like wings behind her head, where it was caught up in a clip. She
looked as though she were made of some substance that was simultaneously white and black and rosy red, like the porcelain head—
was it called bisque?—of a doll my mother had in a cupboard at
home that had been her mother's before her.

The woman's voice was high and very clear and had a warble in
it, like cold milk pouring out into a tin cup, or a small, resonant

ringing bell, and her head sat as gracefully on its upholstered chin and neck as if she were sitting for a portrait. She lowered her hymnbook when she wasn't singing, but she always kept her eyes on the page, and the round curve of her cheek and arched brow swept upward and down again as the book was raised and lowered, and her neck dipped and rose like the neck of a water bird. When she was about to sing again, she would moisten her upper lip with her tongue, draw in her breath, and raise up her book. Her neck and chin trembled when she sang the higher and more sustained notes.

The sun had long set, and the Annunciation window was drained of color, its partitioned sections empty of light, like a page from a children's coloring book before the lines have been filled in. The members of the choir sang together neatly and lucidly, a wellrehearsed flock. I kept my eyes on the soprano throughout the service, feeling a little obsessive, a little mad, but mostly unconcerned. This fixation was surely temporary, another new symptom of the person I seemed to be becoming, or was perhaps an unexpected side effect of a cumulative lack of sleep or too much coffee. It would pass or change into something else, if I waited a while.

I have always been interested in the shifting gaits and gestures of the people around me, enchanted by the often unnoted gracefulness with which they make their way through their days, although I have usually tried to resist staring since I have never wanted to risk seeming rude or overcurious. My greatest temptation, since I was a child, has been to stare for too long at people who interest me, and I have often thought that one of the sacrifices of becoming an adult is giving up the freedom to indulge a good hard stare from time to time. This is doubtless part of my fascination with books, the ability to look intently at the characters in them for as long as I like, unbounded by the conventions of social etiquette. My two sisters, on the other hand, feel little compunction about sizing someone else up, slowly, deliberately, so in some ways the sensation of my eyes locking on the broad, round, calm face of the soprano was a familiar one from years of observing my sisters observing others. I fell, that one evening, into a fixed, appraising gaze on the soprano's face like an expert, like a person tumbling down a flight of stairs, like a star slipping loose from its bearings in the sky, like the tumbler pigeon that tumbles heart-stoppingly backward, beak over claws, while still in flight.

Although they looked unchanged in the mirror, my eyes had been hot and dry for days; they felt like they had been rolled in sand and set back in their sockets, or like rough stones forced into a setting meant for polished jewels. Sometimes, toward the end of the day, simply opening and closing my eyes made me feel as if they were operated by means of rusty levers that badly needed oil. I stared at the singer's face that night, and my eyes and busy mind felt cool, rested, bathed in balm. For the first time in weeks, I could feel a sensation as simple as rest seep into the bones of my skull.

After that night at St. James, the soothing image of the singer's face would sometimes appear on the scratchy insides of my eyelids, like the afterimage from the flash of a camera or the impossible image on the Shroud of Turin, but glowing like the face of a saint in a Russian icon, with a radiant golden halo against a night-black background. Her image never failed to ease my eyes and I began to summon up her face as a substitute for rest. I went to the evensong service another two or three times, but the soprano seemed to have joined the choir for that one night only.

I had a constant sense of changing, or being taken over, in ways that felt even deeper than when I had become an adolescent and acquired an entirely new body over the course of a year or two. As a teenager, I had never felt that the changes went beyond breasts and skin and hair and the new, rounding layer of fat beneath my skin. These changes felt much more profound. Did this second transformation happen to everyone in his or her early thirties, I wondered. Did everyone become someone else altogether in midlife? And, if so, why did no one speak of it? Why was this metamorphosis not discussed or even hinted at in the books I read?

I gave up trying to sleep until close to midnight. Several evenings every week, after dinner, I would leave Rebecca trolling the Internet for facts for her next proposal and drive to Linden Avenue, where Ryan was working on the house that he and my sister Lucy would be living in after their wedding, and I would work with him for a few hours. Ryan always had his favorite music playing very loud—Rachmaninov, Handel, Chopin—on a portable CD player that he carried with him from room to room as he worked.

I knew how to prep and paint a wall from years of helping my father. Ryan taught me how to patch plaster and miter baseboards and crown moldings. Usually, we worked alone on different projects in separate rooms. Sometimes, he called me to provide an extra set of hands or eyes on whatever project he was working on. We passed judgment together over tiny rectangles of color, choosing sage green over butter yellow for the living room, cinnamon red over Stuart gold for the dining room, periwinkle instead of honey for the baby's room. Ryan chose slabs of synthetic stone that looked like Carrara marble for the kitchen counters, and tiles the color of burnt sand for the kitchen floor, although I tried to talk him into something more forgiving, cork or oak laminate, or vinyl.

"Doesn't it bother you that Lucy doesn't mind what your house is going to look like?" I asked Ryan one night when we were packing up. He was carefully arranging the paintbrushes to soak overnight in a pickle jar filled with water.

"Lucy trusts me," he answered. "We agreed that this is how we'll do it. I'll get the house ready and she'll have the baby. I know that she will be happy here, over time, but I also know that it will take her a while to get used to it. One thing at a time seems to be easier for her."

Ryan often played opera music while we worked. By the end of November, I knew "Nessun Dorma" and "La Donna E Mobile" by heart. Ryan would sing along with the CDs, in his loud, cracked tenor, in Italian or in English.

Nessun dorma!	*No one sleeps!*
Nessun dorma!	*No one sleeps!*
Tu pure, o Principessa,	*Even you, oh princess,*
Nella tua fredda stanza guardi le stelle,	*In your cold room, looking at the stars,*
Che tremano d'amore e di speranza!	*That tremble with love and with hope!*
Ma il mio mistero è chiuso in me,	*But my mystery is locked within me,*
Il nome mio nessun saprà!	*No one will ever know my name!*
No, no, sulla tua bocca lo dirò . . .	*No, no, on your mouth I will say it . . .*
La donna è mobile	*Womankind is flighty*
qual piuma al vento,	*Like a feather in the wind*
muta d'accento e di pensiero.	*She changes her tune and her mind.*
Sempre un'amabile	*Always a kind*
leggiadro viso,	*And pretty face*

in pianto o in riso	*Whether she is crying or laughing*
è mensognero.	*She is deceitful.*
La donna è mobile	*Womankind is flighty*
qual piuma al vento	*Like a feather in the wind*
muta d'accento e di pensiero.	*She changes her tune and her mind.*

The face of the singer from the choir sometimes surfaced from the paint pots when I stirred them, or hung suspended in the orange depths of my morning tea. Most often, she appeared in mirrors as I passed by them. Now and then, her face floated in front of my eyes in myriad tiny images, like Andy Warhol paintings or the multiple vision of spiders. But she never appeared in my dreams, which were becoming less frequent. The few hours I slept were dark and formless. There no longer seemed to be time or space in my rare hours of sleep for the luxury and nonsense of dreams.

On the cusp of December, the winter rains arrived in force. The elements are at their most active in Vancouver in the wintertime. The winds bluster and keen, bullying nervous clouds across churning skies. Torrents of rain pound onto the streets and pavements. The water gathers into great puddles, then surges back and forth, as though in search of a sewer grate not yet completely choked by sodden leaves. The waterlogged earth squelches underfoot. Umbrellas sway and clatter overhead, their ribs knocking and jostling against other passing umbrellas. When the umbrellas are taken down, they are shaken firmly in the same brisk, convulsive way that a dog let in from the yard shakes itself just inside the door. The tiny droplets that are flung in every direction are immediately taken up into the air and then into the greedy, incontinent clouds, which release the moisture, transformed into water again, in search of new lawns and heads and feet and umbrellas to soak.

It was now too wet and dark to go out in Charles's boat. Instead, when he picked me up from work, we would drive to some small bar, where I would have a glass of wine with him. He insisted on selecting different vintages for me to try and would never allow me to pay the bill when it arrived. Charles treated me with the kind of old-world respect that I associated with the movies. He always walked on the traffic side of the sidewalk, held my elbow when we crossed the street, insisted on providing tickets to the theater, and art shows, and gave me many small presents of flowers and CDs and books. When we parted at my apartment door, he would press my hands in his two long bony hands and tell me how much he had enjoyed whatever we had come from doing.

One night, we went to a party to mark the opening of an art exhibit on south Granville Street, a pre-opening event, I understood, for serious investors and close friends of the artist. I bought an expensive emerald wool suit from a small shop downtown (where my only previous purchase had been a silk scarf that I had later found did not go with anything else I owned, nor likely ever would, although I kept it wrapped in tissue in my middle drawer against the possible day).

The paintings at the gallery were colossal, powerful, and gleaming. They were made up of rectangles of jewel-like colors bleeding at their edges into backgrounds of iridescent metallic gray. The pictures seemed to throb with force. I stepped into the main room, in my new suit, and with my hair pulled back in a pewter hair clasp, and wearing the bronze pumps I had borrowed from Rebecca. I felt as if I might have stepped out of one of these paintings. I could feel the warm darts of Charles's pleasure in the small of my back, his prideful attentiveness. He was, I understood, the kind of man who liked the woman he was with to fit into her surroundings, whether at his house, on his boat, beside him on the beach, in a small, familiar Italian restaurant, or at an event like this. I felt for the first time in my life like one of those women whose beauty is of the kind that can escape outside her skin and into her surroundings, like the spreading colors from brilliant tissue paper used in a collage.

My Saturday evenings with Leo ended at the door of my building with our hands meeting in a clasp that was closer to a handshake than an embrace, and a kiss on the cheek that placed us in the uncharted territory beyond friendship but not far outside its borders. One night we ran into friends of his when we were leaving a café on Dunbar, a married couple who lived nearby, giddy at being out for a movie without their very young children, and, for that brief slice of time while we stood talking under a green-and-white-striped awning that sheltered the four of us from a light drizzle, in the blurred, jade-shaded pool of light from the coffee shop windows, Leo put his arm around my shoulders and drew me close to him. Under his suit jacket—he had forgotten a coat—he was shivering. With my free arm, I rubbed the small of his back. It felt warm and solid and excessively thick with muscle. The sensation reminded me of the flank of a horse I had ridden for a few weeks at a summer camp when I was fourteen.

Angus's kisses were far more frankly sexual. He held my hand when we walked together, his thumb caressing the soft triangle of flesh between my thumb and forefinger. When we parted, he would push back my hair from my neck and face and press his lips to my brow and mouth with an intensity that reminded me of my relationship with Geoffrey.

I sometimes wondered at how different these three relationships were from others I had been in and, in particular, how different from my most recent short affair. Thomas had come to the door of the apartment I was living in then, over on 12th Avenue, to canvass for a left-wing party. Rain was pouring down outside, and his shoes and tweed jacket and unironed yellow cotton shirt were soaked. He smelled of wet wool and was wearing the hopeful, drooping, damp, unnamable mien of a dog left out in the rain. I invited him in and poured him a cup of tea from a pot I had just made. We talked about politics while his shoes rested upside-down over one of the hot-air registers. I felt crazed with longing for him to stop talking and take me to bed, but he gathered up his pamphlets and put on his shoes and left after an hour or so, when the rain stopped and a watery, pale, half-rainbow appeared in the late gray afternoon sky.

When Thomas had gone, I could not settle or rest, imagining him naked in my bed. He had the compact build and square hands of a laborer, and a face the rich color of clouds in shadow, like one of those ripely sensuous boys in a Caravaggio painting. He was not at all the kind of man I had ever been attracted to; he was gentler, softer, less assertively masculine, with fine dark hair, skin the color of early evening and the texture of upholstered silk, full lips, and, I learned later, a dusky penis enfolded in a monkish cowl of skin. A loud party in an apartment building across the alley began in the early evening and continued all night. The beam of a broken streetlight flickered into my bedroom like a searchlight. At about three o'clock, a desperate, lustful tomcat began to wail in the alley. I felt as though everything in the universe was colluding to mock and thwart and frustrate me.

Thomas and I did have a sexual relationship, one that began and ended quickly, but it was never as intense as that first night of longing had led me to expect. Thomas was comfortable in his loosely fitted skin and hand-to-mouth, romantic, harmless, no doubt useful life. He shared a house with six or seven ever-shifting roommates, took on good works for little or no pay, lived in clothes that appeared somehow when he needed them and that all looked alike, in shades of blue and black and plum, and slept on the floor of his chaotic room in a jumble of blankets and clothes. "Oh, a nest," I exclaimed when I first saw it. Sleeping with Thomas was like having an affair with a badger. Even his penis was molelike: blind and kind and thrusting. There seemed to be no harm in him whatsoever.

This episode ended completely by unspoken agreement, without rancor or injured feelings, after a month or two, when its purpose had been served. I was never clear about what either of us wanted out of it, but I got it, and I am confident that Thomas did too.

That brief whatever it was left me, I think, more conscious of the beauty of men than I had ever been before. The way their hair springs forth jaunty and true from their brows and in an abundant halo around their penises. The mass of shifting muscles in their upper arms, even, surprisingly, in the arms of accountants and bank managers and teachers. The solid ridge of muscle and flesh that separates torso from waist. The stiff swing of their legs in the sockets of their square-cut hips. The tender, attenuated tension strung into their long thighs. The wiry, shifting sinews of their buttocks. The dense, low fur on legs and chest and stomach. Why, I have wondered often, is so much attention paid to the obvious and often contrived beauty of women's uncomplicated curves and fine, downy skin, when men have at least their fifty percent share of splendor and perfection?

But I felt little sexual attraction for Charles or Leo or Angus. I felt as though the passionate side of me had closed over, like a healed wound or a sealed vessel. I didn't long for physical contact with anyone at all. I felt as if I had been freed somehow from needs that are ungovernable and frequently unanswerable.

Kitchen

Rebecca was negotiating with a publisher who had asked her to provide a dozen quizzes for a self-help book on marriage. ("How Well Do You Know Him?" "Should You Elope or Splurge on a Big Event?" "Are Your Fights Destructive or Constructive?") My sisters were busy (Janet) or preoccupied (Lucy). Luba had decided to risk going out with a coworker, a man about whom she had told me little, although noteworthy among the few facts she had mentioned was that he had been stalked by each of the three women he had most recently been involved with, including one, an assistant producer, who had run his garden hose from the exhaust of his car, which she had first started with a key she had stolen from him, into the nearly closed window of her car in the driveway at his house. The woman's intentions were uncertain, however, since she had done this in the morning, a few minutes before the hour that he usually came out to drive to work, and the hose had not been taped or secured at either end so that the hazardous molecules of carbon monoxide spilled uselessly into the air. A coy and thinly dramatic gesture, like trying to freeze to death by lying in your own bed with the window open, or taking two dozen children's aspirin, or wading into a lake with a pocketful of pebbles.

When we discussed this woman, Luba had admitted to me that

she felt that she too had the potential to be a harasser, but she was certain that this man would never rouse her to such a level of passion. She claimed that they didn't even date, really, just met with colleagues for meals or drinks after work, and then went to his place or hers for unconstrained sex.

One Sunday afternoon, I stopped by my parents' house while running errands. From outside, the house had the air of being occupied—several rooms were lighted and a rake and a shovel lay near the front flowerbed as though they were expected to be taken up again soon—but no one answered my three increasingly resonant thumps on the door with its horseshoe-shaped knocker. Finally, I unlocked the door with my own key and stepped into the narrow hall. I could see and hear from the front hall the not entirely unfamiliar scene of Lucy in tears at the kitchen table. Mother was sitting across from her, pouring tea into two clear glass mugs and pulling tissues from a box and handing them to Lucy. Lucy accepted each tissue in turn, wiped her eyes or blew her nose, then tossed it into a pile beside her elbow. Some of the tissues had fallen off the table and were starting to form an untidy pile on the floor. Lucy is not the kind of person who uses anything even remotely disposable more than once.

Both of them were too absorbed to acknowledge my arrival. I fetched a third mug from a hook underneath the cupboard and joined them at the table. It was raining hard outside. Inside, despite Lucy's woe, the kitchen was overwhelmingly its usual, cheerful self. White light spilled down from the six schoolhouse lights that hung in two rows overhead. The clean, milky light resonated around the room like a minor chord, erasing the shadows from the yellow walls. I got up and added milk to my tea from the jug in the fridge, then rejoined the weeper and the comforter at the table. Lucy blew her nose with one hand and reached over with the other and took the cup from me. She began, between sobs and hiccups, to take small sips from it. I picked up the cup that had been sitting in front of her, carried it to the refrigerator, poured in some milk, and then sat down again. Mother put her hand on my wrist.

"There are some cookies in the tin," she murmured. I set the cup back down on the table, got a plate, and piled it high with hermits, the only kind of cookie my mother makes—madeleines to her three daughters. Lucy likes to eat in sorrow and in happiness. She began to nibble on a cookie as soon as I put the plate in front of her. I sat down. Mother placed her hand on my wrist again.

"Go and check on your father," she asked. I picked up my cup and one of the cookies and carried them into the living room.

My father was sitting in the ugly brown corduroy chair beside the window reading. The dim light of the late afternoon was supplemented by the glow of a 60-watt bulb set into a bridge lamp beside his chair. The lamp was a recent addition to the house. Janet had spotted it in a second-hand store. I had picked it up, cleaned the rust from the narrow grooves of its long stand, and polished the metal filigree. Ryan had rewired it. Lucy had dusted the old lampshade.

"Thank you, darling," my father said, looking up from his magazine. He raised his glasses to the top of his head and rubbed his eyes. His magazine fell onto his lap as he reached to take the cup and cookie from me.

"I'm not sure when I'll be able to start dinner. They'll be in there a while yet, from the sound of it."

I sat down on the cracking plastic hassock in front of him and put my arms around my knees.

"What's up?" I asked.

"She's heard from Gian Luigi."

"And?"

"Apparently he wants her back."

"With Ryan's baby?"

"So it seems."

"What is she going to do?"

We sat looking at each other, knowing that, however much we might speculate, what Lucy would do would likely remain a mystery to us all even after she had done it.

My father drank the tea and ate the cookie. We talked about the work Ryan was doing on the house, but both of us were keeping an ear tuned to the ebb and flow of voices from the kitchen.

After half an hour, Lucy stopped crying, and I decided to risk going back into the kitchen to scramble some eggs. Mother and Lucy continued to talk, but they lowered their voices to a murmur. Lucy's tone was plaintive. Mother's was consoling. I took a bowl of eggs out of the refrigerator and cracked two each for me, Mother, and Father and three for Lucy. I found some onions at the bottom of the cupboard under the sink, sliced them thin, and started them over a low flame in a large knob of butter. I cooked the eggs until they were underset and creamy, then divided them onto four plates with slices of brown bread, toasted and buttered, and small mounds of spinach that I had found in a frozen lump in the freezer and reheated in a small pot with more butter. Father came up from the basement with three bottles of cold beer. I reached around my mother and Lucy and set a plate in front of each of them. I handed a beer to my mother and a glass of milk to Lucy, who looked at it dubiously.

I carried the other two plates into the living room, where my father and I ate with our plates on our laps. His eyes stole back to his magazine, *The New Internationalist,* and I picked up a book from the coffee table and pretended to read it. It was about trade patterns in Africa and Asia, the problems of supply and demand, transportation and food preservation. I studied the diagrams and charts, but didn't absorb any information from them. I was still trying to hear what was going on in the kitchen.

At last, when I was on the point of abandoning my father and going home, my mother came into the living room carrying a tray. "Ice cream?" she offered. My father gratefully accepted a dish and my mother's company. I observed how vividly he lighted up when my mother appeared, a man of sixty in love with his wife of almost forty years.

At the end of my relationship with my first love, Chris, I had asked my mother if Dad ever told her that he loved her. "Every day," she told me fondly, touching my cheek, her eyes soft, her pleasure in her husband expanding across her face. "Every day." I remembered suddenly and guiltily the fog of misery I had felt then. It didn't seem possible that I would ever achieve a lasting love like that, one that would guarantee a portion of tenderness every day of my life.

After I had finished my ice cream, I took my dish into the kitchen, where I found Lucy standing beside the fridge, eating with a large spoon from the container of ice cream. Her empty bowl sat on the table.

"Ice cream is a good source of calcium," she said.

"So I've heard. What did you decide to do?" I sat crossways in the chair my mother had abandoned.

"I decided that it's complicated."

"You had better tell Ryan soon, if you've changed your mind."

"I haven't changed my mind." Lucy rubbed her stomach, which was the size of a large squash. "I haven't made it up yet."

"Yes, you have. You made up your mind when you left Gian Luigi, told him it was over, quit your job, moved back to Vancouver, and agreed to marry Ryan."

"That was then."

"What's changed, Lucy? Why would you do this to Ryan?"

"Gian Luigi thinks it might be possible for him to leave his wife after all, that he might be able to talk Ivetta into giving him a divorce."

"Is that what you want? Because if it is, you have to call it off with Ryan immediately. He's making plans for both of you. For all three of you. He's getting that house ready right now."

I felt horrified at Lucy's self-serving reasoning, her careless readiness to set aside Ryan and his plans and work. Poor, steady, adoring, deluded Ryan, dancing and singing around his paint cans, tenderly patching plaster and repairing frayed wiring for a wife and child who might never move in.

"And doesn't Ryan even have a say? This is his baby too, after all."

"I haven't made up my mind, Maggie."

"Well, you are just going to have to. Think, Lucy! There are a lot of people at stake here. Not only Ryan. There are also Gian Luigi's children. How many did you say he has?"

"Three. Claudio, Ugo, and Paula. Paula is five."

"Oh, Lucy."

"I know. I know. But I love him. And he loves me."

"Oh, love!"

"What do you mean, 'Oh, love?' You make it sound like nothing."

"I am sorry, but what could be so irresistible, so irreplaceable, so enduring, so *valuable* about a love for the kind of person that would betray his wife and leave three young children?"

Lucy drew in her chin and filled her lungs with air, but then deflated a little, and let her breath out slowly instead of using it as fuel to turn my question into rage, into an attack, an elaborate justification.

"I don't know. I don't know what to tell you. But I do love him all the same. He makes me happy."

"Oh, *happiness*," I said, half scolding and half mocking—myself mostly, but her as well.

Lucy sat down across from me at the table and smiled. Her right hand strayed to her stomach again.

"Yes. Happiness."

Front Staircase

Sleeplessness did not have any counterpart to anything I had experienced before in life, although, of course, I knew something about it from books I had read. I have always, until recently, felt about books the way people of faith seem to feel about their gods. They form a sturdy wall against which I can lean, a platform from which I can spring. Books alone, among all the diversions and facts of the world, have almost never failed me. They give me perspective, and the sense of belonging and interconnectedness that spiritual people lay claim to.

One night I found in my bookshelf and reread Kafka's story "A Hunger Artist." I wondered then for the first time, although I began to feel it more keenly as the days went on, whether, in the absence of any other art, I was becoming or had become a kind of sleep artist.

In Kafka's strange story, the hunger artist goes as long as forty days without food, fasting not only for the art of it, but for ambition, for fame, for the drama of self-denial. But just when he takes his art to a new level, seeking to magnify himself in complete self-erasure, the hunger artist confesses to a much less exalted motive. He explains that he simply "couldn't find the food I liked. If I had found it, believe me, I should have made no fuss and stuffed myself

like you or anyone else." Kafka is disturbing, claustrophobic reading at any time, but this story made me uncomfortable. I tossed in
my bed and wondered about the links between Rebecca's test and
my sleeplessness, about the ropey connections and inescapable par-
allels between sleep and death.

In the middle of December, a thick layer of heavy snow fell
suddenly during the night. Rain had been predicted, but just before
midnight, the temperature dropped several degrees and the fat
drops were transformed as they tumbled into elegant six-sided
crystals, each a diminutive work of the finest tracery.

Snow is rare on the West Coast, and I could not remember so
much falling so quickly before. The snow was still falling, wet,
heavy, abundant, and dazzling, when I left for work on Monday
morning. Because Vancouver's climate is moderate, the city keeps a
minimal fleet of snowplows, which means that when it snows, only
the roads deemed most essential are cleared. The cars parked on the
street were buried in snow, caught fast in drifts that were higher
than their bumpers. Few of them were likely to be going anywhere
that day or the next.

I joined a growing stream of workers walking to their jobs
downtown. Many of the walkers were mincing between the snow-
drifts in thin-soled shoes. I saw one man who had put a plastic bag
around each of his shoes and fixed them in place with masking tape
around his ankles. His feet slipped and skated alarmingly with each
step. I strode along much more confidently in my hiking boots, the
legs of my pants tucked into the waterproof gaiters that I had
bought for the one or two times a year when Luba and I went
cross-country skiing on the trails at Mount Seymour, warm in a
red wool coat with toggle closures, one of my father's thrift-store
finds.

There was little traffic on Davie aside from a few laboring, slow-moving buses, already overcrowded with passengers who had been forced by the unplowed snow to leave their cars at home. The windows of the buses were steamed over on the inside with the collective breath of the passengers and frozen over outside with long, linked, branching feathers of frost. Every now and then a small area would be rubbed clear by a gloved or mittened hand, but these openings blurred over and closed again immediately like ice reforming on the surface of a frozen pond.

The usual blustering rumble of the buses was gentled by the snow. The sun shone. The other walkers formed a bright moving picture as they made their way along the sidewalks, dressed in vivid Gore-Tex, brilliant fleece and deep-hued wools, wrapped in multicolored scarves, shepherding tiny clouds of warm breath ahead of delighted, inconvenienced, isn't-this-amazing-weather smiles and strawberry red cheeks.

Near the corner of Burrard and Davie, I saw the girl who had once claimed I was a spiritual person. She lay sideways on the sidewalk, in a defeated curve, like a freshly rolled drunk. Her hands were tucked for warmth between her skinny thighs. I could see her face in profile under her lank hair, and I saw a new flatness to her expression, like a partly erased sketch. A dark brown area at the top her head had spread, as the badly dyed red-blond lengths of her hair had grown out, making the top of her head look like the center of a wild poppy surrounded by ragged coppery red petals.

I felt a shock of disquiet. The girl was not dressed adequately. Her blanket was missing. She lay directly against the icy pavement. Her skin was mottled red, blue, and white. She appeared exhausted and ill. I hesitated, then stopped and squatted on my heels in front of her.

"Are you all right?" Ridiculous question.

The girl blinked at me very slowly, but she didn't answer. The surface of her eyes was flat and glassy. Up close, she looked as if she were under water, drowning and freezing both at once, while people hurried past detouring to avoid her twisted knees.

"I am on my way to the hospital," I said, speaking loudly and slowly, as though the girl had gone deaf or spoke a language other than English. "I work there. Why don't you come with me and let them check you over? You don't look well."

She blinked again. Drugs? I wondered. A bad trip? Or had she been beaten, robbed? Her skin had gone dead white; the only color was a pale blue just under the surface, the thin shade of skim milk.

"You can't stay here," I insisted. "You'll freeze to death." My voice was louder now, with the weight of the responsibility I was mustering. Several people passed us on the sidewalk; I imagined their relief at seeing that someone had acted, thus allowing them to walk by without any unpleasant tug of scruple.

The girl's eyes rolled up at me, and I realized with a shock that she was past being able to speak, much less make a decision for herself, that she would not be able to release me from having to take charge. I hesitated. The hospital was only two blocks away. It didn't seem reasonable to ask one of the passersby to call an ambulance. But I certainly couldn't carry her, and she looked too weak to walk, even with my support. I didn't want to leave her. It seemed to me that her presence on the street was no decision, but the result of many betrayals and failures, of the absence of constancy, and I didn't want to resemble even for a few minutes the many people who had abandoned her before.

In a novel or a movie, someone would have come to my rescue, or the girl would have closed her blue fingers around my comforting hand, delivering herself up to my charge, perhaps struggled to her feet to allow me to support her the length of two city blocks, a feral cat tamed by milk and kindness. None of these occurred. After a minute or so of indecision, squatting there patting her cold hand both as an apology and as reassurance to us both, still unsure whether she was sick or letting some substance wear off, I noticed a small patch of red-black under her hip. The stain was growing slowly larger and redder. Blood. I felt my own blood respond by rushing with force into my face and hands.

"I'm going to go for help," I told her. "Don't move." I took off my coat and put it over her.

"You," I held my hand up toward the chest of a woman of about my own age who was about to step to one side to make her way around the girl on the pavement. "You stay here with her. I'm going to call an ambulance."

I sprinted across the street, leaving the woman and girl together. I looked back once and saw the woman obediently standing to one side of the girl's curled up body. She had begun to smoke. Her hand holding the cigarette moved in broad sweeps, her feet shuffled. This girl is nothing to me, her gestures said. She was acting out the scene of a woman who had picked an unfortunate spot to wait for a friend to drive by and pick her up.

I ran to the cashier booth at the gas station on the corner and asked one of the two young boys working there if he would run to the hospital and tell them to send someone to help me get the girl to emergency. He declined, explaining that he was under strict orders from "head office" never to abandon his post, but he did agree to dial 911, and an ambulance soon came at ordinary speed south toward us along Burrard. The distance was so short that the siren let out only a single, abridged admonitory yelp; there was not time enough for it to break into its osculating, full-throated yodel.

The ambulance came to a halt on the street beside where the girl lay. I had returned to her side. To my surprise, the smoking woman stayed put, standing like a sentry at her post, although she moved a small distance off to one side.

Two paramedics dressed in white got out of the ambulance. They were professionally slow and deliberate and serious, and it was all I could do not to urge them to hurry, hurry, couldn't they see that the girl was dying, would die within moments, and weren't we all culpable?

One of them began to examine the prostrate girl, and the other turned to question me. It was rapidly established that I knew nothing of any use at all about the girl. I was discounted, set aside, of no more interest to them than the nearby news box with its batch of fresh papers stacked neatly inside.

The girl was raised up easily between the two attendants, one male and silent, the other female, hippy, murmuring wordless encouragement. The girl was not much heavier, it appeared, than the red-and-white plastic bag that billowed and scudded against the brick wall behind us, then was swept from sight by the brisk wind. She was unresisting except for a despairing, tender, exhaled moan. The girl was inserted neatly between white sheets on a stretcher, bundled under a gray blanket, thrust into the cavern mouth of the ambulance, and carried away under a second short warning blast of noise.

Left behind were the patch of bloody snow, now mostly melted to ice water, and a wrinkled and creased paper bag. I looked inside the bag and found a white comb, a piece of soap, and a small, sample-sized bottle of shampoo. The comb was dirty and broken, the soap a sordid sliver, the shampoo a faint film of gold at the bottom of the bottle, so I crammed the bag into a garbage container.

"All right then," said the smoking woman. She cocked an eye at me, dropped her cigarette butt, and ground it under her heel. "You'll never see that coat again," she observed, then walked away, her shoulders squared in the manner of someone whose job is done.

I brushed my hands together, then thought to check my watch; only five minutes remained until I was to see my first patient. I broke into a jog, but immediately skidded and pitched forward. The loose, churned snow covered a layer of ice that had been laid down during the rains of one day earlier, before the temperature fell below freezing. I slowed my pace. I was freezing without my coat, but knew that I should take care, take my time; everyone would be late today, even the patients. Emergency was the only part of the hospital certain to be busy, filling up with ankle sprains and whiplashes.

I reached the hospital, walked up the main stairs, then surprised myself by turning to the right, toward Emergency, instead of left, toward Radiology. I scanned the crowded waiting areas and the busy corridors in which occupied gurneys lined both walls, like two trains, side by side, come to a halt at a broken switch. I saw no sign of the sidewalk girl.

I tried for a while to get the attention of one of the harried admitting nurses or rushing orderlies, but none of them would allow their ear or eye to be caught. A passing doctor recognized me, but she knew nothing about a homeless girl. Finally I caught the ward social worker, a pink, plump man of thirty or so, who had not heard of the girl either, but he accepted my name and extension number and promised to let me know if he came across her. He stuffed the scrap of paper that I passed to him into the inner pocket of his jacket, which was already bulging with pink memo slips and other small notes, and then turned and scurried away.

I made my way along the hallways to my own office, where three patients were sitting, waiting uncomplainingly in the dark. No one had come to turn on the lights or tell them what to do. I reached behind the reception desk, snapped on the lights, and smiled at them. It wasn't until I turned on my caregiver smile that I realized how deeply my face had been set into anxious lines. The act of smiling felt painful, as though my worried expression had been covered by a thin layer of ice that needed a strong tap to break it apart. I blinked and smiled more broadly.

"I can't wait to hear how on earth you got here through the snow," I said. "Who's first? You can tell me your story while I get things set up."

Bedroom

Because of the late start, and because so many of the patients were delayed, and because one of the other technicians didn't make it in from Surrey, that day ended very late, after seven, and I did not have time to eat either lunch or dinner. I kept going, seeing woman after woman, breast after breast, fueled by cups of milky tea that Ramona, the receptionist for our department, kept pressing into my hands, and by the last two cookies that I found in the package of digestives in a drawer in my desk. I was writing up my last report when the telephone rang, an internal line.

"This is Brian Hinton?" The caller had one of those rare male voices in which each sentence glides a feminine, upward, questioning trajectory. "You asked me to call you? If I had any news about Oriah Burke?"

"Oriah?"

"Your friend? The one you brought into emergency?"

"She's not actually a friend. I didn't even know her name. I found her on the street this morning on my way to work. She seemed very unwell. Is she all right?"

"She was transferred. About three this afternoon? They sent

her over to Women's. They would have kept her here, but, where to put her, eh? You saw this place today, kind of a zoo?"

"What did she . . . ?"

"Miscarriage. She had lost a lot of blood? Ectopic, they said. Women's had a bed open, can you believe it, miracle of miracles, despite the cutbacks, so they gave her a quick transfusion here, then sent her over there. Probably keep her for a few days." He paused. "Look, is there anything else?"

"No. No. You have been very kind. You must be on your way home. Thanks for letting me know."

"No problem. It's my job, eh? Keeping people connected? I was thinking though. It's been a long day. Ummm, if you are free, perhaps we could go for a beer? Or, ummm, a coffee? Share war stories, sort of."

The downward ratcheted shift in the social worker's tone provided a window, or something smaller and more constricted, a keyhole or pinprick aperture into his life. I heard in his vocal hesitancy a man easily intimate with the sorrow of others, at the ready with advice and solutions, but unable to define or resolve or even recognize and acknowledge his own predicament: how to obtain and sustain a passionate life as a man of middle years, median height, unremarkable appearance, no more than standard skill, perhaps substandard wit. He was certain to have some aspect about himself or his life that was a secret source of delight to himself, and would be to someone else, could he find her and show it to her quickly before she looked away. I was certain, however, that I was not this person, and so made an excuse and put down the phone, regretful that I might have hurt him, certain that neither his hurt nor my regret would last too long.

After hanging up, I sat at the desk for a moment. I felt too emptied by the day's labors and demands even to move. On the message pad beside the phone, I had written the words "Oriah Burke? Brooke?" and beside these, I had doodled a rough sketch of the soprano from the choir: plate-shaped face, pastry chin, soft parentheses of hair, mild eyes, round singing mouth. When finally I stood up, my legs tingled and my head felt heavy and echoing, like a cleared-out bank safe. My eyes and mouth were dry, and my stomach moaned and contracted. The phone rang again. I let it ring six times before I sighed and picked it up.

"Hello?" My voice echoed the social worker's hesitant quaver.

"Maggie! It's Janet. You're still at work?"

"Yes, I'm just wrapping up." I cradled the phone under my chin and reached to tear the top sheet of paper from the pad on my desk. I balled it up and dropped it in the garbage. With my other hand, I reached behind my chair for my coat to shrug it over my shoulders. It wasn't there. I couldn't think where I could have left it. I suppressed a sigh of annoyance and deep fatigue and reached forward instead to turn off my glowing computer.

"Can you stay put? Ryan is bringing in Lucy. She's gone into early labor."

Nursery

After Lucy and Ryan had been assigned a labor room and had settled in, Janet and my parents and I found our way to a room marked "Families" at the far end of the ward. The room was painted pale green, with a frieze of storks carrying blue and pink bundles in their beaks. Several posters, faded or bright, depending on how long they had been taped in place, promoted the merits of breastfeeding and inoculations and warned of household hazards to babies and toddlers. Someone had distributed small baskets throughout the room and filled them with balls of wool and knitting needles. Beside them were notices that the Rip and Stitch Club would sew completed squares into blankets for "Newborns in Need."

Both of my parents settled down and started to knit. My father took up a ball of pink wool. His stitches were even and straight and furled from his fingers at a regular pace. My mother chose yellow yarn, but she did not progress. Every half hour, she unraveled most of her work to pick up a dropped stitch.

Janet moved from chair to chair, from window to poster to magazines to doorway. She sat in front of a sprawling jigsaw puzzle for a few minutes, studying the areas that someone else had put together. The box was propped nearby. It showed a picture of the completed puzzle, an English cottage and bucolic fields, complete with lambs and shepherds. Her hand hovered for a while over the tumble of loose pieces. Finally she selected a fragment of blue sky, and turned it round and round for a while, but she let the piece fall back onto the pile without fitting it into place. Several times she strode down the hall to the labor room to check for updates. "Nothing," she reported each time, with increasing irritation. After her fourth trip she announced that things were going slowly and that, since she was certain there would be no change for hours yet, she was going to go home, get the children into bed, and come back later.

"I never came to the hospital until the last minute," she said. She twined a silk scarf around her neck and reached for her coat and purse. "Trust Lucy to dash to the hospital at the first twitch. They're probably just Braxton-Hicks—practice contractions. She's not due for weeks yet anyway." She sniffed and left.

"All right, dear," said my mother, without looking up. She had given up the knitting and had moved to the orange plastic bucket chair that Janet had just vacated. She began to scrutinize the puzzle. My father had finished casting off a neat, pink square. He took up a ball of blue wool and began to cast on, using the method he had learned from his father, who had learned it in the war, with one needle and the fingers of his right hand. His darting fingers looked as if they might be forming the letters in a language for the deaf or casting an incantation using the single needle he held in his left hand as a wand.

My father is tall and dark, with a prominent, lightly cleft chin, a roman nose, broad shoulders, and large hands and feet. He looks strong and a bit exaggerated, like a casting agent's notion of a football team coach, or a senator or newscaster. My mother, who is not beautiful, is noticed far more when she is near him. When she is apart from my father, even an arm's-length away, she is easily overlooked. She is short, just over five feet tall, and has drab, peahen coloring and the figure of a skinny thirteen-year-old boy. My parents buy most of their clothes in thrift stores, but my mother chooses clothes in beige and pale pink and light blue, made from frankly synthetic fabrics, the kind that pill and stretch out and go limp and thin, while my father has a knack for the find—wide-wale corduroy trousers in burgundy, black, or deep brown, well-made shirts, and good woolen sweaters. When they stand or sit or lean together, some of my father's beauty reflects onto my mother, and she takes on a dim gleam, like mother-of-pearl, or a turtledove's effulgent breast feathers, or battered hand-me-down silver plate.

"I don't like this waiting," Mother said after another hour had crept by. She had finished the English pastoral and had started on a second puzzle, a farmyard scene with ducks and hens and geese. "I had you girls at home, where we could be comfortable. Your father kept running upstairs with cups of tea for the midwife and me."

"Can you just imagine Lucy having a baby at home?" I asked her. "Janet said she was demanding an epidural within five minutes of getting here. Lucy's far happier here, with all the latest technology at her beck and call."

At ten o'clock, after Ryan dropped in to report that Lucy was still only five centimeters dilated, my father went out to fetch vegetarian pizza to share with my mother, and a pepperoni one for Ryan and me. By midnight Lucy was still not progressing, so my parents agreed to go home to sleep and wait for me to telephone. I stayed behind and read pages 81 to 114 of *Swann's Way*, which I found on a shelf among the books and magazines, mostly *Reader's Digests* and spy novels. Nothing happened, either in *Swann's Way* or in the hospital. At three o'clock, Ryan came in, haggard and exhilarated, to tell me that Lucy had been started on a hormone drip to get things moving along more swiftly. He got a can of cola from a machine in the hall and went back to suffer through Lucy's next contraction.

I got up, stretched, and worked my way clockwise around the room, reading the admonitory posters on the walls. One, which featured a skull and crossbones and line drawings of unconscious toddlers, warned about the dangers of household poisons, including, to my surprise, several common houseplants. Another illustrated the many ways in which a small child can strangle (drawstrings on hooded sweat shirts, cords dangling from slatted blinds, those looped hand towels in gas station washrooms), suffocate (plastic mattresses, grocery bags, dry-cleaning bags), or choke (hot dogs, popcorn, carrots, ordinary bread).

I sank into one of the ugly orange chairs. What, I wondered, did Lucy imagine she was doing? How would she manage? What hope could there be for the child of such a self-absorbed mother? How did any child survive? Clearly there were dangers in the world against which infants had to be protected. I felt a growing panic at the images the posters cast up on the movie screen of my mind. Harrowing thoughts caught my breath like a fish on a hook inside my chest. Lucy's little baby dangling blue by its neck from the end of a curtain pull. A small shattered body on the pavement at the foot of a brick building, a torn screen flapping blandly high above, as though to make it clear that it couldn't be blamed, an inanimate object, for the tiny tragedy. An infant, dead of crib death or smothered, white and still in its little smocked nightgown, face down on a mattress.

I felt suddenly, intensely, that I had to act, that only I could save this about-to-be child, still only part way through this messy, stormy process of being born. There came to my mind, urgently, a conviction that saving Lucy's child might be the means to save myself as well.

I rose from the chair and stepped purposefully toward the door, then recoiled, horrified, when confronted with an ashen-faced woman, her hair crazily askew, who stuck her head into the waiting room through an opening in the wall. The woman looked worried, urgent, as if she were searching for someone. I put a hand out toward her, and she reached for me in the same instant, for she was, of course, my own reflection in a mirror. I looked around the room. Mum and Dad had gone, and Janet too. I was alone and had fallen asleep. The hands of the clock stood at 4:45.

Outside the windows, I could see a flurry of soft, light, spinning, wheeling movement. The snow had begun again. The driven flakes made pinwheels and spirals and raced in a disordered craze against the black night sky. The sight of the silent, swirling snow calmed me. I breathed in deeply, then out again slowly. The snow would hold the city, and the world, at bay while Lucy and her baby labored through the night.

There were, for some reason, no other anxiously waiting families, and when I reached the hall, I saw the nimbus glow from only one of the birthing rooms, which must be where Lucy and Ryan had been placed. Was no one else being born tonight? I made my way silently down the hall toward the slender thread of light under Lucy's labor room door.

When I reached the room, I could hear on the other side of the door a complicated skein of noise, voices and hissing and electronic humming, tangled together and overlapping. A woman wearing pale green scrubs and soft white shoes padded past me and pushed through the doorway into the room. The heavy door swung noiselessly back into place, its arc controlled by some hidden, slowing mechanism. I pushed against it and went into the room, which was dark except for a pool of light around a bed. A half-dozen people were gathered around a tent of sheets supported by Lucy's knees. Her calves and thighs shivered, blue-white, in the vivid glare of a light suspended from the ceiling and aimed at the mound of her belly. Lucy groaned deeply and panted. Ryan crouched beside her head, his lips close to her ear, murmuring encouragement.

"You're doing great, Lucy. We're getting there. Not much longer now."

"I want to go home," Lucy moaned. "I'm hungry. I can't do this. I can't do it."

Two women in scrubs exchanged terse bits of information with the woman who had come in ahead of me. Another woman clattered metal on metal at the sink, an ugly noise. I could hear, faintly, in the background, the shrill string crescendo of violins. Mozart. Yet another woman crouched between Lucy's legs holding a cotton sheet in her hands. Everyone except me and Lucy wore latex gloves and green scrubs. No one noticed me and I wondered if I might still be dreaming, or if it were possible that the part of me that could observe and think had walked away from my sleeping body in the waiting room. The woman with the sheet issued sharp, short directions to Lucy. She sounded pitiless, although I expected that this must be her job—to direct events according to a familiar script, however unwilling the actors.

"Stop pushing! Shallow breathing now, Lucy. Pant! Like this: huh, huh, huh, huh. Good girl. Don't push. No. Don't push. You will feel a bit of discomfort now, a burning sensation, like a ring of fire, right now, right here. Don't worry. You are doing perfectly. I

am going to ease the skin around ... do you feel that? That's the
baby's head. Your baby's coming now. I can see the top of the baby's
head. OK, I want one more gentle push. Don't overdo it. Now!
Gentle. Easy. Again. Don't push! Short, shallow breaths. Like this:
huh, huh, huh. Good girl. Here it is! It's coming. The head is out
now, Lucy. I can see dark curling hair, lots of it. And now one
shoulder. Can you feel it? Now the other. You will feel a tug now.
Keep breathing. Don't stop now. Pant: huh, huh, huh. Good girl!
Good girl!"

And then, in the same instant, like the moments before a symphony, when the instruments are giving themselves a shakeout and
testing their scales, the noises all came together.

Lucy, screamed, a sound that came from low in her stomach.
"Noooooo," she said.

Ryan said: "Oh my God. Oh my God."

One of the women cried out, "Good for you!"

Another said, "Here we go."

"That's it, then," said someone else in a tone that reminded me
of something, but I couldn't focus to follow the thread of memory.

Someone clattered metal on metal over against the wall.

A young man I hadn't noticed before rushed up with a stack of
blankets.

Someone said, "Ooof."

Someone announced, shaky, giddy, triumphant: "It's a boy!"

A dark shape, slippery and black-red with blood and fluid, and
sinuous as a fish, but bony, helpless, and uncoordinated as a newborn lamb slipped out from Lucy's legs and was caught in the
waiting sheet. I leaned back against the door, felt it give way behind
me, and fell backward, sliding against its weight right down to the
floor. "Oh!" I said. I landed on my bottom. My head slammed into

the door. I sat there and watched while the baby, Lucy's baby, was taken over to a table and examined, carelessly it seemed to me. Its little limbs were pulled and measured, its head felt all over, its skinny legs rotated in its hips. It cried and cried, as well it might, but finally was wrapped up in a light green blanket and brought back to Lucy.

Lucy had raised herself up on both elbows and was leaning into Ryan whose arm was around her. He patted her hair and said to her over and over. "You did it. You did it."

"Never again," Lucy said. Her tone was categorical. "I need a drink. No more of those damn ice chips. A real drink."

I slid myself over to a spot beside the door and stood up, using the wall for support. My head and hip hurt. I was lost in the shadows. No one had noticed me. The baby was laid quivering and wailing on Lucy's stomach and I turned and pushed my way out of the room. I walked down the long, impossibly bright corridor back to the waiting room, found the light switch, turned it off, lay down on my side on one of the couches, covered myself with a knitted blanket, and fell asleep.

Dormer

What happened next was largely my fault, so it is hardly surprising that I felt compelled to act. Gian Luigi telephoned me. He had likely worked his way through the other Selgrins in the telephone book—there aren't too many in Vancouver—and he reached me when he got to the M's.

"Allo, I am looking for Miss Lucy Selgrin."

"Lucy's not here. She's still in the hospital," I said. It was a few minutes before eight in the morning and I was getting ready to go to work. I assumed that this was one of Lucy's Roman coworkers calling. She had mentioned that they often took advantage of the toll-free telephone line at the office to call her and bring her up-to-date on the gossip. "I expect you've heard the news. She had her baby two days ago. A little boy."

Gian Luigi is a smart man. There was no hint that this was the first that he had heard of a baby.

"A boy! *Un maschio!* How wonderful. Hand the name?"

"They've decided to call him Philip."

"Ah, *Filippo!* Exactly like my *padre. Un bel nome.* Hand the father of this *Filippo*, I have forgotten hees name?"

"Ryan. Her fiancé. They are thrilled. He's a beautiful baby. Lots of dark curly hair and the most enormous eyes."

"Ah yes, Ryan. Stupid of me to forget thees. Ryan. Of course. *Senti.* We are wanting to send flowers to Lucy. To send our felicitations. *Auguri.* This is a happy event. But I 'ave lost the address. Can you give it to me please? And the *ospedale?* It is called?"

Of course I told him everything. I didn't think there was anything strange about it. And neither did Lucy when I told her later that one of her friends had called from Rome, although she was annoyed that I hadn't got his name.

"It was probably Roberto," she decided after I described the voice on the phone. "He has a deep voice. And the best English of all the Italian staff."

Philip developed jaundice and was kept in hospital for two extra days while mysterious things were done to him involving needles and lights. Lucy stayed too, relishing the bed rest, television, visitors, flowers, presents, and hot meals delivered by Ryan from restaurants near the hospital, even while she complained about the noise, odors, inattentive staff, and other inconveniences. She had, to my mother's grief and her doctor's undisguised dismay, elected not to breast-feed Philip. Even Ryan, who still appeared oblivious to any imperfection in Lucy, tried to talk her out of giving Philip formula, but he gave up after Lucy pointed out that Ryan himself had been bottle-fed and had turned out perfectly well, while having been nursed for three years by our mother hadn't prevented her from being somewhat highly strung.

I was in the diminutive washroom of Lucy's hospital room pouring the remains of a bottle of formula down the drain on the morning of the fourth day after Philip was born, when I heard unfamiliar voices. Two people were approaching Lucy's bed. A man and a woman.

"Ver is the baby? I insist to see him."

"Gian Luigi! What the hell are you doing here?" I heard Lucy's voice rise. She sounded surprised and alarmed. "And who is this?" I stood still, holding my breath, listening.

"Lucy, I present you my wife. Ivetta, this is Lucia."

"So this is *la bella* Lucia." A dry voice.

"Your wife! What happened to her? She's not fat! And what is she doing here anyway? What the hell are you doing here? No one asked you to come. You're not wanted."

"We have come," I heard the voice of the woman who must be Ivetta, Gian Luigi's wife, announce. "For the baby."

"You mean you came all the way from Italy just to see the baby?"

"Not to *see* the baby. *For* the baby." Ivetta again.

"Listen, Lucy. We have come to talk to you. The baby is as much mine as yours. He's more mine. He's my son. My first son."

"What the hell do you mean! You have no right to just barge in here. This is a private room. Get the fuck out of here, you shithead. You and your damn, skinny wife. Get out of my room. Get out of my life. Just get out."

"Lucy. *Senti.* We have an order. From the court in Italy. The *tribunale* has granted what you call custody, *custodia*, to me and Ivetta. They were very displeased to hear that you left Italy without my consent. And we have consulted with an advocate of law in Canada. He has told me that I have a right to my son. *Ugale* rights."

"*Your* son? You have your own damn children."

"Well, Lucy. Is not so simple, actually. Actually, my wife and I, we have not been able to have children. Is the fault of Ivetta. Her liver. And Ivetta, when she hear there was a child. . . ."

"The child of my *marito*. Even if with an American *putana* . . ."

"*No, no, Ivetta. Lucia non è Americana. Lei è Canadese.*"

"*Pero, caro mio. . . .*"

"*Ivetta, non puoi stare zitta per neanche un atimo?*"

"Ees Italian child. Italian *padre*. Italian *nome—il nome del mio suo-cero. Capelli Italiani. Ho aspetata tanti anni per avere un bambino. L'ho voluto sopra tutto nel mondo. E addesso. . . .*"

"Lucia. *Sentame.* You are young. You will have other childrens. This one, he ees for me. Ees my son. I am hees father. Ivetta and I, when we hear about the baby, eet was like a miracle. We have come to take him home."

"Well, you damn well can't have him. He's mine. You and your skinny bitch of a wife can just get the hell out of here."

"Be reasonable, Lucy. Ivetta and I can give our son everything. I have done my enquiries. This Canadian boyfriend of yours ees not rich. And I am prepared to offer you something, offer you both something. A wedding gift. A substantial wedding gift."

"You want to *buy* my baby?" Lucy shouted. "Are you crazy? *Pazzo?* He's not for sale."

"I was afraid you might not agree with me at first. So, I have brought these."

I heard the rustle of papers.

"You understand, eet was necessary for me to do something un-til you are able to think reasonably. Women after they have give birth, they are not so rational. Thees is well known. I have looked after my son's interests. We have a good Canadian advocate. Very ex-pert. The *tribunale* in Italy has already granted me *custodia*. And your court heard our claim yesterday. Here ees an order, an order *ex parte* that my son no leave, that he stay here, at the *ospedale*, until a final de-cision is made. Our counsellor tells us that we have a very good case, that the courts will give us what he calls 'shared' custody *al meno*. And they will also be displeased to hear that you left *Italia* without consulting me. Lucia. How could you do this? My own *figlio? Sangue del mio sangue. Carne della mia carne.* You should have told me. Why didn't you tell me? *Madonna, Lucia, perque me hai detto niente?"*

The door of the washroom was wide and heavy. It opened outward, into Lucy's room, and blocked me from being seen as I slipped out of the washroom into the corridor. I stood still for a moment. I could feel the blood drain away from the core of my body as though a plug had been pulled, and rush into my hands and feet and throat, urging me to action. I half ran down the broad hall to the bright nursery, where I had deposited Philip, wrapped and fed, a warm, calm, sleeping bundle in his Plexiglas cot on wheels, less than half an hour earlier.

"She wants him back!" I said—gaily, brightly—to one of the nurses, skidding into the nursery.

The nurse pursed her lips and drew down her brow. "He's sound asleep," she pointed out.

"His mother has decided that she wants to try nursing him after all," I said.

"Well, that is very good news," she said. Approval fattened her vowels and spread like a flush across her pink, heart-shaped face. "In that case, he's all yours."

The nurse released the brake at the back of the little glass cot. I wheeled Philip away from the nursery, trying through force of will to remember how to walk normally. My legs were stiff, and my feet as heavy and clumsy as weights. I focused my gaze on the faint tracery of blue veins on the backs of my hands. My hands felt huge and cumbersome. They swam in front of my eyes, too close, then, just as abruptly, they seemed as far away and as disassociated from me as the wall at the end of the ward.

Around the corner from the nursery, I reached a quiet stretch of corridor. I abandoned the cot in a large supply cupboard where I helped myself to three extra blankets from a stack on a wire shelf. I wrapped the blankets tightly around Philip, leaving the smallest of openings for his mouth, nose, eyes, and the narrow band of golden skin in which his barely sketched-in eyebrows fretted and trembled. Philip slept on, oblivious to being plucked from his cot, wrapped in haste. He was sleeping through the unfolding of the second significant event in his life: being snatched away from his mother.

I had left my coat on a hook in Lucy's room, so I borrowed another, a blue hooded parka that someone had left on the arm of a waiting room chair. I shrugged it on. It was too short in the waist and too long in the sleeves, but it fit, more or less. I pulled the hood up around my face. Then I turned with Philip in my arms and walked swiftly in the direction of a side exit. My face burned with heated, urgent blood, and my knees trembled. The baby was a concentrated bundle in my arms, like a small sack of warm, wet sand. He felt surprisingly heavy in the thick layers, and he exuded his own hot, damp heat from which my enfolding hands drew reassurance and strength.

It seemed impossible that no one would stop me, point an outstretched accusing finger at me, raise the alarm, cry out, "What are you doing? Unhand that child!" I slowed my pace again, tried my best to look like a new mother with every right to leave the hospital with her baby. We went out the side door, little used except by staff when they went to smoke cigarettes together, in clutches like geese, beside the dumpsters in the alley. I leaned my hip against the bar to open the door, gave it a hard push, and stepped out into the still, frozen air.

Philip flinched and began to emit a thin complaint, a noise like a whistling sigh. I held him more closely and turned his face inward toward the blue jacket.

"Shhh," I told him. "Everything will be all right. You're going on your very first walk outside. I'm sorry the snow has mostly melted. You would have liked it."

Philip sneezed twice and settled back to sleep. His purple eyelids quivered for a few moments in the bright, cold light.

I took long strides until I reached the street, and then stood still, trying not to feel like a hostage-taker, trying to think of what to do next. My mind was absolutely blank. I had no plan. Cars rushed past. Their tires made wet, sucking noises in the slushy puddles. Black birds circled and called raucously overhead. Steam and the smell of laundry soap rose up in gulps from a cavernous vent behind me. The file of rusted dumpsters in the alley at my back emitted a sour, rotting smell. I wheeled on my heel and headed south.

As I approached the street corner, I saw that the girl was back, sitting in her usual place on the pavement. She had a thick square of carpet underneath her, and she was wearing a coat that was newer and more substantial than the one I had draped over her a few weeks earlier. Her hair was combed and a red knitted hat concealed her grown-out roots. There was color in her cheeks and lips. She looked clean and healthy, like an otherwise normal teenager who had decided, in a bid for attention perhaps, to meditate on a bit of rug beside a busy street. I crossed the street and walked up to her.

"Can you help me?" I asked her.

The girl turned her head to look at me. She stood up. Her gaze was clear. She held out her arms and I handed Philip to her.

"He isn't yours?" she asked.

"No, he's my sister's. He's newborn. A few days old. Someone wants to take him and I need to hide him. Can you help me? Just for an hour or two?"

"Yes, of course. Just tell me what you want."

I fished in my purse and gave her all the money I had in my wallet.

"It's Oriah, isn't it?"

The girl nodded. Her eyes flickered. She hadn't expected me to know her name.

"Go and buy some formula. They sell it in little bottles, already made up, nothing to mix. At the pharmacy over there—see it? And a large bag of newborn diapers. As much of both as you can get. Spend all the money if you can. Then take him into that church over there, the big one. One of the two big doors will be open. Wait inside. I'll be back and I'll meet you there within an hour."

"I understand."

"Are you able to do this? You've been ill. There could be trouble later."

Oriah shrugged. "I'm all right. Sad—but OK. I'll be OK. I can help. You have to hurry."

"Yes." I had decided that I would have to go back into the hospital and create some sort of distraction. "One hour only. I promise."

"I'll be there." The girl framed the bundle that was Philip in the crook of one arm. Her eyes focused on his crumpled face. She reached out and touched the curve of his cheek with a finger—her nails were not exactly clean, but they had been trimmed—then pulled the blanket closer around his head and turned him inward, as I had done, toward her breast. She drew a deep breath that vibrated roughly at the end.

"What about your things?" I gestured toward the scrap of carpet and a large black knapsack that remained on the pavement.

The girl handed Philip back to me and turned and stashed the carpet in a bush behind a nearby newspaper box. She shrugged the backpack onto her thin shoulders and reached for Philip again. I felt an edge of need in the way she took and enclosed him in her arms, and I hesitated, but I relinquished him anyway. I couldn't think what else to do.

I left the borrowed parka where I had found it, on the chair in the waiting room, and looked into all of the other rooms on my way back to Lucy. Four doors before hers, I found what I wanted. A dozing mother, her sleeping baby parked in its cot beside her. I crept into the darkened room, released the brake, and wheeled this baby along the hall to Lucy. On the way, I extracted the card that listed the baby's name and date of birth from its plastic holder, and inserted Philip's, which I had taken before I abandoned his bed. I dropped the other baby's card behind a hamper filled with dirty sheets in the hallway. Although I had been gone for half an hour, Gian Luigi and Lucy were still arguing.

"We must be calm," Gian Luigi was saying, to his wife or to Lucy; it wasn't clear.

Gian Luigi's wife was standing with her back to Lucy and Gian Luigi. She was looking out the window at the dismal, darkening view of the parking lot and the low rooftops of nearby buildings. Clouds were gathering. It looked as if more snow might fall before the day was through. I walked into the room, pushing the other baby in its cot. Ivetta spun from the window and rushed to look at the baby. She was tall and very thin, with black-lined eyes and a great expanse of black hair falling around her narrow shoulders. She had the deeply lined face of a committed smoker.

"Ahhhh," she said. She made a noise like air being released from the tire of a bicycle.

"Let me see him," said Gian Luigi peremptorily. He, too, advanced on the baby in the glass box. He bent from the waist and began to examine it. He did not look pleased at what he saw.

"Don't you dare touch him," said Lucy. She raised herself up on one elbow and glared at me.

"I'll go and get Ryan," I said to Lucy. I grabbed my coat from the foot of her bed and ran out of the room.

I hurried out of the front door of the hospital. It wouldn't take Lucy longer than a second to realize that the fat, fair baby in the cot wasn't Philip. She would check his wristband, which bore the other baby's name. I wasn't sure whether she would play along, or raise the alarm. In any event, the other mother would have her baby back quickly, perhaps even before she woke up.

I joined the stream of people on the sidewalk—office workers out early starting on their way home; shoppers headed for the department stores on Granville and the small shops along Robson, or back to their cars weighed down with bags and packages. I allowed myself to be carried along as far as a branch of my bank a few blocks north of the hospital. I went up to the counter and asked to withdraw five thousand dollars in cash from my account.

The young woman who handed me my money in twenties and fifties had been perfectly trained. She kept her face blank throughout the transaction, her flawlessly plucked eyebrows neither contracting nor rising. After she had counted out the money, and without being asked, she handled me an envelope large enough to hold all of the bills. I stuffed the money inside the envelope, and then squeezed the fat envelope into a pocket inside my coat.

"I'm going to buy a car," I told her. "Used." The teller nodded almost imperceptibly and smiled a thin smile. I turned and walked as slowly as I could manage out of the bank and back onto the sidewalk.

My unease grew larger and more specific with every step I took as I walked quickly back along Burrard toward the church, somewhat against the general direction of the shoppers. I had been too distracted until now to allow my imagination to add details to my fears that the girl, Oriah, could not be trusted.

Terrible pictures began to unscroll in my imagination, like a movie coming into focus. The girl would have run off with Philip and neither of them would ever be seen again. Or she had harmed him, either accidentally or on purpose. Perhaps he had woken up and would not stop crying. The girl might have become fed up and shaken him violently, his heavy head snapping back and forward on his thin, wrinkled neck. He had broken limbs. Brain damage. He had been smothered. Sold to baby smugglers. Traded for drugs. Lost. Dropped. Burned. Drowned. Dead.

I found the girl and the baby both in a pew near the back of the church, sitting at Mary's red-slippered feet. Oriah was rocking the still miraculously sleeping Philip rhythmically back and forth and crooning in a low voice. Her long hair had fallen down around him like a cloak. Beside her on the pew was a large package of disposable diapers and at her feet was a bulky plastic bag. Then I saw the dark man off to the side. The man who knew about the windows. The nephew of Salvatore and Aurelio. He was watching the girl, although he hadn't yet seen me, nor Oriah him.

Ridiculous word, nephew, I thought, irritated to see him there at a time of day when the girl and I and the baby should have had the church to ourselves. This preposterous man was there at this odd, lost hour, doing nothing useful, dressed in black, his hands clasped in his lap, and sitting directly between me and the next part of my life. I stood for a minute watching the man watch the girl, who, in turn, sat gazing at the baby in her arms. She held Philip tightly, as if she was afraid that he might tumble to the floor. I felt a twist of sorrow somewhere under my breasts, a moral ache of some kind. It seemed to me in that instant that it might be a greater crime—for how are such things measured?—for me to take Philip from the girl than it had been for me to steal him away from my sister.

Spare Room

Oriah gave Philip to me without protest, although she did reach out a long, red-knuckled hand and stroke his brow gently, with the side of her thumb, in the manner of a blessing. "I bought him a soother too," she told me, some emotion smoothing her rough voice. "Babies seem to like them."

The man in black stepped forward out of the shadows and insisted on coming with me, to help me with Philip and the bags, although I told him that I would be fine walking home, only a few blocks away. He was insistent and I solved the impasse by permitting him to hail a taxi for me. I was growing increasingly anxious about the time it was taking me to get more than a block away from the hospital with Philip. The man helped me with my packages into the back seat of the taxi and stood on the curb with his absurd black gown whipping and billowing about him, looking down at me.

"That girl," I said, as much to distract him as to help Oriah. "Maybe you could talk to her. She's lost a baby recently."

"Ah," he said, not turning away, keeping his gaze fixed on my face. "Perhaps I will."

"Where to?" asked the cab driver and I had to turn and give him my address, although I was concerned, since it seemed to me that the man in black was listening intently. The taxi started forward with a slight lurch, and Philip startled, but settled again while he and I were ferried the dozen blocks to the apartment to the strains of a particularly plangent Hindi pop song, unmistakably one about a lonely, futile, unrequited love.

"Can you wait?" I asked the driver when the cab pulled up in front of my building. "We're going to the airport. I won't be long." He nodded, sighed richly, and reached to turn up the volume.

Philip began to protest while we were riding up in the elevator. His cries, weak at first, grew steadily louder. When the elevator doors opened, his outrage spilled into the corridor. His crying brought Rebecca out of her closet-office into the hallway as we fell into the apartment. She rushed forward and removed the bags from my hands.

"Is that Lucy's baby?" she asked.

"I had to take him. Lucy's old boyfriend from Italy has come. With his horrible wife. He's horrible too. They have some sort of a custody order. He and his wife are trying to take the baby away from Lucy and Ryan. He says it's his, not Ryan's."

"Is he?"

"No! He's Ryan's. Lucy told me. No, she's never actually told me, but I know, I mean we've all assumed." We were shouting to hear each other over Philip's wails.

"What does Lucy want you to do with the baby? Hide him here?"

"She doesn't exactly know I have him. I tried to create a diversion. But she'll work it out quickly, and she's not the type to keep a secret for more than an hour. Even if she doesn't tell, someone else will figure it out and they'll come here to look for him. I have to take him somewhere else until Lucy and Ryan can get this thing sorted out. I have a cab waiting downstairs. I am just not sure where to go to."

"If anyone's looking for you, you'll be easy to track down. A woman with very long blonde hair with a newborn baby." Rebecca looked at me closely. "A nervous blonde woman with a newborn baby. You won't be that easy to hide."

Rebecca turned her attention to Philip who was continuing to howl. "What about your friend? The one who used to live here? Dana. Can he help?"

"He's all the way in Montreal."

"Perfect. Why don't you see if you can settle the baby. I'll pack."

Philip finished two of the small bottles of formula while Rebecca rushed around the apartment. He fell into a limp sleep only when he had sucked up the last bubble of moisture from the second bottle. He looked absolutely smashed, like a drunk in a ditch. Even after I had pulled out the nipple, which made a slight popping sound as it came free of his mouth, his lips continued to nurse the air. He looked as if he were dreaming of milk. He didn't protest while I changed his diaper. When I had wrapped him up in his blankets again, Rebecca was ready to go. She helped me into my coat and shrugged on her own navy peacoat.

"You don't have to come to the airport with me," I told her. "I have a cab waiting." I couldn't remember if I had told her that already.

"It's no trouble," Rebecca answered. She picked up the two suitcases she had packed and followed me out the door. The driver was still in his cab in front of the building, working a crossword puzzle. He gazed at us neutrally from under his neat turban. Rebecca gave him directions and, when we arrived at the airport, directed me to sit on a bench with Philip while she arranged my ticket.

"I'll put them on my credit card," she said, waving away my thick roll of money. "It would only attract attention if you paid in cash. And you might need that. You can pay me back later."

It wasn't until we were walking toward the security area that I realized what Rebecca was doing. I stopped and turned toward her.

"You can't be thinking of coming too?"

"There's a conference in Montreal just starting that I was thinking of going to anyway," she said. "And you need me for camouflage. They'll be looking for one woman with a baby, not two. Also, since the plane doesn't leave for another two hours, I can do something about your appearance while we're waiting."

We spent the next hour locked in a small washroom marked with a handicapped sign near the gate from which the flight was leaving. By the time we boarded the airplane, my hair had been colored a medium shade of brown, more or less the same tone as Rebecca's, and bluntly cut to just above my shoulders. I was also wearing a pair of Rebecca's large sunglasses. I don't think even Lucy would have recognized me. I kept reaching up with my free hand to feel the blunt ends of hair on my cheeks and on the back of my neck. I hadn't had short hair since I was six and had my last pixie cut.

"It suits you," Rebecca told me. "You look younger, more confident."

Philip wailed when the plane took off, and again when it landed. Apart from that, he lay nested in my lap or in Rebecca's and slept as if he were drenched in sleep. The first time he cried, we tried the soother that Oriah had bought, but found it to be far too large for his small mouth. The package disclosed that it was intended for older babies, eighteen to twenty-four months. Rebecca slipped one of her fingers into his mouth instead, and he nursed at it intensely until he was overcome again by sleep. A few minutes before we landed, we stretched Philip out on the seat between us and changed his diaper.

The airplane, and then a taxi, carried us farther and farther from Philip's parents, from my job, from Rebecca's work, but Rebecca was behaving so matter-of-factly, so calmly conspiratorial in this abduction of Philip, that I might have lost sight of the terrible thing I was doing if it hadn't been for Dana. He was not pleased when I arrived at his front door, in disguise and in the company of another woman and a baby.

"Holy shit, Maggie," he said, when I had explained the situation. "This is just so not cool. I can tell you right now that I don't want to get mixed up in this." He pulled his fingers through his hair and tugged at a few strands above his brow. "You don't seem to realize that there's a lot at stake here. Kidnapping, for god's sake. That's serious. It's in the Criminal Code. It's a major offense. You can't just walk off with someone else's baby. You have to trust the law to sort this kind of thing out. People fight over custody every day. That's what the courts are for."

He picked up his phone and held it out to me. "I want you to call your sister right now. She's got to be going crazy. Then we'll take you to the airport and send you all back home. At this point, no lasting harm has been done."

"Lucy will have figured out that Maggie has the baby," Rebecca pointed out. "She'll know that he's perfectly safe."

"I need somewhere to keep him, only for a few days," I said. I hated the appeasing undercurrent in my voice, was angry with myself for having involved Dana in something he disapproved of so strongly. "Just until Lucy can get a lawyer to overturn the court order. We can't run the risk that Gian Luigi will take Philip to Italy. She'll never get him back if he's taken there. Gian Luigi is a powerful man. He has connections. She could never see him again. It would kill her."

"I know where to take him." Dana's fiancée, Danielle, spoke for only the second time since we had arrived at their front door, at the top of a steep flight of stairs that led up from the street, and where she had greeted us by kissing us briskly on both cheeks and introducing herself.

"My sister's place. In Ste-Anne Desjardins. Everyone there has babies. *Le p'tit Philippe* will be a needle in a stack of hay."

Dana pressed his hands against his cheeks, then slid them apart so that his ears were covered. "I don't want to have anything to do with this."

"You are right," said Danielle. She reached up and patted Dana's shoulder. "The less you are knowing will be the better."

Danielle did the driving. Philip sat with me in the back seat in a molded-plastic car seat that Danielle had dug out from behind a set of skis and a hockey bag in a closet. Rebecca sat in the front seat with Danielle. Danielle and Rebecca talked the whole way, a four-hour drive, while I held onto one of Philip's compact feet and willed for him to be OK, for me to have done the right thing, for Lucy and Ryan not to panic, and for Rebecca, Dana, Danielle, and the girl on the street not to get into too much trouble. When Philip cried, I popped one of the little bottles of formula into his mouth and he opened his lips wide to accept these like a fledgling in its nest, although it seemed to me that he drank them with more and more reluctance.

As we neared a town called Annonciation, Rebecca fell asleep, her head bouncing lightly against the inside of the car door. Philip woke up a few minutes later. His eyes flew open and his face screwed up into a purple, wrinkled mask of dismay. He drew a

deep breath. In the same instant, Danielle, in the front seat, began
to sing:

> *Ils étaient trois garcons.*
> *Ils étaient trois garcons.*
> *Leur chant, leur chant emplit ma maison.*
>
> *Leur chant, leur chant emplit ma maison.*
> *Amis, où allez-vous?*
> *Amis, où allez-vous?*
> *Je suis si triste et si las de tout.*
>
> *Je suis si triste et si las de tout.*
> *Ami, viens avec nous,*
> *Ami, viens avec nous,*
> *Tu connaîtras des plaisirs plus doux.*
> *Tu connaîtras des plaisirs plus doux.*

Philip released his anxious breath. His face relaxed and he appeared to shift his attention subtly in Danielle's direction. How
much could he see or hear? His thumb bumped against his mouth
and miraculously, accidentally, found its way into its pink folds.
His papery eyelids flickered, opened, closed, opened again, then remained shut, while he sucked, furiously at first, then more slowly,
on his tiny, perfect, purple thumb. I marveled at this demonstration
of so many talents all at once. He seemed to me to be the smartest,
ablest, cleverest baby alive. I held onto his warm foot, which felt as
sturdy as the head of a walking stick, and as warm as a bun, and listened with him to Danielle's lulling song.

Tu connaîtras la paix,
Tu connaîtras la paix
Bien loin, bien loin de ce qui est laid.

Bien loin, bien loin de ce qui est laid.
Ils étaient venus trois,
Ils étaient venus trois,
Quatre partaient le coeur plein de joie.
Quatre partaient le coeur plein de joie.

The scenery had changed. The thronged, slushy streets, and bill-boards and neon advertising and street signs of Montreal, with its two-level brick houses tucked in tight, one against the other, to con-serve materials, energy, and space, each with iron-railed steps leading down to the sidewalk from modest stoops, had fallen away. We passed first through snowy neighborhoods of modest single and two-storey suburban houses, with siding in cheerful shades of pink and blue and yellow, then through fenced fields and woods, where the snow bil-lowed light and high in drifts, with unpaved roads leading off at reg-ular intervals from the secondary highway we were following.

The next road sign pointed toward the next town: "L'Ascen-sion—50 km."

Box Room

$\mathcal{W}e\ arrived$ in Ste-Anne Desjardins a few minutes before midnight. Danielle drove through the town, which was dark, unlit even by streetlights, aside from the occasional desultory glow from an all-night gas station and *dépanneur*. We followed straight, quiet streets to a white house that was set off to the back at one side of a large lot. A clothesline bare of clothes ran from the right side of the house to a stand of six or seven birch trees, thigh-deep in snow, huddled together beside a one-car garage that leaned at a friendly angle toward the house. Danielle stopped the car and turned off the motor. Philip started awake in the sudden quiet. He stiffened and launched instantly into a concerted, anguished cry. "I'm hungry!" I understood him to be saying. "Where is my mother?" "Who is my father?" "Why am I so far from home?"

We opened the car doors, and his lamentations poured out into the sleeping street. Danielle released Philip's car seat from the seat belt. "*Oop-la!*" she said. She lifted him up still strapped into the plastic seat, carried him to the front door of the house and balanced him on her knee while she felt for and rang the bell.

It was difficult to tell whether the bell was working around the din of Philip's screams. Philip had kicked his blankets loose, and he was beginning to turn purple and stiffen with rage. He was hardly taking the time to draw breath. His body shook and his complaints multiplied with each gulp of air that he pulled in to replenish his lungs. I began to believe that it might be possible for him to choke to death in his own rage and dismay.

The door was thrown open all at once by a thickset woman in a white nightgown with a disordered mass of curling brown hair around her round, red face.

"*Qu'est-ce que vous...*" she began, her round, thyroidal eyes bulging into the dark night. She stared first at the screaming baby, then shifted her gaze to Danielle. "*Danielle! Qu'est-ce que tu fais ici? Et avec ce bébé?*" She stepped back and spread her arms wide in an embrace and welcome, gesturing for us all to come in out of the cold night.

The house was warm, and had a comfortable smell, like toast or fresh ironing. We followed the woman down a narrow hall to a sitting room that was crowded with furniture and decorated with doilies under plastic and religious figurines and pictures. There were several wooden plaques on the wall depicting folded hands and prayers in French. The couch and the two armchairs were strewn with knitted afghans, in alternating zigzag stripes of yellow, brown, orange, and gold.

"*Assoyez-vous,*" the woman said. "*S'il vous plaît.*" She nodded sharply toward me and Rebecca. "Please. Sit down." Then the woman looked at Danielle and turned her palms upward, inviting an explanation.

Danielle began speaking rapidly in French, gesturing from time to time toward me, Rebecca, and Philip. Philip continued to cry, his tone becoming even more urgent. I rummaged in the bag that held his things, found a bottle of formula, pulled off the top and stuck a nipple on the end of the bottle. I handed it to Rebecca, who pressed the nipple against the purple O of Philip's mouth. He turned his head from side to side in rejection, and released a new wave of outrage.

The woman continued to murmur with Danielle, but she was distracted by Philip's outpouring of dismay. She glanced sideways at him, then down at the rejected bottle of formula. Her lips pursed and her forehead wrinkled. She turned her full attention to Philip and frowned, as if she were silently working through the many steps of a complex calculation.

"*Attendez*," she said at last and picked up the phone.

"*Non, non*," said Danielle. She placed a hand on the woman's plump arm. "*Ce n'est pas nésessaire, Silvie.*"

Silvie ignored Danielle. She spoke rapidly into the phone. No more than five minutes after she put down the receiver there was a ring at the door. Silvie left the room and returned shepherding a yawning young woman with pale, unlined skin and short, thick dark hair. She was wearing a wrinkled pink nightgown, a purple velour robe, and pink fleecy slippers.

"Eh! *C'est celui, ci*?" asked the young woman, pointing with her chin toward Philip, who had stopped screaming, and was now crying in his car seat softly and steadily in a way that scraped against my heart. The dark-haired woman released Philip from the straps of the car seat and gathered him into her arms. She sat down on the couch beside Danielle, opened her gown, and positioned Philip against her round, rosy breast. Philip's mouth softened, he fell silent and butted his head once, twice against the woman's chest. Then his lips fastened around her nipple and he began to pull at it. I sat forward, alarmed.

"I'm not sure this is a good idea," I said to Rebecca.

"It can't hurt him, Maggie," she said. "Look at him."

I watched Philip nestle closer to the dark-haired woman. He relaxed his suction on her breast every few moments to take a deep shuddering sigh. His nose still bubbled with his past grief and his forehead was damp and red, his dark curls flattened against his hot head.

"Listen," said Danielle. "It is all organized. Nicole has a girl who has two months. She said she can take the boy for a few days until this affair with the husband of your sister is resolved. Silvie, she says that he has need of *lait maternel*. This other stuff," she gestured toward my bag with its few remaining jars of formula. "She says it is not good for him. This is better until he can go back to his own *maman*. You can stay here if it pleases you, with my sister Silvie, or you can come back with me to Montreal. And Rebecca, too. You are also invited. In any case, it is not necessary to make a decision tonight. We can all decide what we will do tomorrow. For now, we sleep."

Although I objected, there was no strength in my protests, and Nicole left with Philip wrapped in her arms. Danielle and Silvie pointed out her house to me—it was only four doors away, down the street, past the family of snowy birch trees and contentedly tilting garage.

Silvie steered Rebecca and me into what appeared to be a spare bedroom with a small, pink-tiled bathroom attached. We brushed our teeth and fell into the high double bed beside each other. Danielle disappeared down the hall with Silvie; I had the impression that they would share Silvie's bed and likely not for the first time in their lives. I made myself comfortable under the pile of quilts and was asleep within the first minute. Rebecca was asleep even sooner and her ruffled breath was like a lullaby.

I started awake in the very early morning, and lay quietly listening to Rebecca's steady breathing. I willed myself to asleep again and plunged back into sleep headlong, like a diver, realizing as I fell that I had found that knack again. Something gained and something lost.

Attic Stairs

I began to resurface to wakefulness in the same moment that daylight began to lighten the night sky. I lay quietly for a few minutes in the bed beside Rebecca, whose lips still fluttered together in a hypnotic, motorial rhythm. I repressed an impulse to put an arm around her. I was so fond of her, so gratefully glad that she had taken charge. But I also felt an urgent need to appropriate some of her warmth. My muscles were tight, my teeth locked together, my jaw clenched. I was in, I recognized, a state of shock. What on earth had I done?

I was reminded of the weeks after my friend Rachel died, when I was in high school. To the extent that I had anticipated her death, I had expected her absence to be more or less the same size and shape as her presence, as if someone were to have taken a pair of scissors and snipped her out of a photo. But that wasn't the way it was at all. A person present is in one place, knowable, embraceable, contained. Her loss, I discovered, was both nowhere and everywhere. It shifted size and shape and density and form. It became a different thing from hour to hour: a sharp needle imbedded in my thoughts, rancid bile on my tongue, sandpaper on my spirit, a cold, heavy weight in my stomach, a dancing phantom, a damp fog, a sudden malaise, an icy headache, a searing lance of almost over-whelming regret, an overall, generalized ache like a flu.

I felt somewhat the same way then, lying in bed beside Rebecca, as realization seeped in, at about the same rate that the morning light began to pierce the lace curtains at the window. What had I done so precipitously in Vancouver? My fears and anxieties, which were not quite regret—which I was certain even those despairing moments was what I would have been plunged into had I *not* snatched Philip and ran—grew, diminished, hardened, softened from one instant to the next. I felt cold with distress, then, in the next moment, flushed with a kind of shame. My crimes felt heavy, then weightless, meaningless. My only two absolute certainties were that Philip was being tenderly cared for in the house down the street and Rebecca's very solid presence was beside me.

My thoughts turned to my parents. What would they be doing to help or reassure Lucy? Would they blame me or think I had done the right thing? Then I thought of Leo, Angus, and Charles. What would they think of me if—when—they knew what I had done? Charles, I suspected, would be appalled. He liked order and be-lieved that rules existed because it was generally a good idea to fol-low them. Angus was a father himself and bound to see things from a father's point of view. I couldn't guess at what Leo might think. He was a lawyer, compelled to respect the law. But he had a gentleness to his nature that might, I thought, ameliorate his point of view. I had no reason to imagine that Charles's perspective would be the one I would never learn.

My blinking gaze drew Rebecca's eyes open. She smiled and raised her head from her pillow and tilted her chin toward me.

"How does it feel to be a kidnapper?" she asked.

A half-hour later, we were eating cornflakes and drinking café au lait from thick china bowls at Silvie's kitchen table. Danielle provided Silvie with more details of our flight with Philip. Silvie, listening, moved about the kitchen, making satisfying tsking noises and murmuring softly sympathetic imprecations. At the end of the story, she swept her arms wide, as she had done when we had first arrived, noisy and late, at her door the night before.

"Here, is safe. *Tranquille. Faites comme chez vous,*" she said smiling. "*Vous avez trouvé ici un havre de paix!*"

Over Silvie's objections, I washed the breakfast dishes while Rebecca made a telephone call to an old school friend who lived in Germany. Her friend agreed to send an e-mail from an Internet café to my sister Janet's husband John at his work e-mail. We agreed on the text of the message: Philip is safe. I would return in a few days when I thought it likely the legal wrangling had produced a satisfactory result. I also asked if Rebecca's friend would request that John contact my supervisor at the hospital and tell her that I had been called away unexpectedly and urgently, a family matter, and would return as soon as I could. We heard back from Rebecca's friend within an hour. John had our message and would call Lucy to reassure her as best he could.

After the dishes were done, Rebecca and I made up the bed we had shared and tidied our small room. Then we went with Danielle down the street to the house of Nicole, the woman who had taken Philip home in her arms the night before.

A girl of four or five, dressed in jeans, a red sweater, and red socks, opened the door of Nicole's house. She stood and stared at us, clearly thrilled.

"*Elles sont arrivées, maman,*" she called back into the house—both sentinel and messenger—"*Danielle et les deux dames anglaises sont ici.*"

The little girl spun around and thundered up the steep stairs that led from the narrow hallway. Danielle and Rebecca stepped into the hall and I followed the girl's flashing red-stockinged feet up the stairs. She skidded to a stop at an open door on the second floor and adopted quite suddenly an air of exaggerated quiet.

"Shhhhh," she said, a finger at her lips. She motioned downward with the flat palm of the other hand.

Nicole was in bed, asleep in a mound of sheets, blankets, and pillows. The pages of a newspaper, *Le Journal*, were scattered around her, along with an empty mug and a plate littered with crumbs. There was a sleeping baby on either side of her. One baby was blond and fat and pink. The other was Philip. The muscles in his cheeks contracted once, twice, and a vestigial smile trembled on his lips. I stood in the doorway beside the young girl, who stood still, in the manner of a deer, as if she thought any motion might make her visible, and together we gazed at the messy bed and three sleepers.

Philip's outflung hand rested alongside Nicole's encircling arm. Against Nicole's pale rose skin, Philip's hand was red-gold. His dark hair curled like waves on his brow. His lips were dark red, a shade very close to purple. He looked—there was no way I could, even striving, fail to notice this—as Italian as if he had been born in Palermo or Venice or Naples instead of downtown Vancouver. Shit, I thought. Shit. And then: But this is no reason for Gian Luigi and that hideous Ivetta to get him. He's as much ours as theirs.

"*Ils dorment*," the girl at my side said in a loud whisper.

"*Comment t'appelles-tu?*" I whispered back.

"*Marie-France*," the girl said. She wrinkled her mouth and nose together. "*Mais je n'aime pas beaucoup mon nom. Je préférerais qu'on m'appelle Brittany.*"

"*Alors, enchantée, Brittany*," I said, extending my right hand. Marie-

France took my hand in hers and pumped it up and down several times.

Danielle and Rebecca must have begun to wonder what we were doing. They had made their way silently up the stairs and now joined us at the bedroom door. Nicole opened one eye, then the other.

"*Il était très sage,*" she said, struggling to sit up without waking the babies. "*Il a bien dormi, et bien mangé. Ils viennent d'avoir leur dejeuner et moi aussi, comme vous voyez.*"

With Danielle assisting where Rebecca's and my French broke down, it was agreed that Rebecca and I would take Philip with us and come back with him when he was next in need of milk. Nicole loaned us some clothes for him and a pink snowsuit and a kind of sling that slipped over my shoulder in which Philip could nestle. Rebecca and I took him back to Silvie's house and put him down to sleep in the middle of the big bed we had shared the night before.

Nicole and Marie-France came over to Silvie's house for lunch a few hours later, and Nicole woke Philip up and nursed him until he was drowsy again. She reassured us as she fed him that she didn't mind feeding Philip along with her daughter, that with all of her children—this new baby girl was her fourth—she had produced enough milk for a village and had always had plenty to spare.

"It runs in the family," she explained, Danielle serving as translator. "My *grand-mère*, Agnès, told me when I had my first child, my son Antoine, that she was a good milker too—*une bonne nourrice.* They used to keep the women in hospital for a good two weeks when they gave birth in those days. Not like today when you're in and out as fast as they can rush you. I didn't even get a meal last time in; Emilie was born at ten at night and I had to go home at eight the next morning. My husband was late getting to work at the mill because he had to cook my breakfast before he left.

"My *grand-mère* had eight children and each time they kept her in the maternity ward for as long as a month—once even longer. Some of the women had problems with their milk. It came in late, or not at all, or their nipples cracked and bled so the babies got as much blood as milk when they suckled, or their baby turned up their nose at it, or they just couldn't get the trick of it. There wasn't much else to offer. Cow's milk or goat's milk, and that was still sometimes unpasturized. They added corn syrup, or even maple syrup to it and hoped for the best. But my grandmother had milk enough for all the babies there. And so she was encouraged to stay on. All her meals were provided. No chores. She would lie in her bed propped up on pillows and feed baby after baby and talk to the other women and to the nurses. It was a closed world. Women only, except for the doctor of course, *le maître*, who came in once in the morning. No visitors allowed. The women would hold their babies up to the windows in the evenings to show them off to their *papas* down in the street. Do you know what my *grand-mère* told me?"

We all leaned forward over our plates.

"She said her milk came out with so much force that she could hit the wall at the end of the ward! As far away as over there," Nicole pointed to a spot outside the kitchen door on the far side of the hall. "That's what she said."

We all gazed at the gold-flocked hall wallpaper and marveled.

"My mother always said that a drop of breast milk would cure warts."

"Yes, that sounds possible. It's filled with antibodies, isn't it?"

"I saw a few drops of Mary's milk in a church in France once.

It was a blue-gray color, and it was still sloshing around in a little glass sleeve after two thousand years. The nun who led the tour said that it never dried up like ordinary milk. It remained liquid. A miracle, she said."

"It was a miracle anyway—virgins don't produce milk!"

"I've heard that mothers who adopt can sometimes get milk to come in by putting the baby to their breast."

"A friend of mine lived in Sweden for a year when her husband went there to manage a construction project. She couldn't get a work permit, so she volunteered at a breast milk bank. It was like a blood bank. You could make deposits and withdrawals. Like your grandmother, Nicole, but more organized."

"Did you know they used to think that breast milk was made in the uterus, out of redirected menstrual blood. That was the reason they thought women didn't get their periods while they were nursing—the blood was sent up to the breasts. I saw a picture once in a textbook of how they thought it worked. There was a duct leading from the uterus upward and it branched to the two breasts."

"You'd think that the first time they did an autopsy, they'd see there wasn't any connection."

"Maybe they thought that it shriveled up when it was no longer needed."

"I was breast-feeding when I got pregnant with my second. . . ."

"It used to be the fashion for women of any means to send out their children to be nursed."

"I've heard that children from different families who were nursed together were considered milk-siblings, almost related."

"I once met a woman who nursed her son until he was four. He would walk over to her, lift her shirt, and latch on to her breast."

"Two is old enough. Once they can eat regular food."

"That long?"

"You want to do what's best for your child."

"My mother fed my sister and me canned milk with corn syrup, and we turned out fine."

Silvie sniffed and stood to clear the table. "Well," she said. "There are mothers like that even today. Too busy or too proud to feed her own child."

Rebecca and I went for a walk through the town, while Philip napped and Danielle visited with Silvie. There was an *hôtel de ville*—the town hall—a small volunteer fire hall, two churches, three blocks of stores and businesses, and several small neighborhoods of houses. A frozen river looped through the modest downtown like a gray thread following a needle through cloth.

We saw women with knitted scarves over their heads pushing strollers along the cleared sidewalks and guiding young children, clumsy and splay-footed in their winter boots and bundled up so that only their red, runny noses poked out, back to school for the afternoon. There were women behind the counters at the post office, the bakery, the bank, even the hardware store. Ste-Anne was a town run by women. The men, it seemed, all worked at the sawmill south of town. Steam from a stack at the mill telegraphed its location a kilometer or two downriver, at the spot where the railway track crossed the highway. Trucks loaded high with logs drove along the main road in the direction of the mill, the long, orange-ribboned log ends bounding and recoiling jauntily with each turn of the wheels.

Over the next few days, Rebecca, Danielle, and I fell into a kind of dreamlike interlude, an unintended and virtually complete escape from our usual lives. Rebecca took a holiday from her quizzes, the first break she had taken in several years, she admitted. Danielle had already set her students' examinations, and was able to arrange by phone for an invigilator to oversee them. I was fairly certain that I no longer had a job to go back to and found that I was able to keep from worrying by electing to live entirely in the present.

Philip spent more and more of his time with Nicole and her daughter Emilie. He was discernibly happier with them than he was with either Rebecca or me. He cringed in the cold outside air and relaxed into the warmth of Nicole's house. He would pull at Nicole's plump breasts until he fell into a milk stupor, and then fast asleep. Even after the nipple fell free of his mouth, his red lips pursed together like a kiss, nursing at air molecules. He took his naps with Emilie in her crib, one baby at each end, their feet turned toward the middle. When he was awake, Nicole often laid him beside Emilie, who would turn her head and gaze at him. Sometimes one of Emilie's exploring hands would happen onto one of Philip's and the two babies would cling together like castaways, their fingers knitted together so that it was difficult to tell where one baby ended and the other began. When Nicole was busy, she would pass both babies along to her cousin Françoise, who had begun to wean her one-year-old, but who was able to nurse Emilie and Philip if they became desperate for milk and Nicole had not yet returned for them.

Rebecca and Danielle and I took Danielle's little car and followed the roads that led to and from Ste-Anne in every direction. We were passed on the highways by trucks stacked with logs bound for the many local mills, or headed away from the mills loaded with lumber, woodchips, plywood, or strandboard. Noise-belching snowmobiles often kept pace with the car as we drove, following trails that ran alongside the road, swooping and dipping and soaring in brief bursts as the drifts rose and fell. We drove past solitary men sitting in lawn chairs in the middle of frozen lakes, fishing through the ice, beside huts built of scavenged lumber and plywood, stacks of beer cans at their feet.

Whenever we reached another town, we stopped and got out in search of a cup of coffee or to stretch our legs. We walked on orderly streets, through different neighborhoods, along stretches of windswept lakes and rivers, through snowy parks and cemeteries. We brushed the snow from cenotaphs—every town had one—and read aloud the lists of names: Blanchard, LeBlanc, LaSalle, Martel, Levesque. We saw women everywhere, walking, shopping, talking, or working. Older women picking their way along the sidewalks with canes or walkers. Younger women leading their flocks of small children.

Each community was similar to the last, but also, in greater or lesser measure, different from the one we thought of as our own. Rebecca called one of these other towns, as we walked through, Ville Déjà-Vu, referring to the sensation it inspired of blurred familiarity. We had just turned a corner confident that the next block would include a Dunkin' Donuts store and a Dépanneur Silvain, but found instead a Patisserie Rocheleau and a Quincaillerie Montagnais.

One day, under a hard, cold, watery-yellow winter sun, we walked far to the north of the town and came across a frozen blue fan-shaped pond, its rough surface scattered with wisps of snow. The narrowest point of the pond was close to our feet at the edge of the road. There was a quiet, rushing sound; the water underneath the thick skin of ice seemed to spill from an underground culvert below the road. Danielle stumbled on a boulder hidden under the snow on the bank edge, and one of her boots kicked loose a chunk of ice the size of a lemon, which shot out and skittered across the surface of the ice. *Thuck. Thock. Thock. Thick. Thick. Thck.* It bounced and rebounded six or seven times, like a flat rock skipping across summer water, but with more spring and covering a greater distance, and the ice reverberated loudly with a higher tone each time ice glanced against ice. There may have been a layer of air between the ice and the water that formed a chamber in which the glancing sounds reverberated, creating music of the oddest sort, a natural, amplified glockenspiel. The ringing noise resounded again in the air, echoing against the leaning trees, white birch, feathered pine, and naked maple, rising in pitch as the sound waves expanded, clear, exuberant and ridiculous, like solitary laughter. We stood there for a full hour, taking turns tossing pieces of ice onto the frozen surface of the pond, making it ring and chime, and drinking in and echoing the hilarity of the cold ice music.

We allowed ourselves to speculate over our morning coffees, and as we drove or walked, about what might be unfolding back in Vancouver. We had, of course, heard nothing; the silence was unsurprising but disconcerting nonetheless. Rebecca logged onto the Internet every day, miraculously connecting her laptop computer to the eventful outside world through the umbilical cord of Silvie's slim telephone line. She scanned the newspapers available online, and searched in all the search engines, but she found no mention of Philip's disappearance. This kind of case must not be uncommon, we concluded, although we were mystified about a world into which a baby could be so easily mislaid or borne away with so little fuss or comment.

It was just remotely possible that Lucy had accepted that her son was safer with me, knowing that the alternative was for him to be snatched away by Gian Luigi. I found, however, that I couldn't hold this acquiescent image of my turbulent sister in my mind for longer than a minute. It seemed far more likely that Lucy was trying to find Philip, that she was working to track me down. But if she was, it was also impossible for me to believe that Lucy wouldn't find her son if she truly set out to do so. She had always known how to get what she wanted. Lucy was extraordinarily resourceful. And those years working in Italy had honed her skills. I believed on balance, though, that I was safe for the moment, that Philip was out of harm's way, and that my sister and family must be working to solve the problem presented by Gian Luigi, and that all I needed to do was correctly judge when to reappear with Philip.

I slept the sleep of the blameless those long winter nights in Silvie's deep bed, surrounded by fat feather pillows, nested as if I were hibernating under drifts of quilts, with Rebecca's sonorous nighttime noises as a lullaby. I began to describe to Danielle one morning over breakfast what this was like, the return of sleep after months as an insomniac, how sleep felt like water poured into a dry bucket of sand, how it seemed to soak into every part of me, my brain, my bones, my breast, how every morning I woke saturated, filled to the brim.

Danielle listened intently, and then nodded and said, "This is a good comparison, water and sleep. It happens that the material that I teach to my engineering students is concrete, a significant material. Many important things are made of it. The ingredient most critical in making concrete is the water. It is the water that makes the powdered cement react and absorb water to itself, to make a *pâte*—a thick paste. The *pâte* covers all of the surfaces of the aggregate and sand and makes them to bond. Too much water makes the material more easy to work, but the concrete will be poor and weak. The right measure of water makes the concrete very strong. Not too much, not too little. This is like sleep, is it not? You need the right amount, but not too much."

I felt the hermetic seal of the bubble in which I had taken shelter give, just a little, but that was enough. A rush of anxiety found the opening, small as it was, and broke through. Danielle had not intended any criticism, but her words surfaced a current of unease that had formed an unacknowledged background or frame to my sense of peace. I couldn't hide here in Ste-Anne forever. This wasn't a rest cure or a vacation. A child's future and my sister's happiness were at stake. A feeling of apprehension began to expand inside me like a spreading stain. My thoughts were pulled to the people I had left behind. They appeared before me at first like ghosts or negatives. I could see through them. If I concentrated on Danielle, they shattered and shimmered like water when an oar is pulled through it. But it became more difficult to push them away from me. Their faces took shape and form and expression. I began to consider the events that had brought me here and to imagine what might happen next, and what might follow after that. Being in Ste-Anne had been much like being asleep, and the time was coming soon for this state to come to an end.

Attic

"*It's time to go back*," I said to Rebecca the next morning as soon as I heard her breath break from its regular nighttime rhythm. Her eyelids flickered and parted a fraction.

"I'm not sure," Rebecca said, considering. Then she sighed. "I can't judge it one way or another. But it's your family. We'll have to trust your instincts."

I had been awake for hours, waiting for morning and considering the options that might be open to us. I had ruled out remaining in Ste-Anne. Danielle had promised us that we were welcome for as long as we wished to stay, that Silvie loved the drama we had brought with us and was enjoying our company. But I knew that a week was long enough for any guest to stay, however welcome. I was just as confident that a week was not long enough for Gian Luigi to have retreated from his mission to secure Philip for himself and his wife. I thought of going somewhere else but could not come up with any other place that would offer refuge to a small baby in the final wintry days of the millennium in a cold northern country. I had never played chess, but several times when I woke during the night it had occurred to me that it might have been useful if I had, that I might have benefited from some understanding of the tactics that chess masters used to break out of a difficult spot, to buy time or gain an advantage.

The night that I lay awake in Silvie's house and pondered what next to do began as the waning hours of December 21 and ended as the dawn of December 22. I had lost track of the days, but Rebecca had kept assiduous note of them, since she had taken on the task of checking the news every day. We had arrived in Ste-Anne Desjardins about a week earlier, in the final minutes of December 15. During the very few hours of that late December night when I did sleep, so lightly, so uneasily that I did not dream, a fire started back in Vancouver, in the apartment next door to the one that Rebecca and I shared.

The tenant in the apartment next door, a single man of slight stature, someone we had encountered rarely, but who always managed to gave us the impression that he had no employment, plenty of money, and an intemperate social life—a modern version of a remittance man was what we had concluded—had noticed the day before that the upholstery on the wrought iron furniture that he kept outside on his balcony had been soaked through in a recent winter storm. He brought the cushions inside, propped them up in front of the gas fire that he had recently had installed in his living room, showered, dressed, and went out for dinner. He had planned the evening as a seduction, and he was so successful that dinner progressed into a stay overnight at the *bijou* apartment in Yaletown owned by the object of his affections.

Meanwhile, the cushions that he had left at home before the hearth dried steadily, but unevenly. Little by little, they began to curl toward the heat. Finally, at just past one o'clock in the morning, the cushions, scorching on the side nearest the fire, still sodden on the other, tumbled together, slowly, preposterously, irrevocably, headlong into the fire.

A heavy pall of black smoke was drawn from the roasting foam and cotton and plastic like a spirit from a bottle, but the dark, toxic cloud expanded throughout his apartment, pressing against the walls and doors and windows, without triggering the alarm, because, unfortunately, the alarm had been disabled. Our neighbor had removed the batteries from his smoke detector a few weeks earlier, after they ran low and began to beep ominously and, more important to this story, annoyingly. He removed the spent batteries and tossed them in a drawer and had not got around to replacing them. So his alarm did not sound and the smoldering cushions were soon glowing with heat.

Because the cushions were made of urethane, the smoke cloud contained lethal amounts of hydrogen cyanide and carbon monoxide. At about one-fifteen, our neighbor's ancient tabby cat, Judy Garland, dozing on her pillow in the kitchen, drew in three or four shallow breaths, sneezed, coughed, and died where she lay.

The acrid smoke poured, too, into my bedroom, which shared a common air duct with our neighbor's living room—where the cushions were fully alight now and beginning to release dirty orange sparks into the air—and spilled down the white wall onto my empty bed. It churned and twisted its inky way across my blue-and-white-striped pillowcase and pale blue bedspread, leaving a film of gray as it passed, then seeped into the hall that led to Rebecca's room, where it finally came into contact with and touched off the alarm in the hallway ceiling.

The cushions in our neighbor's apartment were now frankly, merrily, ablaze. They burned with such great heat that everything around them caught fire—the mantle over the fireplace, the lacquered wood floor, the furry throw rug. The fire reached the couch and two armchairs. They burst into flame instantly and it was at about this point that the escaping smoke and heat reached the building's other alarms and sensors and caused the valves of the building's sprinkler system, which was almost but not quite up to code, to open. Because of an undiagnosed fissure in the system that fed the sprinklers with water, the spray was weak, half-hearted, so by the time the fire trucks arrived at one-forty-five, in a glorious explosion of speed, light, urgency, and noise, smoke was pouring from the windows on the upper floor of the Beach Avenue building, flames could be seen behind all of our neighbors' windows, and the asphalt shingles on the roof had begun to smolder.

The other tenants, pulled from sleep by shrieking alarms, falling water, and chaotic shouts, streamed out of all four of the apartment building's exits. They were dressed in pajamas, housecoats, sweatpants, winter coats, jeans, leggings, whatever they were wearing or had taken the time to pull on when the alarms sounded and sprinklers began to spurt. They carried in their arms such of their possessions as they had the presence or absence of mind to take hold of before they hurried to get out of the burning building. Not one of them thought that this might be a false alarm; they could all smell the bitterness of the burning foam, drywall, and electric wires, mixed with the campfire scent of burning wood and the classroom odor of scorched fabric and old dust. And they could feel something different in the night air, which was charged, somehow, as if with extra ions. All experienced a general, unnamable sensation that something serious was happening, something momentous and irreversible, even before they saw the confirmatory smoke and flames.

One man, short in stature, with very white close-cropped hair, wearing quite an elegant scarlet smoking jacket–like bathrobe over red-and-cream-striped pajamas, walked out onto the front lawn brandishing the water glass that he always kept half-filled on his

bedside table. He had snatched up his water glass, he advised anyone who would listen to him, and many who would not, including
the fire chief himself who was just arriving, and had brought it
with him in case he encountered open flames on his path down the
hallway toward the exit, which he had not, although this did not di-
minish to any degree his interest in his tale of the half-full water
glass, which was really, of course, a story about himself and his
qualities of foresight and preparedness, of which he was quite
proud, although they are the type of trait that are often overlooked
or underappreciated.

Another man emerged holding his treasured black cat tenderly
in his arms, and he murmured into its naturally sooty ears fond
words of comfort and solace (words that of course he intended
mainly for himself) as they stood in the most inconvenient very
middle of the chaotic too-ings and fro-ings of the other tenants
and of the valiant, yellow-booted, hard-hatted firefighters with
their heavy hoses and thick breeches and authoritative shouts.

A woman tenant, young, naturally blonde, single, soft-chinned,
smooth-browed, known to her friends and family to be not terribly
clever but exceedingly kind, thinking to reach for something to take
with her only as she passed across the threshold of her apartment
door, came out holding her sisal doormat with its pattern of three
sunflowers, which she knew was ridiculous—of all the things to
save!—but she refused to relinquish it even when the Red Cross arrived and pressed on her a cup of coffee, with cream and sugar already added, and an egg salad sandwich. She consumed these
awkwardly but avidly, although she took her coffee black and didn't
like onions, huddled with the other dazed and dazzled residents on
the sidewalk across the street from the burning building, solving
the problem of the sisal mat by placing it under her slippered feet.

Finding that the mat protected her feet nicely from the cold damp ground, she offered to share it with another evacuee, a quite good-looking young man from down the hall. Everyone escaping a fire should have one, they agreed, leaving the woman with the mat elated that fate had led her to take from her apartment precisely the right thing. Which she had, as it turned out, since the young man, a personal trainer at the YMCA of Italian heritage, with a romantic flair as wide and deep and substantial as his mother's unbound bosom, was smitten with her then and there and married her six months later on the semi-anniversary of the fire. All the tenants were invited, including Rebecca and me, although we had missed the fire, and the fire crew as well, and the Red Cross volunteers.

Another woman, the tenant who had resided in the building the longest, since the early 1940s it was rumored, heard the alarm and telephoned 911 on her bedside phone, which was the kind no one else has anymore, high and black and solid, with a round, slow-moving dial. She gave extremely precise instructions as to her location and condition, and was found and carried down into the street by two fire-fighters, who locked their arms together in a kind of sling under her antique bum. The residents let out a cheer as they saw her being borne in this manner through the front door. She added an indisputable flair to their otherwise fairly blandly attired group on the far sidewalk; she wore a red satin nightgown and a black negligée; her abundant white hair was swept up in a black lace mob and she wore on her feet a pair of red mules, the kind with high transparent heels, and feathery fluff at the toes. A Red Cross worker opened out a folding canvas stool for her, draped a coarse gray blanket around her narrow shoulders, and placed a paper cup of muddy coffee in her hands, but her presence was undiminished—she was a bird of paradise who had deigned to land among the sparrows.

The amazing, efficient firefighters cordoned off the burning building with swathes of yellow tape that twisted and glittered and shone like ropes of gold in the streetlights and headlights. Ambulances arrived, and well-organized teams of paramedics alighted— they looked like old-fashioned carhops in their eagerness and starched, pressed uniforms. They assembled and then examined a long queue of displaced residents, assessing them one by one for possible burns and the side effects of smoke inhalation. A few evacuees were given tiny vials of eyedrops that they were told to instill (wonderful word!) into their stinging, dilated eyes. All were pronounced fit and free to go.

At about four o'clock, a glorious blossom of sweet, pungent odor rose up over the crowd, discharged through an open window in one of the basement apartments. Someone's sizable marijuana stash was ablaze. The fire had traveled through the walls of the building to the underground room where an entire crop had been spread out on newspapers and left to dry, ready to be cut, weighed, packaged, and sold. The watchers—tenants, reporters, newscasters, neighbors, friends, and family—burst into applause or laughter or words of reproach, depending on their perspective on such things.

By dawn, all of the residents had found shelter with friends or family, or in the nearby Lydia Hotel, which had generously opened its doors and offered free breakfast to all, as well as rooms at discount rates for the displaced. There remained only the fire crew and cleanup workers, a bleary-eyed insurance adjuster in a suit with his frayed tie loose around his neck, an arson investigator, also in a suit, but with his cuffs shot and his silk tie perfectly knotted and draped, and a few die-hard observers, including Luba, who had received news of the fire from a friend at the radio station where she worked and had come to watch on my behalf. It was from her that I learned all of what I relate here, since I was far away tucked into Silvie's bed in fitful, unsettled half-sleep, unaware of what I had missed.

It was a night of miracles, starting, of course, with the fact that no casualties were suffered aside from the loss of our neighbor's incontinent tabby cat. A firefighter lifted her bony, curled-up body from where she lay and carried her out, leaving behind him a badly burned room that was greasy and black with soot except for the spot—perfectly round—on the cushion on which she had been resting. This one place in all the building was unspoiled. Everything else, from attic to crawlpace was ruined, by smoke or fire or water or the firefighters' axes exploring the walls and ceilings for hot spots and other hidden trouble.

Luba snapped a photo of the firefighter who carried poor Judy the cat out from the still smoldering building, and she caught in her lens the modesty and strength of the worker, his yellow jacket slick under the dim orange light, and the defeated grace of the victim, soft and small and wilted, carried like treasure in the firefighter's upturned calloused hands. Her amateur but artful picture was carried in newspapers around the country. This is how Rebecca and I learned of the fire and the loss of our home. Rebecca came across the shot as she trawled the Internet in the morning, and she read the story out loud to all of us gathered at Silvie's breakfast table.

"You would have been killed, you know," she said, lifting an eyebrow in my direction over the beige clamshell of her open laptop. "Your bedroom would have been the closest to the fire."

I wrapped my hands tight around my brimming bowl of café au lait and looked around the table at Silvie, Danielle, and Rebecca, who all looked back at me fondly. I closed my eyes and smiled.

Pitched Roof

There remained the problem of how to go home, coupled now with the further difficulty of having no home to return to.

Gian Luigi and Ivetta Potenza, meanwhile, had established a temporary residence at a small downtown hotel owned by the ex-wife of a former business associate. The location was central, and the hotel was luxurious, discrete, and close to restaurants, shopping, and other diversions, and, most important, only a block or two from the Vancouver courthouse. From these comfortable quarters, Gian Luigi attended on his team of lawyers, and with them crafted affidavits and supporting documents of great complexity, persuasiveness, and credibility. His lawyers launched their case on the shortest allowable notice to Lucy and the lawyer she had hired, a young woman, a friend of a friend of a friend.

The application was heard in the morning on December 22 by a single judge of the Supreme Court, a man of approximately Gian Luigi's size, shape, age, tastes, background, and temperament. Gian Luigi and Ivetta presented themselves as the ideal couple, caring, loving, successful, well-to-do, able to offer Philip every advantage that his feckless mother demonstrably could not. Lucy was unemployed and possibly unemployable, for what skills did she have? Her carelessness was obvious; she had misplaced the baby within a matter of hours after his birth. She had no assets to speak of and no settled home. Her marriage plans were uncertain; in light of Philip's disappearance, she and Ryan had put their wedding plans on hold. She had a demonstrable pattern of short-lived, stormy relationships. She had, in short, virtually nothing to offer an infant. What might have been her trump cards had been squandered. Courts are reluctant to separate a nursing baby from its mother, but Lucy had, for selfish reasons of her own, elected not to breast-feed her child. Courts are also likely to lean in favor of the status quo. The status quo was that Lucy did not have the child.

The Potenzas were everything that Lucy was manifestly not. A picture-book couple, tall, handsome, educated, active—a mother-and father-in-waiting, lacking only a child. They were stable, having just celebrated their twentieth anniversary. They were established, well-regarded, sophisticated, and prosperous. Their extended family was large, close, and warm. If Philip were to live with them, he would have many first and second cousins. He would reside in a sprawling Roman apartment not far from the Coliseum during the school year, and would spend his summers fanned by cool breezes at the family's sea-side summer villa at Forte dei Marmi, an Italian coastal resort town.

The judge didn't even pause for a recess before rendering his decision. If Philip were to be found, and, provided blood tests confirmed that Gian Luigi was his biological father, which no one had seriously argued before him might not be the case, then custody would be granted to Gian Luigi, with generous access to Lucy, details to be worked out by counsel.

Lucy's lawyer walked out of the courtroom, went directly downstairs to the Court of Appeal registry, and filed an appeal. Her argument that the Court of Appeal should, in the circumstances, grant a stay of the decision of the Supreme Court immediately, was unsuccessful. During the winter break, the Court of Appeal would hear matters of only the utmost urgency. Anything else would have to wait until the New Year. And, since there was no baby, where was the urgency?

You need to find the baby before he does, Lucy's lawyer told Lucy.

You need to find the baby before she does, Gian Luigi's lawyer told Gian Luigi.

Lucy and Ryan tried to get into my apartment that afternoon to search for clues about where I might have gone. They were turned away. All the entrances to the building had been secured. The watchman at the front door told them that the building was unsafe and might soon be condemned. The top storey in particular, where the apartment I shared with Rebecca was located, was unsound; the roof could come down at any moment, or the charred floors might collapse. There were ashes and dust everywhere, probably contaminated by asbestos from the ancient insulation, and lead from the melted layers of old paint. It was impossible to be allowed access to the building pending completion of a thorough engineering report. No one was working over the holidays, so nothing would be known and nothing could be done until the New Year.

Gian Luigi had, it came out later, made arrangements for Lucy to be kept under careful watch in case she might lead him to the baby, so her visit to the building on Beach Avenue was closely observed. In exchange for a gift of a carton of cigarettes and fifty dollars toward any Christmas purchases he might choose to make, the security guard posted at the front door shared the small amount he understood of the reasons for Lucy's attempt to gain access to my apartment. What little he knew was enough. That night, Gian Luigi and Ivetta made their way through a poorly secured rear door and up an unlit stairwell to my apartment. They stepped over and through what was left of our door, which the firefighters had smashed through with their axes.

Gian Luigi and Ivetta enjoyed this adventure immensely. They had gone shopping first, at one of the department stores on Granville Street, and were dressed in matching black outfits, including black knitted caps, and flat-soled, silent, black canvas shoes. They carried slender, powerful flashlights, the kind with a brilliant, pin-prick, laserlike beam. They tested the broad floor boards carefully as they crept about the apartment, and they each kept a wary eye on the ceiling.

They found little, however, to help them. I had left my address book locked in a drawer of my desk at the hospital. The hard drive of my computer had melted in the fire; the keyboard was a puddle of letters, set into a solid blob of alphabet soup. Gian Luigi found letters and business cards on Rebecca's desk and took notice of her name. When they had given up poking in the dark in the burned-out apartment, he suggested to Ivetta that they take a look around in the darkened lobby. There, well away from the nodding watchman, behind a very large potted palm still green and glossy under a layer of ashes, they found a cardboard box containing batches of mail for the tenants. They took away mine and Rebecca's, which they found secured cozily together inside a fat, blue rubber band. Once they were back in their suite, they methodically went through the bills and brochures and Christmas cards. Quite quickly, they came upon treasure: a Visa bill and an Air Canada frequent flyer report.

Ivetta made a call to the Air Canada ticket office. She had enough of Rebecca's information and was able to project a sufficiently convincing facsimile of charm to secure the critical information. Rebecca had booked two flights for Vancouver, leaving from Montreal at noon on Christmas Eve day.

Chimney Pots

Rebecca booked the tickets. We were to fly together back to Vancouver from Mirabel Airport, leaving in the middle of the day before Christmas. Because Vancouver is three time zones behind Montreal, it was possible, even probable, if the flight was on time, that we would be back home in time to join my family for dinner. In any case, we would wake up under my parents' roof on Christmas morning and this felt to me like the right next place to go. I reasoned that clever Lucy and steady Ryan must have worked out by now some way to keep Philip safe from Gian Luigi and Ivetta. Rebecca and I could contact our insurance companies, work out what needed to be done with our burned belongings, and Rebecca and, less certainly, I, could settle back into our work. Life would return to normal.

There was very little time to prepare. It took us less than an hour to pack up our few belongings. We decided that we should keep Philip with us for our last night in Ste-Anne, so that we would be able to leave as early as possible in the morning. With luck, he would sleep during most of the drive to Montreal. Rebecca went to the drugstore to buy supplies for Philip for the trip, and I went over to Nicole's for Philip.

"*Il n'est pas ici,*" Nicole told me. "*J'ai laissé les deux enfants avec ma cousine Françoise.*"

Philip wasn't at Françoise's house either. Françoise had gone out, her neighbor told me. She might be over at Stephanie's.

I found a group of four or five women at Stephanie's, all having coffee together, but none of them had seen Françoise. Perhaps she had gone to exercise class at the community hall. They had a child-minding service there where she might have left the babies.

A young woman at the community center pointed me down the hall to the nursery. There were a dozen children there, from small babies to boys and girls about eight or nine. I knew none of them.

I was beginning to feel a sense of unease, with a sick edge of desperation. And of course my growing concern was shot through with guilt. How had I allowed it to happen that I had no idea where my nephew was? He was vulnerable, wholly dependent on me, and I had left his location and welfare entirely to chance, to the hap-hazard goodwill of people I barely knew.

I tried the fellowship hall next door to the church next. It was dark and locked. I was frightened then, standing there pulling at the unyielding, solidly bolted doors. My knees began to rattle, and I began to pray in the manner of the godless. "Please let him be all right. Please let me find him."

I couldn't think where to go next, and I ran back to Silvie's house more from instinct than thought, to ask someone to help me. I charged through the front door, not even taking the time to push it closed behind me against the cold wind that had chased me along the street. I followed the thrum and harmony of female voices en-gaged in vigorous conversation down the hall to the living room. Silvie, Rebecca, and Danielle stared up at me as I burst in. Philip lay curled like a cat in Silvie's great, red arms. His dark eyes wheeled in my general direction, and he emitted one of his random quivering smiles. I dropped down on my knees, put my head in Silvie's wide lap beside him and cried and cried. I felt shattered with relief and remorse and undeserved fortune. Waves of sweet nausea pushed against the hard knot that had lodged in my chest like a stone during the hour's panic. Silvie stroked my hair, and said tsk, tsk, and everyone else waited patiently for my fit to pass.

"I could have lost him a hundred times over since we've been here," I said to Rebecca a few hours later. I was sitting up in our shared bed, the covers tucked over my knees, watching her brush her hair. Rebecca was sitting on the small chair beside the dressing table. The chair had a plastic seat, coppery metal legs and a low back made out of the same red-orange metal twisted into a bow shape. The dressing table had a long ruffled skirt made of some synthetic material that appeared both ancient and impervious to age.

"No one should be expected to look after a newborn infant all on her own, you know," she said.

Rebecca turned around in her chair to face me. She continued to pull the brush through her hair, her arm moving in sure, rhythmic arcs.

"You're being too hard on yourself. It's unreasonable to expect that you can do everything on your own. Babies are enormously demanding. They make regular life just about impossible. Humans wouldn't have survived the move from trees to savanna or made it as far as we have if mothers didn't always have a lot of help. Think of it. The very earliest people: the father might help out with some hunting, but what if he got hurt or killed, or didn't acknowledge the baby was his, or found another female he liked better? And why would any other man help out? He'd devote his energies to his own children. Mothers must always have needed other women to help them—sisters, grandmothers, great-aunts, older daughters, and cousins. Caring for babies has always been communal. A new baby is terrifying. It's so vulnerable. A shock to the system. Then you have all these expectations imposed on top of everything. There are a few women who can do it all. Most of us can't, that's all. It's too much. No one can ever measure up."

Rebecca got up and came over to inspect the top of my head. She parted my hair with a few bristles of her brush.

"We'll have to touch up this color soon. Your hair must grow a lot faster than mine. The roots are already showing."

"You don't think I'm a monster? What kind of a person am I to let my own nephew be passed from hand to hand by strangers like luggage?"

"Not strangers, friends. And anyway, however we've managed it, we seem to have done a fine job. Just look at him."

Philip was sleeping and performing a trick I hadn't seen before, a diminutive, ruffling snore, like a scaled-down version of Rebecca's. Nicole had come by at bedtime to feed Philip. He had nursed for a thirsty hour, and then fallen into a limp, satiated stupor. He would have one more visit with Nicole's generous breasts in the morning, and then we would have to rely on formula and prayer for the rest of the trip. Rebecca and I had discussed how he would cope, but in the absence of any alternatives, we had decided just to try to make it home as fast as we could.

Nicole came by in the morning as promised, just before dawn, and we tickled Philip's feet to rouse him enough to drink. He took the daintiest of draws on Nicole's breasts, which were, I noticed, bulging and blue with the milk that had accumulated overnight. When Philip pulled back his head, milk spurted out in every direction, like a wonky showerhead. Philip lolled back into sleep a few times, and we shook him gently, urging him on with the task of drinking as much as he could hold. He sighed each time, with a resigned and wise expression, like an old man, and opened his mouth to receive the offered nipple.

"You'll have too much milk for just Emilie, after we go," I pointed out.

Nicole shrugged and Philip, in the crook of her arm, rose and fell with her motion, like a small boat on a great maternal sea. "Only for a day or so," she said. *"Ce n'est pas grave."*

I gave Nicole a gold chain with a locket on which I had asked the local jeweler to engrave two letters, E and P, entwined. "He is her milk-brother, now," I told her. *"Son frère de lait."* I had also bought a pair of gold earrings for Nicole, thick, heavy loops with a vinelike design running around them. We wrapped Philip up and deposited him, drowsy and full, in the car seat in which he had arrived at Ste-Anne eight days before. Nicole bestowed a kiss on his brow. Then she yawned, drew the lapels of her housecoat up around her neck, said *"Au revoir"* to Rebecca and me, and *"A bientôt"* to Danielle. She turned and made her way carefully through the ice and drifts back up the street to her own small house where her husband and children were still sleeping.

We drove through silent streets toward the highway. The low red sun cast long blue shadows on the drifted snow banks. At the edge of town, Danielle swung the car in the direction of Montreal. We stopped just once, to fill the tank with gas and buy coffees and patisseries at a service station near L'Ascension, and we drove along after that without talking. Danielle kept the radio on low, and we listened to carols sung in French, the chatter of radio hosts, and sprightly advertisements for the kinds of things that other people were rushing out to buy now that Christmas crouched a relatively few hours away. The coffee was hot and bitter, and the pastries flakey, sweet and filling. Philip dozed, his nose and lips emitting a fine rumpled purr of sleep and trust.

I held on to Philip's warm foot, as I had on the drive to Ste-Anne, and wondered whether the fact that it felt larger in my hand was a hopeful trick of my imagination. There was no doubt that he looked fuller and rounder after the days on Nicole's good milk, more filled out, less provisional, less newly arrived. His movements, when he shifted his head, or swung a balled fist, or kicked a leg, were smoother, more practiced, more assured. Eventually, this small, tender, untested foot would walk, run, skate, kick a ball, carry him through schools, to his life's work, to his life's partner, through children, pleasure, and illness. Eventually, his moon-white toenails, perfect flakes of mica, would thicken and yellow; perhaps someone now unborn would trim them for him, gently, lovingly, as he lay past caring in his final bed.

An hour after we had finished our coffee and pastries, I was roused from a drowsy daydream by Rebecca, who said to Danielle, "Why isn't she moving over?" Her tone was sharp, edged with alarm.

I looked at the road ahead and saw that a car some distance away, headed in the other direction, had swung into our lane in order to pass a long truck ahead of it. It was moving quickly and, although it passed the truck easily, it remained in our lane, headed straight toward us.

"I don't like this," said Danielle. She tightened her hands on the steering wheel, eased her foot off the gas, and began to steer our car as far to the right as possible, which wasn't very far, since a snowplow had recently passed and the snow that had been cleared from the highway had been pushed onto the shoulder. The approaching car was less than a hundred meters away by now, holding steady in our lane, overtaking cars that were where they should be, in the single oncoming lane. The errant vehicle continued to rush toward us. We could see now that the car was old, low-slung, and rusted, with one broken headlight, and then in another instant we became aware that a collision was all but inevitable. Danielle's knuckles whitened against the steering wheel, and Rebecca reached forward to brace herself on the dashboard. I closed my eyes and leaned sideways, curling against Philip in his car seat.

It was over in a moment, although it was a prolonged and disordered sweep of time as we experienced it. The old car passed us in a whoosh in the nonexistent third lane that had been created in the space between the oncoming lane and our car, a space that Danielle had called into being by moving as far to the right as she dared. The right wheel of our car crunched a couple of times into the icy banked snow, which made the car slip and jolt and shudder and caused the wheels to fight to tilt the car even further toward the right. Danielle held her grip on the steering wheel and fought back. I caught a glimpse, as the other car swept past us, of its driver, an ancient woman, with a tangle of white hair, dark brows, and a misdirected streak of bright lipstick slashed across her mouth. She was scarcely taller than the dashboard and was hunched over, glaring between the knots of her fingers, which were gripped at eleven o'clock and one o'clock on the steering wheel.

I imagined that I heard a click and I thought I saw the smallest glint in the half-second that the other car rattled past us. Philip gave a yelp and I realized that my hand had clenched itself tightly around his foot. I relaxed my grip and patted his foot reassuringly. "Sorry," I said to him. "Sorry."

Danielle pulled the car to a halt a hundred meters farther along the highway, where a half-moon-shaped turnout had been left clear, and she turned off the engine. For a while, not one of us said anything except for Philip, who grizzled softly. I could feel the roadway tip and shudder under the still car.

"She must have been confused," I suggested. "Maybe she thought it was two lanes in her direction." My voice sounded hollow in the silence, lost inside a thin ringing in my ears and a static haze inside my head.

Rebecca opened her door and stepped out, pulling her coat closed around her. "My knees feel like water," she called back to us. "I can barely stand up." She walked around to Danielle's side of the car. "Come and have a look at this," she said.

Danielle and I got out and joined Rebecca. She pointed to a fresh scratch and a dent in the middle of the driver's side of the car.

"It was the handle on that woman's car," I said. "It was the older kind, the kind that sticks out. I thought I heard something; that must have been when it hit us. I saw a spark, too. I thought I imagined it."

"We should make some sort of report," Rebecca suggested. Since none of us had a cell phone, we agreed to stop and phone in a description of the ancient driver at the next gas station. But we knew it was hopeless. None of us had noticed the licence plate and we couldn't even agree on the color of the car. White, I thought. Silver, Rebecca guessed. Or blue, Danielle ventured.

Rebecca put her gloved hand on the sleeve of Danielle's parka. "Do you want me to drive for a while?" she asked.

"No, no, I'm fine," Danielle protested, but, after she sat back in her seat and reached to switch on the ignition, she hesitated.

"You are right," she admitted. "Better for you to drive for a while. I need to refind my nerves."

Rebecca exchanged places with Danielle, took the wheel, and started the car. She scanned the road for a break in the traffic, and, in another minute, we rejoined the stream of cars and trucks headed southeast toward the city.

Philip turned his gaze to me and blew a series of bubbles between his pursed lips. I reached over and folded a hand over one of his clenched fists, which, after a while, relaxed and went slack as he fell back into sleep.

Back Path

Rebecca drove all the way to the airport, following Danielle's directions. At one point, when we were stopped at a light that seemed to have become stuck permanently on red, Philip woke up and began to cry his hungry cry, a pinched and plaintive wail that spilled over with sorrow and need. His cheeks reddened. His chin trembled. His fists flailed. I pointed the nipple of one of the bottles of formula into his mouth, but, after a few strong pulls on it, he thrust the nipple out of his mouth with his tongue and gave me a textbook look of disgust—nose and forehead wrinkled, brow lowered, eyes narrowed, lips pushed outward and pulled down at the edges. I switched to a bottle of sugar water that Silvie had prepared. Philip drank this down, watching me suspiciously all the while. When he had finished it, he sighed and began to knit his fine fingers together while his gaze followed nothing in particular in the space in front of him, floating air molecules perhaps—who knows what babies see?

All of the lanes leading up to the departures level of the airport were filled with cars dropping people off for holiday flights. We were forced to double-park a long way from the entrance. A tall van promptly triple-parked beside us; its many doors flew open and it began disgorging an extensive and noisy family with an endless number of children in colorful knitted sweaters, aunts in saris, uncles in tweed jackets, suitcases, bags, and parcels.

"*Eh bien,*" said Danielle. Then, "You are certain?" She was not convinced that returning to Vancouver so soon was a good idea. She had invited us to stay with Dana and her until after the holidays. "Just a little more of time," she had said. "Until the New Year."

"Thank you, Danielle," I told her, when we had unloaded our two suitcases and Philip, who looked solemn and regal in his car seat, which we were taking with us. He raised his right hand, fingers partly unfurled, in the manner of the Christ child in a Renaissance painting.

"I'll say you a secret," said Danielle. She unfolded her right hand and pressed it against the middle of her stomach. "A baby. Following another seven months."

"Does Dana know?" I asked her after Rebecca and I had given her hugs and congratulations.

"Not yet," said Danielle. "I am going to tell him tonight after I am at home." She smiled. "Maybe we call him Philippe."

Danielle embraced us both, then placed a kiss on the fingers of her right hand, and deposited it on Philip's forehead.

"*A bientôt,*" we all promised. Rebecca took a suitcase in each hand, and we turned and fought our way through the throngs to the entrance of the airport and, once inside the airport, toward the ticket counter. Philip began to cry and my purse, which was hanging on its strap on my arm below his car seat, thumped uncomfortably against my thigh as I struggled to keep up with Rebecca. We weren't certain where to go, but eventually joined the end of a long queue that seemed to be snaking toward the right counter. I stood and jostled Philip's carrier back and forth, trying to soothe him, but I resisted offering him a bottle of formula, reasoning that he would be more likely to accept it when he became genuinely desperate. The tone of Philip's crying increased in woe and intensity, and, when we hadn't advanced after ten minutes, and no one had validated our choice by electing to stand behind us, Rebecca decided to go to see if she could find someone who might take pity on us and suggest another way to get our boarding passes.

The terminal was a chaos of bright lights, rushing people, and amplified Christmas music, overlaid with announcements and messages that could scarcely be heard above the general noise and confusion. I kept imagining that I heard my name being called. Carts heaped with luggage loomed and then receded. Dogs in travel cages woofed and whined. Children called for parents. Parents admonished children. People lamented to each other or to themselves about the heat inside and the weather outside, which was about, it was rumored, to turn dramatically for the worse. A blizzard was sweeping in. All flights east were being canceled, a woman worried. Not so, said a man, the weather system is out west; it's the westward flights that can't get out. We'll be stuck here through the holidays, another man prophesied.

I resorted to Rebecca's trick and offered Philip a forefinger to suck on. He was plastered with hot, wet grief. Where was Rebecca? How much time had gone by? She had taken the tickets with her, and I couldn't remember the time we were meant to be leaving or our flight number. Was that a Vancouver flight that had just been called? Were they paging a Ms. Selgrin or a Mr. Pellegrin? I could feel pressure building in my brow and throbbing painfully down into my right eye.

At last Rebecca reappeared, one hand aloft waving a fan of white boarding passes. Relief eased my headache. I popped my finger out of Philip's avid mouth and bent down to pick up my suitcase. "We have to move quickly, she said. "This might be the last flight out. They are terribly overbooked because some earlier flights were canceled, but they took pity on us because of Philip."

An hour later, we were, miraculously, being borne upward, into the early evening sky. Philip, worn down, accepted a bottle of formula, which he drank thirstily. He then fell into a light sleep, his fists drawn up tight against his cheeks like an infant pugilist. The jangling approach of the drinks cart woke me from a dreamless doze a few hours later. I accepted, gratefully, a shallow cup of deep orange tea and a package of shortbread cookies nested together in a plastic wrapper printed with a pattern of red and green bells. Through the window I could see the night sky, vast, dark, bottomless. Below were fields of snow. The farms were divided by black roads laid out in a grid, evidence of the scale of the land grants to the farmers who first settled this area and staked these neatly ruled-off quarter-section claims. The lights of small towns shimmered icily in the distance. I could see as far as an incandescent fringe where the fields met the star-specked heavens and I was suffused with a sense of the earth turning slowly, serenely, safe and sleeping, tucked in like a child beneath the infinite, uncaring skies. The finely engineered airplane, with its rows of identical seats, riveted metal walls, tempered glass, and tirelessly droning engines, felt like another medium, outside of time and neither of the world nor of the skies.

We stumbled out of the plane, exhausted, into the middle of another seething scene. Vancouver's airport was as hectic as Montreal's, with the same level of frantic chaos. Rebecca went to find our luggage while I tried to reach my parents on the phone. The line was busy, and they don't have an answering machine, so I was unable to leave a message. I tried Janet's number. No one answered. I left a message that Rebecca and Philip and I would be at Mom and Dad's house soon.

"Is Margaret, yes?" A tall, dark-haired man wearing an impressively luxurious wool navy coat approached me as I set the receiver back in its metal collar. A half-step behind him was a woman wearing a similar coat, but with a fur collar.

This must be someone from the airline, I thought, stupid with the time change and the sudden expulsion from the airplane's warm, stale air and rhythmic, mechanical thrum into the loud, bright airport. A new service, perhaps, or one laid on for the holidays; a smart woman in public relations must have dreamed up the idea of having someone to help with infants and young children and awkward items of luggage. The man thrust an authoritative navy wool arm out toward the handle of Philip's car seat.

"I take the baby from you," the man said. I hesitated only an instant, then realized that what he must have meant was "I take the baby for you." My head pulsed. I glanced down at Philip. His eyes fluttered under his red-blue eyelids, which remained determinedly closed. He looked resigned. I handed over the carrier. The man gripped the handle of the carrier professionally, coolly, but the woman behind him lunged forward and brought her face in close to Philip's.

"Ahhhhh," she said.

I had heard that sigh before, a sound like the air being let out of a tire, a noise that flew the tall man and the thin woman up and out of the crowded airport and deposited them in Lucy's hospital room, into the exact center of my memory of the argument over Lucy's baby.

My heart swelled, trapped inside the bones and muscles of my chest, which suddenly constricted, one or more sizes too small for

my lungs. My limbs buzzed and trembled. I was electrified, unable
to draw breath. My arms reached stupidly for Philip; I could see, as
if from a great distance, my hands moving clumsy and slow
through the thick, silent air. Gian Luigi swung Philip easily out of
my reach and somehow his navy wool shoulder and Ivetta's arm
came between me and the baby carrier. Ivetta thrust herself forward, all dark hair and angles and elbows. She was wearing blood-
red gloves made of kid leather, exquisitely sewn.

"No!" I cried. And then, "Stop!" I was confident that I would
be rescued, that this scene would be obviously what it was—a kidnapping—to the hundreds of milling travelers. Someone would in-
tervene.

The cleverest place to commit a crime can be in plain view of as
many people as possible. Just think of that scene at the end of
Muriel Spark's novel *The Girls of Slender Means,* when, in the midst of
multitudes celebrating the end of the war, a sailor slips a knife between the ribs of his girlfriend. Even before she can fall, so en-
meshed is she in the pressing horde, her lover is away, swimming
against the surging mob, and you know that he will never be found,
and even if he is, nothing could be established against him, there
will be too few witnesses, or too many, each with conflicting stories.

Because my protests could not be heard in the general commo-
tion, and because the airport was already a stage for countless major and minor scenes of irritation, impatience, and unwished-for
partings, and also, to some extent, because, out of a natural and
lifelong and classically Canadian aversion to causing a scene, I delayed making more than the most reasonable remonstration by a
critical few moments, Gian Luigi and Ivetta were able to turn away
from me, with Philip suspended in his plastic container in Gian
Luigi's robust arms, and make their retreat rapidly through the

crowd; powerful Gian Luigi in the lead, opening their way, with fe-line Ivetta flowing along behind him. They left no gap that I could follow in their wake. I pushed rudely against people and was pushed just as rudely back. I grabbed arms, begged and explained, in short, gasped phrases: "My baby. That man. Let me through. I have to catch. Did you see a man and a woman just pass? With a baby? A small baby." Some people I spoke to shook off my hand, shook their heads brusquely. Others stared at me quizzically. No one it seemed could make out what it was I wanted in the very short time I was before them, crazed, disheveled, distraught.

I pressed on until I found myself in the center of a kind of hub, from which several hallways branched off in different direc-tions, toward a choice of exits and gates. There was no way of telling which way Gian Luigi and Ivetta had taken Philip. I groaned and sank to the floor, flushed, out of breath, weighted with a sense of failure too oppressive to be borne. A flash of red caught my hopeful eye; not Ivetta's incarnadine gloves but a telephone on the wall with the word Emergency printed in white letters above the headset. Even then I hesitated. Was this an emergency? My body decided for me. Before my mind could become in any way engaged in a debate of the point, I rose, picked up the phone, and said to the woman who was summoned instantly at the other end of the line, "Someone has taken my baby," and I provided a full description of barrel-chested Gian Luigi and his whippet-wife, right down to the buckles on Ivetta's narrow, spike-heeled navy shoes and the crested brass buttons on Gian Luigi's substantial navy coat.

Miraculously, they were found. They were spotted on a security camera in the parking garage, struggling to work out how to fasten Philip's car seat securely into the seatbelt of their rented car. I had been led by then to a small, featureless room with beige walls. A lumpish and only mildly sympathetic security guard had provided me with a Styrofoam cup of tepid water and a box of tissues. I dabbed my eyes and cheeks, and was surprised to find them wet. Rebecca had not yet appeared, although she had been paged. The telephone on the table blurted an electronic bleat. The security guard answered, and, as he listened, began to eye me with greater interest. But he declined to impart any information to me after he hung up.

After another few minutes, two police officers came to the door, a man and a woman. They nodded for the security guard to leave the room, and he complied, making no effort to suppress the sigh of someone who has been managing perfectly well but who has been displaced nonetheless.

"We have located the baby, ma'am," the male police officer said. He used the term "ma'am" not as an honorific but as a means of reinforcing his authority, nailing it tightly like a notice into the thick air between us. "But we have, I am afraid, two very different stories." He paused, providing me an opportunity to speak. I could not think what to say. "Just what is your relationship to the child?" he asked after a long pause and in a tone that implied disappointment that I was withholding information to which he was entitled, that I was willfully making his job more difficult.

"Philip is my nephew," I said. "I am bringing him back from a trip to my sister, his mother."

"Mr. Potenza asserts that he is the child's father," the woman officer said. "He has shown us various documents that appear to establish this fact. It appears also that he is in possession of a valid Italian custody order, and papers for the child. You should be aware that he and Mrs. Potenza are urging us to lay charges against you."

Rebecca arrived at the door as the other officer was reading aloud from a small blue card that he held stiffly in front of him. ". . . to retain a lawyer of your choice. . . . The right not to say anything, but anything you do say will be taken down and could be used against you in a court of law." He read it all the way through, quite quickly, without looking up until he was finished. "Do you understand?" he asked.

"I guess," I said. "But, I can explain the situation."

"No, Maggie. Don't say anything," Rebecca prompted.

The male officer rose to his feet, squared his shoulders, hitched up his pants, and hooked his thumbs around his belt. "I am afraid, ma'am, that I am going to have to ask you to wait outside," he said to Rebecca. "I'll call Leo," Rebecca said. She rolled her eyes and pursed her lips toward me and delivered a short shake of her head toward the officer as she left.

The two police officers seemed about the right age to have young children of their own, and it seemed to me possible, even likely, that the story of what had happened would persuade them that I had done nothing more than preserve Philip from being removed from the country and from the arms of his mother by someone whose rights were murky at best. So I laid out most of the story of the past few days, but leaving out Rebecca and providing only the vaguest indication of where I had stayed in Quebec, while the two officers took notes on page after page of their small lined notebooks. When I had finished, the woman read her notes back to me and I initialed every page and signed and dated her record of what I had said at the bottom of the last page. I was hoping that my ready cooperation would buy me something and I asked for it when we were done.

"Please. I need to take my nephew to my sister now. I am sure we can sort this out tomorrow."

"The child welfare authorities are attempting to reach the mother," the woman officer said, not unkindly. "She will have to see whether she can come to an agreement with the child's father on what should be done with him. If an agreement can't be reached, it is possible that the child will be taken to a foster home until the question of custody can be decided. That is the usual practice in this sort of case."

"Fathers have rights too," the male officer said. His voice was thick with something more than authority. I glanced at him and saw that his mouth and brow had hardened into an aggrieved expression. His partner shot him a complicated look and he didn't say anything more. The woman told me that I was being released on my own recognizance, and I signed a paper promising to be in court at ten o'clock on the morning on December 27.

Rebecca was waiting for me some distance down the corridor. "Lucy's on her way," she said. "She should be here in half an hour, and she'll have her lawyer with her. I couldn't reach Leo." She touched my arm. "There's nothing more we can do, Maggie. It's out of our hands now."

Hearth

My parents have never seriously challenged the decisions that Janet and Lucy and I have made in our lives. They believe in the gentlest of guidance, and that knowledge comes from the spirit as well as the head, from practice more than from instruction, from mistakes and trial and error and self-correction. To some extent my mother and father also consider that boundaries are designed to be put to the test, that a wealth of information about ourselves and the world can be found at and slightly beyond the margins. When we were girls, Janet and Lucy and I were usually permitted to work through issues and problems in whatever way we saw fit, and encouraged to measure our efforts and achievements for ourselves, rather than by reference to a grade or judgment or assessment conferred by someone else. So my parents accepted Rebecca's and my arrival at their front door very late on Christmas Eve with an embrace, and a glass of wine, a plate of crackers, nut pâté, Edam cheese, and white apples sliced thin, a few questions, and certainly no recriminations. We arrived almost in the middle of a very clear, cold night, so cold that, outside, each molecule of air felt still and distinct and individually coated with frost. The house was warm and smelled of home, of cooking, rest, kind words, and well-being. A very young Bob Dylan was whirling on the ancient

turntable singing of your sons and daughters "beyond your command." The overhead lights were switched off. My parents had
been sitting together beside the fireplace in which old wood
burned—odd-sized boards and planks from one of my father's
failed fencing projects—drinking herbal tea and listening to Dylan
and each other.

My father pulled the cork from the neck of a bottle of wine,
and Rebecca and I sat and ate and talked with them until long past
one in the morning. The house had cooled, the fire had died down,
and the telephone had not rung with news. I tried calling Ryan's
number, but there was no answer, so we all went to bed hoping for
the best, rationalizing that we would surely have heard bad news
since it was more likely to spread wider and faster than good. I refused to allow fears for Philip to undo me, and forced away any image of him alone or frightened or untended. He was in good hands.
He must be in good hands.

I was in the kitchen washing breakfast dishes when Lucy arrived
the next day, Christmas morning. My mother had risen early and
made coffee and pancakes and applesauce; we were both keeping
busy against apprehension. I heard the front door slam and Lucy
call out: "Maggie!" Her tone was weighted with accusation.

I put the dishcloth down and went to meet her. This was the first
time that I could remember walking toward Lucy when she was in one
of her rages, rather than trying to flatten myself into the background.

Lucy was striding along the hallway toward the kitchen. I
stopped when I saw her, my nerve failing, but she came right up to
me and pointed her finger in accusation.

"Why did you do it?"

I didn't know how to respond. Which of my many efforts and
failures was she referring to?

"Where's Philip?" I answered.

"What the hell did you think you were doing?"

"Is Philip all right?"

"You've completely screwed up my chances to keep that baby, do you know that?"

"Where did Philip go last night? Who has him?"

"If I had had the baby, the judge would have let me keep him. That's what he said, right in the courtroom. Now we're completely fucked."

"When can I see him?"

"How could you just hand him over to Gian Luigi?"

"Oh, God. Gian Luigi doesn't have him, does he?

"Bloody typical, Maggie. Whatever you were trying to do, you did a piss-poor job of it."

"Lucy." My mother's voice interrupted. She and Rebecca had come down from upstairs. "You know perfectly well that Maggie was only trying to give you and Ryan time to try to fix this thing, to sort it out. She didn't plan to keep the baby forever, just for a few days. She had no way of knowing that man would be waiting at the airport."

Lucy's eyes glittered. "I just want—" she said. Her voice failed and she paused and drew a fresh breath. "I just want Gian Luigi to go back home with his stupid cow of a stupid wife and leave Philip and me alone."

"And I want to know where Philip is." I raised my voice. "I've spent a week taking care of him. I think I am entitled to know who has him and whether he is all right."

It took a few minutes longer for my mother to persuade Lucy to sit down at the kitchen table and tell us what had happened at the airport. Lucy described a boisterous conference involving Lucy, Ryan, Gian Luigi, Ivetta, the two police officers, and a child welfare worker who had been pulled from bed to help decide what should be done with Philip. Neither Gian Luigi nor Lucy would allow the other to have Philip overnight. Nor would Gian Luigi agree to permit someone else—a friend or relative of Lucy's or Ryan's—to take Philip until the appeal was heard. Gian Luigi had the advantage of custody orders from two courts and would not accept any arrangement that might weaken his lead in the contest. Lucy was working from the primal strength of a mother whose child has been taken from her. They were thus perfectly balanced in their intensity and conviction, the kind of draw where it is perfectly possible for neither side to win. It hadn't taken long for the welfare worker, whose first priority was to go home and back to bed, to conclude that resolution was impossible and that Philip should be taken to a foster home for the few days until the appeal court could be persuaded to hear Lucy's application on an expedited basis.

In Lucy's analysis, everyone and everything was either at fault or a participant in a scheme of conspiracy against her interests— me, Gian Luigi, Ivetta, the justice systems of Italy and Canada, the police, the child welfare system, even Ryan, whose errors were unspecified. Lucy alone was, on her telling, without failing, a blameless young mother, whose conduct was misunderstood and whose perfectly legitimate needs had been utterly disregarded by all.

Rebecca always tries to understand the essence of a matter. "May I ask a few questions?" she said, when Lucy's torrent of words and indictments finally slowed.

"It isn't clear to me yet whether you are upset with Maggie because she took Philip in the first place, or because you believe she has harmed your case against Gian Luigi, or because she gave Philip to Gian Luigi instead of guarding him with her life. Also, you are clearly very angry at Gian Luigi and his wife because they want to take Philip away. Can you tell me, though, whether Gian Luigi is Philip's father? This is bound to come out sooner or later, and I expect it is going to be important. In fact, everything will likely turn on it."

Lucy opened her mouth and closed it again.

The telephone rang. No one moved. We were all waiting to hear what Lucy would say. It rang again. I moved toward it. "That might be Ryan," I said, picking up the receiver. "He'll want to know what's going on."

The call was for me. I put my hand over the receiver. "It's my friend Charles's daughter, Sarah," I explained. I carried the phone into the living room.

"Oh, Maggie. I'm so glad I found you. You've been hard to track down." Sarah was a calm, gentle woman in her mid-twenties. She ran a successful veterinarian practice with her brother Roger in West Vancouver.

"I have bad news, I am afraid." I sank down onto my father's ottoman; it exhaled slowly under my weight.

"Listen. I am sorry to have to tell you like this, over the telephone, but I knew you'd want to know. Dad died over the weekend. It happened quite quickly. He drove himself to the hospital and had a cardiac arrest in emerg. His dad died of a heart attack at about the same age, and his grandfather did too, but we never thought..." She started to cry. Her sobs were small, polite, subdued, brave.

My heart filled and teetered. I opened my mouth, not sure what words would come. "Oh, Sarah," I said. "I am so terribly sorry. Your dad was a wonderful person. I was very fond of him."

An image came to me, of Charles rising from the table after lunch that first day we met. He had held my hand in his for an instant before helping me on with my jacket. I could recall the cool pressure of his fingers as they cradled mine.

"What an awful, sudden loss for you and your brother and your mother," I said into the receiver. I could hear Sarah struggling to recover her voice. "Your dad never said anything to me about being unwell."

"He didn't tell us, either," said Sarah. "Roger and I, we think he didn't want us to worry about him."

I resisted making Sarah an impulsive offer of the loan of my own father any time she liked; I couldn't imagine what her life would be like without her father to anchor it. Then I thought of how gentlemanly Charles had always been—gallant was the word that fell into my mind like a stone into a pond. An old-fashioned word. A good man.

"Your father was so fond and proud of you and your brother," I told Sarah. "I am just heartbroken for all of you."

I wondered for an instant whether my heart might be broken for myself as well, but realized that it would take a while longer to think through what Charles had meant to me, and to understand my own loss. He had, I realized, been a part of my imprecise vision of the future. His solidity, his decency, even his absurd self-assuredness had made me desire to fall into him, to lose myself a bit in his expansiveness.

Sarah promised to let me know when the memorial arrangements had been made, and we hung up. I sat on my father's broken-down old hassock and wondered if I would lose my courage, whether I would be unable to find my way back to an ordered, commonplace life, whether it might all become too much to bear, until my mother called out: "Maggie! What's become of you?" I put my feet under me, and rose up and stood. My knees held. I breathed in and out.

The telephone rang again almost immediately; this time the call was for Lucy. "Someone named Harold Gordon," said my mother, handing Lucy the receiver. Rebecca tilted her head, interested. "The newspaper columnist?" she asked. My mother raised her hands to signal that she didn't know.

"No," said Lucy, firmly. "No." A pause. "No." Another, longer pause. Then another "No." And finally, briskly, "Yes, all right." She hung up.

"Gian Luigi has gone to the newspapers," she said. "And he's got some fathers' rights group involved—Fathers Against Custodial Treachery, or something like that."

"That is definitely not good," said Rebecca. "Those guys are obsessed. They've dropped water balloons from the galleries in Parliament and they go around picketing judges' houses to protest guardianship decisions. There was a story about one of them in the paper a few days ago. He broke into a courtroom and tried to place the judge who had awarded custody of his children to his wife under citizen's arrest."

"He wants to hear my side of the story," Lucy said. "I said I would meet him in a half-hour at the coffee place on Twelfth."

"Shouldn't your lawyer be there?" I asked. But Lucy could not be dissuaded from meeting with Harold Gordon by herself. "He's going to publish a story anyway," she argued. "He might as well get the facts right. Gian Luigi *lied* to me. He lied to me about everything. That's what people have to understand. It was all under false pretenses."

Janet arrived a few minutes after Lucy had left. She was taking the twins skating at a nearby rink that was open over the holidays and had dropped by to borrow hats for them, and to see if she could leave Marie with Mom and Dad. John was at his bookstore getting the post-Christmas sale displays set up.

"Shit, Maggie," Janet said when she saw me. "Look at you. A bad haircut and a bad dye job; you went all out. Lucy is so pissed. She'll probably never speak to you again." She gave me a light hug, and exhaled a plosive "mwah" into the air near my ear. "Then again, that might be a good thing, eh?"

I went along to the rink with Janet and held sleeping Marie in her carrier sheltered against my stomach while Janet got Claudia and Thomas started taking shaky forward steps on their new, two-bladed skates between battered orange plastic cones at one end of the ice rink. Every now and again, Janet left the twins to stumble and bump along on their own—they clung together hand in hand—and glided off for a rapid turn around the rink. She had taken figure skating lessons for years, and she still looked steady, swift, and confident. She took the turns efficiently and precisely, blade over boot, and, on the long run down the boards, she tilted forward at an angle calibrated for speed and grace. After a few circuits, she would return and explode to a stop beside the twins, sending up a shower of ice from the surface of the rink into their blinking eyes. The blades of her skates made a slick, carving sound as she turned them crisply to one side, as if she were engraving her name upon the ice. Janet continued to circle the ice and practice crossovers and turns for almost an hour after Thomas and Claudia grew cranky. I helped them off with their skates and bought them cardboard cups of weak hot chocolate and paper bags of popcorn at the concession, and we sat together in the wooden seats and watched their mother speed and spin. I ran my hand over and over along the small dome of Marie's head; it felt warm, hard, busy, and functional, like the rounded top of my mother's ancient mixer just after it has been put to use.

"I wonder if you'd be interested in this?" I said to Janet, when at last she came over to sit with us. She looked up from loosening her gleaming white skates, and I handed her a notice that I had found pinned to a notice board. "Women's morning drop-in hockey. You might be good at it."

"Maybe," Janet shrugged. She tossed the flyer into her sports bag. "I'll think about it."

Basement Stairs

Against everyone's advice, I pleaded guilty. It seemed the simplest, most straightforward thing to do and, by doing so, I avoided implicating Rebecca or anyone else. Guilty with an explanation, was how I thought of it. Once he understood that I could not be persuaded to change my mind, Leo made an appointment with the prosecutor to negotiate a deal. "He's asking for three months' house arrest," Leo reported afterward. "Way too much, but the press is watching this case closely to make sure the system doesn't go easier on women than on men. He says his hands are tied."

My case was scheduled for early May. The hearing took only a few minutes in the morning in a crowded courtroom on Main Street. The judge, a woman with a tired brow, and intelligent eyes, asked the prosecutor whether he really believed that three months was warranted, but gave me the agreed sentence after he assured her that defense counsel was in agreement as to the fitness of the term.

That afternoon, Sukhinder Singh, the adult probation officer who had been assigned to me, came to the house to attach an electronic monitor to my ankle. It was an oddly intimate moment. I took off my shoe and held my foot out to her, toes pointed, and she clasped the lock shut, briskly but not unkindly.

The device was small, discrete enough, larger than a bulky wrist-watch, but much smaller than the time-honored ball and chain.

Sukhinder straightened immediately after fastening the monitor, and asked me to sign what she called "a personal agreement, Maggie. A personal agreement between the two of us."

She handed me a four-page document to review. It required that I abide by the monitoring conditions that were attached and comply with a twenty-four-hour curfew except for permitted purposes (medical appointments, education, any counseling that may have been ordered) and as may from time to time be approved in writing by Sukhinder, such permission to be carried on my person at all times when not in my place of residence. I was also to agree to permit staff members of the Corrections Branch to enter my place of residence at any and all times, whether with or without notice, in order to permit them to verify that the equipment had not been tampered with, and that I remained in complete compliance with all terms herein referenced. I signed.

Sukhinder was also responsible for what are called home visits, and she telephoned me between visits, less and less often, but at unexpected hours, to ensure that I was complying fully with the conditions of my sentence. When she came to visit, I usually made a pot of tea, which we drank sitting at the painted kitchen table. By design or chance, Sukhinder's appearance mirrored her personality, or what she let me see of it. She bundled her long, graceful body into severe jackets and trousers. Her clothes were made of unyielding synthetic fabrics and were kept tightly closed at her throat and wrists and waist with buckles and belts and buttons—a jailor's wardrobe. The impression she gave, of great strength of will in spite of her slender build, was reinforced by the weight of hair she balanced on her slender neck. Her glossy hair was scraped away from her face into a tight mass at the back of her head and contained in a circle of navy netting held in place by several dozen pins. After her visits I always found escaped hairpins on the floor. Once or twice I witnessed one of the pins launch itself from the taut surface of her head and spring out into the air, a small, isolated mutiny. In a dozen visits I collected twenty-seven pins. I kept the hairpins like talismans leaning together in an eggcup on the windowsill in the kitchen, miniature soldiers on furlough. She must go through hundreds of them.

Sukhinder exuded professional pleasure in her job. During one of her early visits, she told me that electronic monitoring was invented by a judge in the United States who had been reading a Spiderman comic in which someone, perhaps Spiderman, was being tracked through an electronic bracelet he was wearing. The judge was intrigued by the concept and had a prototype designed. But what was a judge doing reading comic books in the first place, I wondered, after Sukhinder had left. A picture floated into my mind of a brightly colored comic book, printed on cheap paper, propped up and hidden behind a massive legal tome, illicitly absorbing the judge's interest while a trial went on. An unsatisfying image. More likely the book belonged to one of his children, and he had glanced into it idly, while tidying up the living room. But this was not entirely believable either. Do judges tidy? I wondered. More likely the judge, a wise and mature man, had been flipping through the book in a fit of nostalgia, interested in no more than a short, sweet, intense rush—a sentimental return to the joys of his childhood—and came across the idea in this way. However it happened, a comic book source makes sense to me; this form of punishment is flat and two-dimensional at best, and childish—the grown-up equivalent of being sent to one's room.

During the early weeks of my three locked-away summer months, I wandered the house from room to room, getting to know it, touching wood, plaster, door frames, windowpanes, tiles. I ran my hands along moldings, fixtures, stairs, and light switches, brushing them with my fingertips, the way I've seen women shop for clothes, pressing the fabric against their palm, inspecting for permanence, warmth, worth. I examined each room with the pads of my fingers, with the soles of my feet, and with the outer curved edge of an upper arm and the sharp leading wedge of a shoulder as I brushed against walls and furniture, up and down the stairs, and through doorways.

I listened to the radio—talk, music, facts diced small, teased away from their context, and served up as bulletins—and I sent and received e-mail from the computer on the desk in the office. News from the world seemed almost infinitely remote; most events struck me as ludicrous for the most part, improbable at best. So much strife and random force, such mean passions and evanescent glories.

Three newspapers were delivered, a ridiculous number, but I put off canceling any of them; I liked the dense, frank sound they threw off when I dropped them onto the kitchen table. When I first moved into the house, I had to clear away a mass of them, yellowed and curling, stacked like lumber against the front door. I read the papers in a fitful way throughout the day before tearing them into strips for the evening fire. Burning the newspapers felt like a small service to the world outside—exchanging the worst part of the day just past for a modest pile of fine, clean ashes that I carried into the backyard and dug into the garden. Surely the world benefits from even such small acts of destruction and resurrection, history stirred back into the dark earth, the worms devouring short-lived fragments.

Over the decades, smoke from burnt logs—alder and dogwood, to judge by the stumps of trees that have been taken down in the backyard—has seeped around the mesh fire screen into the living room, shading the bricks around the fireplace into a darkened nimbus, like the negative of a halo. In the evening, when I knelt to light the kindling and crumpled newspapers in the living room fireplace, the white bow of the plaster mantle hovered over me like the outspread wings of a well-meaning custodial angel.

I was able to go to the front yard as far as the gate since this is where the papers and mail are delivered, each into their own white wooden box, one labeled "Mail" and the other labeled "Journal" for some reason. The newspaper box is a simple long box, open at the front, closed in the back. The mailbox is more intricate. It has a roof covered in miniature shingles, a protective flap over the slot at the front and a hinged rear wall where the mail can be removed. Some days were so silent, I was startled by my name, Maggie Selgrin, on the envelopes—a reminder that the world continued to be aware of my existence. Occasionally mail arrives still for Mrs. Agnes Penny, who lived here for thirty years. I send these on to Mrs. Penny's son in care of his Toronto office, although I have reason to believe he throws them away unread.

The back of the property was also open to me, as far as the gate beside the blackberry canes at the bottom of the garden. The berries have just begun to turn from red to purple although they are still too sour to eat. The back gate is where I leave the garbage cans once a week. The garbage men—their job must have another name by now, not sanitary engineer, which I think was only a joke anyway, but something their children can declare comfortably in school—collect along the other side of the alley first, then turn around and do my side, one driving, the other heaving the cans. They set them down neatly, respectfully, with the lids repositioned on top, and as quietly as they can manage.

My parents visited me, and my sister Janet and her children. One or two others. Friends. Charles's two grown children, Roger and Sarah, came once or twice.

If anyone comes to see me who hasn't been before, I always offer a tour of the house, and invariably my offer is accepted.
Through the rooms we go, with me in the lead, explaining.

We start here on the front steps. Next the front porch. Then the
hall. Living room. Dining room. Kitchen. Study. Small bathroom.
Staircase. The white bedroom. The green bedroom. The yellow bedroom. Large bathroom. Staircase. Kitchen. Back porch. Backyard. End.

This house has seven rooms arranged in an immutable order
that strikes me most days as almost unbearably hopeful. Living
room, dining room, study, kitchen, and three bedrooms—one yellow, one pale green, and one white, the one I sleep in. These rooms
envelop me in a way I have not felt since I was a very small girl in
the house of my mother, father, and sisters. This house breaks my
heart and mends it over and over. Walking through these rooms has
become a conversation, an exchange of histories. My footsteps are
my side of the discussion. The response is in the creaking floors
and settling joists and slow shifts of shadow and sifting currents of
dust. It is only a house, but it has become a consistent and reward-
ing friend. Its enfolding walls, responsive floors, honest corners,
and hovering ceilings protect me. It has like me, a history, an archi-
tecture, and, I like to think, a kind of soul.

My parents came one July morning bearing bundled gifts that
they held clumsily and tenderly in the cant of their arms. They
parked in the graveled area at the back of the lot, behind the fence,
just off the alley, and came in the back way, through the kitchen door
with its paint worn thin where it has been pulled, pushed, kicked, or
nudged by unknown hands and feet on both sides over many years.
My mother's gift was a quilt, handmade for me by the members of
her Healing Touch group, squares of green and pink and yellow
stitched together and surrounded by a calico border. At first, bundled

in her arms, it looked far too large for my bed, but then my mother gave the quilt a shake and a turn, and a blue-gray kitten with narrowed, cautious eyes emerged from its folds. The kitten was small and fine-boned, with a sharply pointed chin, eyes oblique and watchful, and the softest possible downy coat the substance and color of a fleeting regret. "Something for company," my mother said.

My first reaction was affront. I had become, I realized as I felt my face stiffen, stubbornly proud of my isolation, and almost jealous of my solitude. I could feel the severity of my seclusion crack and splinter as we watched the animal nosing its way around my kitchen, and I felt then a kind of heat seep in, gladness it could have been. I saw my mother watching me closely, my expressions clear as water to her, and I provided her with a smile. "Yes," I told her. "A good idea. It will be good for me to have another creature around."

The quilt is startlingly ugly. The adjacent patches have little relationship to each other in texture, scale, or color. They were made independently and bound in an attempt at harmony in mismatched strips of calico. The Healing Touchers used pens to write expressions of support on each of the squares and in many places the ink had run and bled. I read a few of the blurred messages aloud for my mother's benefit: Strength. Peace. Truth. Justice. Healing. Happiness.

My father's package was long and angular and awkward. I unfurled several lengths of brown paper wrap to reveal a paper kite in the shape of an orange fish with a gaping yellow mouth and many overlapping golden scales. "From Chinatown," he said, and he pulled from his pocket a new spool of white string, tightly coiled into a perfect pattern of nesting Vs. "I thought it would give you a sense of freedom. You should be able to fly it from your backyard if you get a reasonable bit of wind. Screw the buggers, eh?" The strongest language I have ever heard him use.

I took the kite outside an hour after they had gone, although the wind was languid, and there did not seem to be enough space, either side to side or from the house to the end of the yard, to collect enough of a gust to catch the fish's wide, orange fins. When at last I turned with it in my arms, to take it into the house and put it away, an unexpected burst of breeze got caught like a gusty hook in the fish's great yellow mouth. Its stomach trembled and began to swell. The rows of scales flickered, rippled, and then surged like pennants in an undulating orange flutter. The fish's long, gold tail filled with air and began to swish and sway from side to side. Up, up the fish rose. It pulled free from my hands and up it sailed, swimming through the air, its mouth dipping and gulping, rising and tugging on the unfurling string. I felt like a fisher, fishing backward, playing out the line, letting my catch swim farther and farther away, allowing the distance between us to lengthen as it made its way up, out, into its own airy element, reaching up toward the troposphere.

That night I woke up and heard in the dark the sound I seem to have been waiting for since the day I moved in. A rhythmic subterranean rumble. A thumping pulse. In every direction, the walls and floors and ceiling, furniture, books, and dishes were resounding to a rumble in the air. At last, I thought, at last. After so many weeks of practice, I had become attuned to the solid thrum, thrum, thrum of the beating heart of the house. I held my breath, lay still, and listened. Gradually, I came more fully awake into consciousness of a slight weight and warmth on my feet. I held on as long as I could to my aural vision, of the house as a responsive, breathing thing, alive and, like me, at ease inside its skin.

But in another moment the illusion had lost all substance and escaped like a puff of breath into the air. I raised my right foot under my quilt, testing, and heard or felt a responsive vibration. The kitten. She rose to her feet, delicately shaking out first one paw, then the next, and so on, until all four had been attended to. She walked up the pathway of my shin, thigh, and stomach and paused on my chest, her eyes wide now in the dark. A single, cold, whiskery touch on my cheek, a contact spark of responsive electrons, and then she curled up just below my breasts, kneaded my flesh for a moment with her paw and cheek, and fell asleep. She had no weight at all, more like a bird than a cat, a scattering of down and a handful of insubstantial bones, like a sparrow, more song than substance.

At the end of July the heat of the summer settled in. The sun baked the grass around the house to a pale green-yellow; the blades became thin and brittle, scarcely able to conceal the dry dusty earth. The air at night was still and dry. All of the windows in the white bedroom were painted shut years ago, so I began sleeping in the green bedroom, which has a bank of twinned windows in a long row along the outside wall. The lower half-windows can be pushed up so the room can breathe; they are heavy, substantial, and deliberate on their ancient sashes. Hector Wong, a widower and my neighbor to the west, came over to introduce himself and I took him around on the usual tour, which interested us both equally, since his house is, except for variations in color and in the different deletions and accretions over the years—a different front door, window boxes on his house, shutters on mine, a gable over his back door—essentially identical to this one. He explained to me that my green bedroom, like the same room at the back of his house, was once an open sleeping porch, that our houses date from a time when illnesses, often fatal or permanently disabling, could strike without warning, and it was imagined that exposure to the bracing night air might strengthen the lungs and build up resistance to germs and bugs. In later years, as families grew and notions of what was healthful changed, these rooms were invariably closed off to be put to better use. Hector showed me the places where the lines and materials of the original house gave way to construction that was simpler and rougher. "In the war years," he sniffed. "No one took pride in their work."

I sat outside on the front lawn yesterday after dinner, with a book and a tumbler of beer. The night was a long, slow time coming. At about eight, a translucent moon, round and blank as a mirror, rose up in the bright sky, a scrap of chalky lace floating in a bowl of milky blue. I pulled at a desiccated dandelion and its large, brown, carrot-shaped root came up in my hand, easily twice the length of the shriveled, pale-green stem. Under the tutelage of Hector Wong from next door, I have been weeding the front flower beds, working to free the rampant wisteria and tumbling peonies and spiky rosebush from the invasive green tentacles of morning glory. The morning glory vines, with their innocent white trumpet flowers, appeared out of nowhere in early June, and spread rapidly to smother the other plants. "Bindweed," Hector calls it. "You have to pull out every last root and sucker from underneath the soil," he told me. "It is necessary to be very thorough; you can't leave even a centimeter behind."

We found a heavy, wooden-handled, rusted hoe leaning in a dark corner of the shed at the end of the backyard, and Hector showed me how the sucker roots of the bindweed run like a complicated nervous system under the soil. The suckers are rubbery, ropey, cold and disgusting to touch, but pleasurable to pull at, like pulling perforated paper apart along the serrated tear line, until, invariably, they snap and I plunge my hands into the soil to search for the broken end. I have spent hours up to my wrists in dirt, overturning ants and woodbugs and displacing worms and slugs from their snug, dark homes for the kitten to snap at.

In this last week, the number of visitors has begun to increase.

People brought the outside world with them when they came. It was caught in their clothes and hair and conversation and interests, carried in under their fingernails. Their breath was laden with it. My seclusion of the past few months was irrevocably breached; it sprang countless pin-prick leaks. Light, activity, motion, and purpose forced their way in, displacing the stale, unsatisfactory temptations of self-absorption.

Three women came on Monday morning from the church, the one I used to drop into during my morning runs in the city last fall. I was surprised to see them at my door, and concerned that I was about to become the target of a salvation mission, some well-meant effort to raise up a fallen sister. But it was not like that at all.

"We read about you in the papers," one of the women said. "And we were worried that you might lose heart."

"We have nothing to offer, really," the youngest of the three added. "Except curiosity—we have been wanting to hear your side of things—and our own stories, if you would like to hear them."

I had tea made and cooling in the yellow pitcher, and we sat in the backyard on folding chairs drinking from sweating glasses in which the ice cubes jostled and fractured. I was out of practice as a speaker, so I mostly listened. I found the fluidity of the conversation astounding. Each woman opened her mouth in turn, and words spilled out like rows of knitting, sentences within stories, perfectly strung together and leading, like a clew, to other worlds.

The eldest woman, Ruth, surprised me by revealing that she was a retired pediatric oncologist. To the extent I had considered her at all, I had thought of her as a generic church lady, old, a grandmother several times over, and useful in domestic matters such as how to prepare crustless sandwiches and other dying arts like tatting and the making of tea cozies. She spoke of how quickly they had lost children in the early days, when treatments were few and doctors often limited to alleviating such pain as they could.

The youngest woman, aptly named Merry, was a theological student in her final year and considering a posting to Peru, to a village without a well, a school, or a church. "Think of the thirst," she said, marveling, and she gave the liquid in her glass an emphatic jostle.

The third said that she was just a housewife, but Ruth and Merry protested. They held up their hands and counted off on their fingers all of the other ways she could define herself, as a mother, a volunteer, a musician, a singer in the choir. I recognized her only then as the soprano whose face had for many days floated inside my former buzzing, sleepless head. Her bakery-made chin and cheeks had disappeared. "Oh," she said, holding her hands up to frame her face. "I gained sixty pounds—imagine!—when I was pregnant with Gideon."

The kitten sprang up to my lap and tested her sharp claws against the thin fabric of my skirt. I tipped her back down onto the grass and she landed lightly, shook quickly from nose to tail, jumped sideways twice, and snapped toward a dandling cluster of barnyardgrass. "What is her name?" the middle woman, Merry, asked, and I opened my mouth, realizing as I drew breath that I had not yet thought to provide her with one. "Dogbane," I answered. The name of a weed that Hector had pointed out to me the day before leapt from my mouth with the same lightness and agility as the kitten tumbling from my knees to the ground. A successful landing. Ruth tipped back her blue and ivory and pink head, unfolded her mouth like a fan, and laughed. I smiled and felt the warmth of the day seeping from the sun-drenched grass and soil through the thin soles of my sandals and rise up into my bones.

Basement

I have begun to explore the basement, which is primitive and dark, with a cement floor, cinderblock walls, and small, high-set windows encrusted with dirt and cobwebs. There are shallow shelves and cupboards along the north wall. Inside one set of cupboards I found dozens of bottles of preserves lined up by kind and color. Two shelves of raspberry jam and three of blackberry. A long row of yellow peaches, with the curved edges of the fruit turned outward, mooning me through the thick, pale blue glass. Jars and jars of yellow relish flecked with green, pink cherries suspended in red liquid, cucumber pickles cut long or in disks, baby onions gleaming like dentures, green beans and yellow, marmalade, plums, and pears. Months of labor over hot caldrons invested then forgotten, like the earned and unspent riches left behind by someone hardworking but miserly. The food bank told me decisively on the phone that they could not accept home canning, so I spent an afternoon carrying the jars upstairs, emptying the contents, and washing the jars in the sink. They were the old-fashioned kind, with heavy glass lids secured by a hinged metal clasp. Angus came by with his truck, loaded the empty jars in the back, and took them to a Salvation Army thrift store to be resold. I kept behind a dozen jars in case I should ever have a yearning to can tomatoes or make mango chutney.

Yesterday I dragged and bumped an old table up the narrow basement stairs and into the backyard so that I could get a closer look at it and see if it was worth saving. It had several layers of paint, green over yellow over cream. Much of the paint came off readily under the prying blade of a putty knife. I worked until the early evening stripping it clean of the last remnants of paint with solvent, steel wool, and sandpaper. I uncovered a solid pine table with a drawer and pretty carved legs. The top is scarred and gouged from years of use as a workbench. It is made up of only two wide boards carefully fitted together. The legs have a pattern of long parallel lines capped at the top with a crude rosette.

The drawer was painted shut at first, but I was able to pry it free. Something had been rattling inside while I worked, and I found and fixed with two nails a bit of wood that had come loose, a wobbly runner. Inside the drawer were several handfuls of paper. Bills and letters and postcards and shopping lists, notes, and clippings. Someone's accumulation of unassociated scraps over several years, dated, mostly, in the early fifties. Three letters were from Dudley Worthy to Irene McKay, and the others, and the postcards, from friends and relatives sent to Irene and Dudley Worthy. The bills were for coal, oil, and electricity. The shopping lists listed flour, milk, soap, raisins, potatoes—nothing out of the ordinary. The newspaper clippings all gave tips for raising roses, except one, a recipe for a kind of cookie made from peanut butter, icing sugar, cornflakes, and shortening. Still, I was thrilled as much by this prosaic time capsule as by the softly scarred, yellow pine table.

Irene and Dudley. Dudley and Irene. Imagine, I thought, loving a man named Dudley. He would be tall and self-assured; anyone named Dudley would have to have developed a carriage of confidence. Irene would be rounded, softer, more lively than calm Dudley, a reader and a listener, a gardener of roses the size of dinner plates—excessive roses—and someone who could remember and repeat a good story, emphasizing its singularity with arching gestures of her freckled, thorn-pricked hands. Irene would have provided practical, solid Dudley with what he most needed without quite ever realizing it—an inner life.

Yesterday was the last day that I was required to spend here but I decided that I would not walk out the front door and down the steps and onto the sidewalk at the first possible moment. I decided instead to sleep by choice on a cool, ironed white sheet in the narrow bed in the green room, another white sheet on top of me, with all of the windows wide open.

The early evening's lacy moon fattened into a full, gold disk and its gleam bathed my face like a remedy while I slept. A pancake moon was what we called a full moon in my family when I was a child. My younger sister Lucy asked my father once, when she had first started school and was having an antagonistic time of it, "What if Saturday had a fight with Friday and refused to come?" My father told her that the moon, who observes all, would simply mix up a batch of pancakes, and the fragrance of the sizzling batter and the promise of maple syrup would entice greedy Saturday to come out from wherever she was hiding.

I am driving with Angus to Tofino for a few days, and then coming back to live here in this house and take up my old job again. The hospital where I work was persuaded that I should be permitted a leave of absence for compassionate reasons during the months of my sentence. Rebecca, who has been living temporarily in Janet's basement, will stay here in the house and take care of the kitten while I am gone. She has been looking in this neighborhood for a house of her own to buy and has found one or two that seem promising not too many streets away. Luba has moved her father into a care home down by the quay, and she and her mother have bought a two-bedroom condo nearby. Her mother can walk to see her father. Luba keeps them both under a careful, respectful eye.

The custody hearings and my trial were widely covered both here and in Italy, one of those odd human-interest stories that catches the public mind and eye for some reason. All of us—Lucy, Gian Luigi, skinny chain-smoking Ivetta, and I—attracted defenders and detractors, most of them more interested in the causes we were considered to stand for than in ourselves. Lucy, articulate, opinionated, undaunted, became a favorite of the more liberal media, and she now writes an oddly illiberal weekly column for the local newspaper. Her columns are about women, the workplace, raising children, any brewing political or social topic that catches her interest. She produces mostly chatter, as this kind of writing tends to be, but her columns can be fierce and each one has a crystalline core, a solid, well-thought-out, defensible idea or thought, and this gives them a certain weight.

Early on in the debate over who should have Philip and in what country he should be raised, I came across in one of the papers a braying op-ed by a local conservative clergyman. The Reverend Shane advocated a return to traditional values—mother in the home, father providing, children doing as they are told. Just as Jesus heads the church, a father is head of the home, he wrote. A son especially needs a father; too great a price is paid when fathers are absent. Violent criminals are overwhelmingly boys who grow up without fathers. Girls who lack a father are more apt to become promiscuous or worse. Children from a fatherless home fail or drop out, exhibit antisocial behaviors, commit suicide, display the classic indicators of abuse or neglect. In short, the presence of involved fathers is unconditionally decisive if we as a society are to raise God-and-state-fearing children. He finished by issuing a direction to fathers from one of the letters of St. Paul: "If anyone does not provide for his relatives, and especially for his immediate family, he has denied the faith and is worse than an unbeliever."

The accompanying photograph showed a handsome man in a clerical robe and collar standing in front of the broad front door of his church. He held his large head upward at an earnest angle, as if he was addressing his remarks to a rapt audience somewhere between heaven and earth. His mouth was half-open, displaying his fine, white teeth. I recognized him as the man who had explained the stained glass windows to me that time that I drifted into the church next door to the hospital, and who had hailed a cab the day I fled with Philip.

I took a short trip with Luba to the village of Tofino late last April, the final weekend before my case came up for sentencing, and I am going back there with Angus, who has spent, in the past few weeks, one or two illicit nights here with me in the house. We will throw ourselves against the wide embrace of the Pacific Ocean and invite the brisk, salty winds that sweep in from the water to scour us of staleness, inactivity, and any other lingering malaise. The climate on the west coast of Vancouver Island is infinitely changeable. During the brief half-hours when the sun comes out, it bears down hard and brilliant on the shore, and we will throw off fleece and waterproofs. But the scattered clouds soon pile up together, like sweepings under a broom. They muster and bluster, threaten and spit, then let loose a squall of icy rain, or hail the size of infants' teeth. The rain is soon pushed over the headland by the hardworking wind, which forages in the stands of trees and shrubs as it passes, calling and searching for something that it has misplaced and wants urgently.

In the woods of cedars, hemlock, fir, spruce, and alder, and the undergrowth of salal, red huckleberry, salmonberry, and blueberry, the colors are as variable as the weather, but within a narrow, infinite palate of greens and browns. The flashes of shapely yellow beside the paths look like oddly shaped lilies from a distance, but reveal themselves to be odorous skunk cabbage up close. A forest of cedars, tall as ships, as vast around as giants' pudding bowls, festooned with epiphytes, rises up only meters from a boggy marsh in which trees just as venerable—hundreds of years old—stand no taller than my mother, crabbed by the acid soil.

At the shore, sharp-edged shells are buffed by the wind and salted water until they take on a softly fluid gleam halfway between sand and water. Rough-hewn cedar logs are tossed and polished by the waves to a slippery, animal-pelt sheen. Sea lions, ponderous as pianos, move with the grace of ballerinas on the rough rocky outcroppings. Standing, watching, and listening in the midst of all these fervent doings, it becomes abundantly clear that we will become who we will, and we will be as our nature guides us no matter how hard we may strive.

During our stay in Tofino last spring, Luba and I were standersby when an accident began to unfurl in front of us. It was at the end of a day of whipsaw weather. We had after some deliberation decided that the early evening sun would go unchallenged for at least an hour and we set up Luba's small portable barbecue at the First Street Dock to cook fresh halibut purchased from a fisherman who was selling his day's catch from the side of his boat. Another family was picnicking in the same spot. One of their children, a disaffected girl of fifteen or so, went to listen to the local radio station in her parents' minivan, and she somehow dislodged the gear shift. The van began to roll down the sloping parking lot toward a steep embankment that dropped directly into the cold, deep, black water.

"Jump!" everyone shouted to her, but there was no time and, in any case, providence played its trickster hand. The van had only half completed its backward climb over the concrete barrier at the bottom of the lot when the open driver's door struck and dug itself deep into the side of another parked car. The van came to a precarious but final stop, its rear wheels overhanging the barrier by a good half-meter. Only metal and dignity were hurt.

Had we all benefited, I wondered, from the benediction Luba and I heard earlier that day on the car radio as we listened to the local station during a drive from Tofino to Ucluelet. The young man who was serving as d.j., and who was playing music as casually as if he was in his own bedroom, announced between songs that a young Cuban boy had been snatched away from his relatives in Miami so that he could be returned to his father in Cuba.

"It was really rough, man," he mused. "Guns and everything."

"Well," he concluded, after a long and brooding pause. "We send loving peace to them all."

I will be leaving at nine this morning with Angus, and now I am half-dressed, sipping from half a cup of tea and keeping half an eye out for his car. I've been up since first light and have gathered a collection of documents of various kinds, including Irene and Dudley's correspondence and newspaper clippings about the custody battle and my sentencing. They will all fit into a single cardboard banker's box, which I'll seal shut with packing tape and store on one of the empty shelves in the basement.

I found seven more jars on a dark bottom shelf when I was cleaning the basement yesterday, all of them filled with buttons. One jar had a hundred or more small, neat, trim, two- or four-holed buttons, the kind that are used on men's dress shirts. The face of each of these was a variant shade of white, but on the other side the plastic was flecked with random dots and streaks of color— tiny, round metaphors I thought for the way men so often conceal their characters beneath a conventional surface. The other jars held buttons that had been classified by color—black, red, blue, yellow, green—except for the last, which held a miscellany of buttons that could not be easily sorted. I poured these out onto my bedspread and admired them and play-acted a miser, heaping them in my cupped hands, letting them trickle through my fingers, delighting in their profusion, savouring the rich feeling of abundance and a bolt of joy that sprang from nowhere I could precisely pinpoint. I'll put this last jar of buttons in the box, as well as Sukhinder's hairpins and the plastic sandwich bag, still sealed, that holds Janet's long-ago gift of three multisided little pills. The pills are beginning to crumble and will soon be yellow dust, but the sympathy of her gesture still makes my heart contract.

I will step out of this house, which, like the final jar, is full of small, commonplace, abundant riches. The key will turn under my hand and the tumblers in the lock will jostle and shift and spill. At the moment, I do so, it will be just possible that I and most of the people I know well are happy, even my two malcontented sisters.

Lucy is at her word processor, waxing acid this week about mid-wives and doulas and the birthing practices of the self-indulgent.

Janet is in the middle of a morning game, striking the ice impatiently with the blade of her hockey stick, signifying her readiness for a pass. She has joined a hockey team that plays in a women's house league, and she has as a result, at least in my opinion, cut back on her pills. "They didn't seem to be working any more," was all she told me.

My parents are considering swapping their house for a suite at a new cohousing community over on Main Street, one that has rain barrels, a rooftop vegetable garden, solar panels, and a composting and recycling program. Lucy and Ryan just might buy my parents' house from them and are already talking of dormering the upstairs.

I am certain that Oriah alone, who I have not seen or sought, is not happy, and I wonder if she is of a different tribe, one for whom happiness is trivial, and thus despised, or who have a kind of allergy to contentment, and who feed on sorrow and discord like those bacteria that feed on tarry oil spills.

I've had several letters from Leo, who moved to Kosovo in the spring to take up a position as a legal adviser to the peacekeeping force there. He has recently been transferred to Bosnia-Herzegovina, where he lives in a trailer and has, some days, a single functioning phone line for calls and faxes. In his letters, he sounds worldly in a wide-eyed way, committed and exuberant, optimistic and disillusioned, juggling an excess of demands with purpose and joy.

Even this house seems happy to me this morning. For the few hours after I leave and before Rebecca arrives, it will have its rooms and shafts of light and creaks and imperceptible entropic forces to itself. Dust will fall in random whirls, producing its own minute music. The glass in the windows will creep downward into vitreous puddles that will not become apparent for another thousand years. The floorboards will enjoy a vacation from my tread. The house will delight in the pleasures of my absence as it found contentment in my arrival after a time of emptiness. I think of the happiness it has contained and imagine that its joys parallel my own. Delight in family members and pleasure in their departure. Serenity in times of quiet and elation in the midst of music and laughter and talk. The bliss of being admired. The thrill of going unnoticed.

Happiness is more ephemeral than thought. It can't be observed without changing its nature. Its ingredients are subtle, and there is no guarantee that a formula or recipe for joy can be written out or passed on or repeated even once again. Happiness evades capture, dissolving like a melody into the air, eluding even the most delicate, careful grasp. It frustrates any systemic search, responding better to random fossicking and oblique approaches, and its rewards are infuriatingly arbitrary, stingy or abundant by purest chance.

Life is perhaps after all simply this thing and then the next. We are all of us improvising. We find a careful balance only to discover that gravity or stasis or love or dismay or illness or some other force suddenly tows us in an unexpected direction. We wake up to find that we have changed abruptly in a way that is peculiar and inexplicable. We are constantly adjusting, making it up, feeling our way forward, figuring out how to be and where to go next. We work it out, how to be happy, but sooner or later comes a change— sometimes something small, sometimes everything at once—and we have to start over again, feeling our way back to a provisional state of contentment.

I used to float along in all of this, like a leaf on a coursing stream, but I am heavier now, less easily moved, more resolute and steadfast. I am no longer in pursuit of happiness. As I stand here at my front door, key in hand, I think it is just possible that happiness, at least for now, today, this hour, may be in pursuit of me.

COURT TO DECIDE
WHETHER ABDUCTED
CHILD SHOULD BE RAISED
IN CANADA OR ITALY

Gian Luigi Potenza has come all the way from Italy to claim custody of his newborn son, a child he has yet to meet.

The baby's mother, Lucy Selgrin, denies that she had anything to do with the child's disappearance on the day that Potenza arrived in Canada wanting nothing more than to hold his infant son for the first time. Selgrin alleges that her sister went into hiding with the child without her knowledge when it became known that Potenza was seeking custody.

The baby at the center of the dispute is tiny Philip—or Filippo, as his father prefers to call him. The Court of Appeal will be asked this week to decide who should have custody of him.

"This is a test case," says Duane Classen, spokesman for Fathers Against Custodial Treachery, a small group opposed to what it asserts is systemic bias against fathers in the justice system.

"Judges almost invariably ignore the facts and award custody of children to mothers," Classen claims. "In this case, the father, Mr. Potenza, has demonstrated that he is by far the better parent. For custody to be awarded to the mother in this situation would be yet a further blatant example of the unfairness of our courts and our laws. Our members are planning to be in court to support Mr. Potenza in his quest for justice. We want the court to know that fathers matter too."

Potenza and his wife Ivetta ease their anxiety with espresso and cigarettes as they wait in their Vancouver hotel room, and hope against hope that they will be permitted to take Filippo home to Rome. He would be their only child and an answer to years of prayer. For Ivetta Potenza, Filippo would be the baby she never expected to have.

Although Filippo is less than three weeks old, he has already slipped through the Potenzas' fingers twice.

The first time was when Selgrin left Italy without telling the Potenzas that she was pregnant. Filippo is the product of a brief relationship between Selgrin and Mr. Potenza, an indiscretion for which Ivetta Potenza says she has forgiven her husband. "Italian men!" she says, raising her hands in a charming shrug, and gazing fondly at her husband of twenty years.

The second time was when Selgrin's sister, Maggie Selgrin, left the province with the baby in breach of two court orders granting custody of Filippo to the Potenzas. Maggie Selgrin now faces criminal charges in connection with what Classen calls "kidnapping, no more and no less."

Potenza agrees. "I contacted the authorities here and in Italy only to be told I must find my son myself and bring my claim to the Canadian courts," he says. "I am a simple man. My wife and I must place our faith in your courts."

Faith that Classen asserts is misplaced. "The courts start from the premise that children belong with their mother. Fathers are routinely labeled as aggressive, violent, sex offenders, or worse. I am just one example, but there are thousands more like me. Just because I lost my temper once or twice with my ex-wife over her overly permissive parenting style, I have a restraining order against me and I can't see my own children. The fact is that there is no justice for fathers."

"Every day, my emotions run the gamut, from heartbreak to rage to sorrow, and back to rage. It never stops," Classen says from the kitchen table in his trailer home just outside of Abbotsford.

"But they'll never break me. Everything I've gone through has just made me more determined. I'll get my kids back if it is the last thing I do.

"And I am committed to helping other fathers so that they don't wind up like I did, with an empty home and an empty heart."

Word has spread both locally and in Italy about the Potenzas' fight to regain their stolen son, a battle that has received extensive coverage in the Italian media and is beginning to gain notice here.

"Will justice be done?" Classen asks. "Don't hold your breath."

COURT OF APPEAL
for
BRITISH COLUMBIA

BETWEEN:

Gian Luigi Massimo Potenza
Petitioner
(Respondent)

AND:

Lucinda Joanie Selgrin
Respondent
(Appellant)

BEFORE: *The Honourable Mr. Justice Judson*
The Honourable Mr. Justice Oriel
The Honourable Madam Justice Yu

Reasons for Judgment of Madam Justice Yu:

[I] This appeal is brought on an urgent basis by the mother of the child, Philip Magnus Selgrin, from the order of Findlaysen J. granting custody of the child to his father, Gian Luigi Potenza, the Respondent before this Court. The urgency is compounded by the season, by the facts that the child is only a few days old and has been taken into care temporarily, and by the stated desire of the father to remove the child permanently from this jurisdiction.

[2] The case is somewhat complicated by the fact that the child was removed from this province, his place of first residence, by his maternal aunt when the child was a few days old. Counsel for the father argues that this transfer of residence leaves the child's place of ordinary residence for purposes of application of the Hague Convention on the Civil Aspects of International Child Abduction open to dispute.

[3] The Hague Convention on the Civil Aspects of International Child Abduction is designed to ensure that abducted children are returned to their country of habitual residence. It presumes that custody and visitation disputes are properly resolved in the jurisdiction where the child habitually resides. The Convention applies in cases where both the country of the child's habitual residence and the country where the child has been taken are signatories to the Convention, the child is younger than 16 years of age, and the child has been wrongfully removed or retained in breach of rights of custody under the law of the state where the child is habitually resident.

[4] It was forcefully and, in my view, creatively argued on behalf of the father before us that, although the child has now been returned to this jurisdiction, because he resided in this province for only four days before the removal of the child to the province of Quebec, there should be no presumption in favour of this jurisdiction as the child's state of habitual residence.

[5] It was further argued that the child will suffer grave

risk of psychological harm if he remains in this jurisdiction and is deprived of exposure to his Italian family and culture, which counsel for Mr. Potenza characterizes as his "birthright."

[6] Philip was conceived in Italy last year during what the father describes as a brief extramarital affair. The mother relocated to her family home during the summer, and Philip was born here on December 12th of last year. He and his mother resided in this city for only four days, during which time his father obtained a custody order from the Italian courts, apparently without notice to the mother. When the father arrived here and sought to enforce the Italian custody order, the child's maternal aunt, Maggie Selgrin, is alleged to have absconded with him to Quebec, apparently in an attempt to avoid removal of the child to Italy.

[7] I am in agreement with the appellant that, notwithstanding the removal of Philip as a very young infant from this jurisdiction to Quebec, his state of habitual residence was and remains Canada. Accordingly it is my view that the burden is on the Respondent to establish that there is a grave risk that leaving the child in this jurisdiction would expose the child to physical or psychological harm or otherwise place the child in an intolerable situation.

[8] The matter came before us on an amended Notice of Appeal and fresh evidence was adduced with leave given by Mr. Justice Shaw. The fresh evidence goes to the issue of illegal acts alleged to have been committed by the father and his spouse. The mother has provided an affidavit concerning statements made to her by the father, Mr. Potenza, which she in her affidavit characterizes as "boasts," concerning the

manner in which Mr. Potenza obtained information about the child's whereabouts and concerning subsequent attempts by Mr. Potenza and his wife to take the child from his aunt and remove him from Canada.

[9] I conclude that the Hague Convention has no application to Philip. I find that he has been and remains a habitual resident of Canada for the few short days of his life and that there has been no wrongful removal of the child from Canada. I further find that the father has not discharged the burden of showing that there is a grave risk that leaving the child in this jurisdiction would expose the child to physical or psychological harm or otherwise place the child in an intolerable situation. The cultural loss referred to in the affidavits by psychologists, sociologists, and others concerning deprivation to the child if not exposed to his Italian heritage speak to arguments about the child's best interests, which is for the court to determine, and ignore the fact that Philip is half Italian and half Canadian. He is entitled to exposure to the cultures of both his parents.

[10] In making these findings, I do not condone the child's aunt's actions of removing the child from this province without notice to the child's father. I understand that this matter will be dealt with in separate proceedings.

[11] Having considered all of the evidence, it is my view that the best interests of the child will be served if the custody order made in the court below is overturned and custody of the child is granted to the appellant, Ms. Selgrin. I am of the opinion that this situation requires appellate intervention.

[12] The trial judge concentrated on the backgrounds,

characters, personalities, family environments, and economic means of Mr. Potenza and did not give sufficient recognition to Ms. Selgrin's upbringing, family support, education, marriage plans, and parenting skills. He seems to have accepted with little reservation that Mr. Potenza would be a better parent, notwithstanding that Mrs. Potenza, and not Mr. Potenza, would in fact be the primary caregiver. We have had the benefit of a report that describes Mrs. Potenza as somewhat narcissistic and lacking in emotional maturity.

[13] The trial judge also discounted the Selgrin family's strong family ties, in preference for the Potenzas' family situation. While a grant of custody to Mr. Potenza will permit Philip to join what appears to be a warm and extensive family in Italy, by the same token if custody were awarded to Mr. Potenza, the child would be deprived of a full relationship with his relatives on his mother's side: his uncles and aunts, cousins and four grandparents.

DISPOSITION

[14] For the foregoing reasons, notwithstanding the respect due to the experienced trial judge in this case, I am of the opinion that he erred in his determination that Philip's best interests required that Mr. Potenza be his custodial parent. I would allow the appeal and award custody of Philip to Ms. Selgrin.

[15] While I do not think it is appropriate to finally establish the specific conditions of access at this time, I do grant Mr. Potenza generous access on the general terms set out below. If counsel are unable to agree on the transition or

access arrangements, they should apply to the Courts for further direction.

[16] While the child is under the age of eight, he is to reside with his mother in Canada. The father will have supervised access to the child as often as he might reasonably wish to exercise it. He may exercise his rights in Canada or, if the mother agrees and at the father's cost, the mother and child may travel to Italy so that the child can spend time with his father. After the child reaches the age of eight, or earlier if the mother consents, the father shall have unsupervised access to the child in Italy for one month of every summer and two weeks during the school year.

[17] I think it appropriate that the parties each bear their own costs.

I AGREE: "THE HONOURABLE MR. JUSTICE JUDSON"
I AGREE: "THE HONOURABLE MR. JUSTICE ORIEL"

GLADSTONE, LUI & DAWES
Barristers & Solicitors

January 20, 2000

Dear Ms. Selgrin:

Re: Estate of Charles Edward Addenbrook

May we extend our deepest sympathies on the recent death of Charles Addenbrook.

I write to advise you that Mr. Addenbrook had recently revised his will to name you as one of his beneficiaries.

I would be grateful if you would kindly contact me at your earliest convenience so that we may discuss Mr. Addenbrook's bequest.

Yours sincerely,

Christine Dawes
cd/er

Lucy Selgrin

and

Ryan King

Invite you to share their happiness

as they exchange

vows of marriage

and begin their

new life together

Saturday, September 16, 2000

at 3:30 p.m.

At the home of Jack and Jean Selgrin

3990 West 16th Avenue

Reception to follow

p.s.

Ideas,
interviews
& features ...

About the author

About the book

Read on

A Talent for Double Happiness

Louise Tucker talks to Anne Giardini

'We would make different choices from those
our parents made, and have lives different from
theirs in ways we were certain of but could not
predict.' How does your life differ from your
parents'?

Until I was ten years old and in grade five, I
imagined that I would do exactly as my
mother had done: have five children and
do bits and pieces of work from home. I
was ten at the end of the 1960s, a period of
great change and disruption, a time when
commonly accepted ideas were turned inside
out and held up to critical scrutiny. Some
of this percolated through even to children,
and one day at school I had one of those
moments of realization and clarity that I
wish came more often: that I might well
have to fend for myself and that I should
have a career. I think, from then on, I never
questioned but that I would live differently
from my parents. And in fact, I did marry
later, have fewer children, and have things my
mother didn't have, at least when my sisters
and brother and I were children: an office, a
boss, a briefcase, a pay cheque, a secretary.
Looking forward at ten years of age, all of this
seemed marvellous and exotic and
adventurous.

*Your mother was also a writer, and, like you,
started long after her youth. How did she
influence your decision to write, if at all?*
I always absolutely knew I would write. And I
always knew I would write a novel. As a child,

I liked to tell long, complicated stories to my three sisters – the most attentive and astute of audiences. Whenever my Manchester-born sister Catherine thought that a narrative needed more drama, she would urge me to 'put a fire into it', and I would conjure up a dramatic blaze that threatened but never consumed the heroes and heroines of the story. I have included a fire in *The Sad Truth About Happiness* for Catherine's benefit.

For several years, I wrote a weekly column for one of Canada's national newspapers, the *National Post*, and this was the best possible experience. Having to write from scratch on a regular basis forced me to pay attention and react quickly and authentically to life, and to people and events. My mother's advice – and I have seen other good writers do this – was to always produce my best work. Nothing should be held back or saved for later. Writing is like drawing from the most abundant aquifer – something new and interesting always wells up to replace what has been taken. When I stopped writing the weekly columns, I realized that just enough time might have been opened up for me to undertake something more sustained.

My family had also been ambushed by my mother's diagnosis with an aggressive form of breast cancer and this led me to think in a new way about happiness and its central difficulty, which is that it can't be sought directly and can't be grasped securely. The novel contains much of my thinking about ▶

❛I always absolutely knew I would write. And I always knew I would write a novel. As a child, I liked to tell long, complicated stories to my three sisters – the most attentive and astute of audiences.❜

3

Author photo © Bracken-Horrocks Photography

LIFE
at a Glance

Born in Toronto in 1959, Anne has lived in several Canadian cities and in England, France and Italy. She now lives in Vancouver with her husband and three children where she writes and practises law and the violin.

A Talent *(continued)*

◄ happiness over the two and a half years I spent writing it, as well as other issues and ideas that interest me.

What was the inspiration for The Sad Truth About Happiness *and how did you start writing it?*
I had as one of my starting points an encounter with a single friend in her late thirties. We were seated together at a dinner party. We had drunk a bit too much and had begun to have a quite amusing talk that led to the topic of pain – she had just run a marathon. She asked me about childbirth and I told her that, for much of labour, the pains come and go, so there is respite. To emphasize the point, I squeezed her knee quite hard, and then relaxed the pressure. I was surprised to see tears come into her eyes and I said, 'I can't have hurt you, can I?'

'No,' she said. 'It's just that no one ever touches me any more.'

I felt that this was the most intimate insight into what life can be like when you are yearning for love. I realized as I began to write that, as the author, I could provide Maggie with someone to love. In fact, perhaps because I was so fond of her myself, I found that more than one of the men I introduced her to became quite taken with her too.

Maggie says that she wants 'to do something manifestly practical'. Do her choices echo your own, to be a lawyer first, then a writer?
I see myself as very much the blended product of my gentle, creative mother and

my resolute, engineer father. Once I had realized I would have a career, I thought I might be an actress, but eventually I learned I had absolutely no talent. When I went to university, I very consciously took a broad spectrum of courses but, in the end, law had what it seemed I needed – rigour, challenges, the creative use of language, and many stories. I have a fairly rare combination of careers, but I am not surprised at all that so many lawyers I meet write or want to write fiction. The law is all about stories. It contains thousands – millions – of individual narratives and it creates from all of these narrative threads a good part of the cloth, the stuff, that we call society. On the other hand, I am beginning to believe that novels are a form of advice, so my two careers may be more closely linked than might be obvious at first glance.

The book lovingly describes Vancouver in all its colours and seasons. Why is it so special and could you ever imagine living (or have you ever lived) anywhere else?
I have lived and been happy in many other places, including England, France, Italy, and other cities and towns in Canada. Vancouver was wonderful to write about, however, because it is still a young city, and not terribly well known, and because it has so many interesting neighbourhoods and moods. My next novel is set in Ontario, in an Italian-Canadian working-class suburb, and I am having fun capturing a very different community. I think the place where I have been happiest is Rome, and I would love at ▶

FAVOURITE AUTHORS

Carol Shields

Alice Munro

Jane Austen

Virginia Woolf

V.S. Naipaul

John Updike

Nicholson Baker

Vladimir Nabokov

Muriel Spark

Barbara Pym

Colson Whitehead

A Talent *(continued)*

◄ some time to live there again. Maggie's sister Lucy lives in Rome before she returns to Vancouver and I have given to her some of my love for that city.

'Something to love, something to do, something to hope for . . . these are the essentials of happiness.' What is, if anything, the essential 'sad truth' about happiness for you?
Of course the sad truth about happiness is that it is entrancing, desirable and maddeningly elusive. The moment you say the words 'I am happy' some of it leaks out. You can't aim directly for happiness, or, once you attain it, hold on to it for long. Happiness is replete with paradox; hard work can make you more genuinely happy than rest, and difficulties can provide fertile ground for the seeds of future joy.

Do you believe that happiness is the key to longevity?
A happy life feels longer because it is richer. Happiness is a prism in which a moment's joy reflects and shines and expands into infinity. I understand that scientists have discerned many more dimensions than the four we are familiar with and perhaps happiness will be discovered to be yet another dimension, with its own laws of time-bending relativity.

The chapter headings all refer to parts of a house and, for Maggie, a house must have a heart to be a home. What or who makes you feel at home?
I have used the central metaphor of home in

❛ My mother's advice – and I have seen other good writers do this – was to always produce my best work. Nothing should be held back or saved for later. ❜

6

the book because it is the location of our deepest joys and conflicts. I wanted to have Maggie, my protagonist, describing the events of the months just past in the way that someone in a new home takes a visitor on a tour through it. This impulse to give guided tours fades, so I have come to believe that showing someone through one's home is really a means of getting to know it for oneself by seeing it through different eyes and from different angles, and that this must lead to a deeper knowledge and understanding of where one is – in all senses. Our homes enfold us; they are a refuge, a place for the kinds of routines and nourishment that steady and ready us for creative work. I don't think a home needs to be complex to serve. In university, I lived in a succession of well-designed rooms that held all that I needed: a bed, a chair, a shelf for books, a place for my cup and spoon, ideally room for a visitor. I have a larger space to live in now, but I share it with a husband, two teenage sons, my daughter, and their nanny. Sometimes I catch myself longing for a simple room with chair and board. Maybe this return to simplicity is what people strive for when they seek out a cottage retreat.

Having lost your mother to cancer, was anyone that you met during her treatment the particular inspiration for Maggie?
What a wonderful question. This is not something I have ever actually considered, but I think you are right. My mother's cancer brought me into contact with many people whose focused intelligence and ▶

❝ As a lawyer, I have a fairly rare combination of careers, but I am not surprised at all that so many lawyers I meet write or want to write fiction. The law is all about stories. ❞

A Talent *(continued)*

◄ understanding and warmth reaffirmed my belief in the essential goodness of people. I think of Maggie as someone who makes mistakes, and who is cautious by nature, but who, like her eccentric parents, is driven by an instinct for goodness.

Was it difficult or therapeutic to write about an illness that has affected you so closely?
My mother's lengthy illness and death were devastating to me, as they were to many others of her family and friends. Even today, two years after her death, I am still struggling to understand her loss. It doesn't seem quite possible. I miss her constantly.

But I also found this process through pain and loss to be fascinating. I was deeply interested in how my appetite dulled or quickened in sympathy with my mother's; in how sorrow differs so profoundly from depression (although it can lead you there and sometimes leave you stranded); in the etiology of cancer and in its spread and in its treatments; in the physicians and caregivers and hospice workers and in other patients and their families; in the intense bursts of laughter and wild jolts of joy in a chemo treatment wing, beside a hospital bed, at a memorial gathering. I felt and still feel strongly that none of us is immune from life's most profound sorrows, but we can go through them unthinkingly, or we can proceed fully conscious that all of life is brimming over with many different experiences and we can experience them narrowly or fully at our will.

I was determined to find interest and

❛ Of course the sad truth about happiness is that it is entrancing, desirable and maddeningly elusive. You can't aim directly for happiness, or, once you attain it, hold on to it for long. ❜

passion and joy in my mother's illness and death in part because she was determined to find them too. In her last few days she was reading and thinking about apples and bee keeping, and sonnets – she compared them to cutlery drawers, the words lined up in rows – and Iceland and the Swedish neighbourhood of the Chicago of her childhood. And she was sick! How could I do less? Writing provided me with the opportunity and the privilege of working through some of this and was in the end, for me, the best kind of therapy for sorrow.

How did writing this book change you, if at all? Most obviously, writing this book made me a novelist. I see the world now through a novelist's eyes. Everything is material; everything is weighed for its narrative possibilities. I think of novels as enormously capacious and I am always looking for interesting ideas to appropriate. ■

A Writing Life

When do you write?
Whenever a moment presents itself.

Where do you write?
Anywhere I happen to be when opportunity
and ideas coincide.

Why do you write?
To tame the words and thoughts that swarm
inside my head.

Pen or computer?
I prefer a computer but do use a pen or pencil
from time to time.

Silence or music?
Usually a fair amount of background
household noise, to which I am oblivious.

How do you start a book?
The shape, tone and central idea come to me
pretty quickly, then it is a matter of setting
down the first sentence, and the one after
that, and the one after that . . .

And finish?
When I feel I am only gilding and that the
pith and substance of the story have been laid
out.

**Do you have any writing rituals or
superstitions?**
None.

Which living writer do you most admire?
Alice Munro.

What or who inspires you?
All of life in its noisy tumble. People, words,
the music of sentences and phrases, the allure
of ideas and the need to wrestle with
questions and problems.

**If you weren't a writer what job would you
do?**
What I do now; I am a mother, wife, sister,
daughter, friend and, secondarily, a lawyer.

**What's your guilty reading pleasure or
favourite trashy read?**
Home decorating magazines. But don't tell
anyone. ■

The Truth About Happiness

by Anne Giardini

HAPPINESS HAS MANY aspects and comes in more guises than we may readily recognize. Contentment is a purring, low-maintenance kind of happiness; it is happiness without the energy to aspire to joy. Glee is hopped-up happiness, happiness on a tear. Nostalgia is the craft of discerning happiness in the past, just as hope is all wrapped up in happinesses that are anticipated in the future. A commonly cited short cut to happiness is to strive only for the powerful experience of present happiness. Thus we are counselled to live in the moment, to take the time to stop to smell the roses, or – advice I heard once on the radio – 'When you stir the pot, you should *stir* the pot.' I understand the intent behind this kind of instruction: even in the wake of great sorrow, the world is saturated with cause for joy, if we can only open ourselves fully.

Oddly, one of literature's experts on happiness experienced long periods of deep unhappiness and killed herself in the end by filling her pockets with stones and striding into the River Ouse. Virginia Woolf wrote often of the intense pleasure she and her characters took in all of life's experiences. In a short story titled *Happiness*, she describes a man whose talent for contentment is envied:

> *In happiness there is always this terrific exaltation. It is not high spirits; nor rapture; nor praise, fame or health (he could not walk two miles without feeling*

done up) it is a mystic state, a trance, an ecstasy which, for all that he was atheistical, sceptical, unbaptised and all the rest of it, had he suspected some affinity with the ecstasy that turned men priests, sent women in the prime of life trudging the streets with starched cyclamen-like frills about their faces, and set lips and stony eyes; but with this difference; them it imprisoned; him it set free. It freed him from all dependence upon anyone upon anything.

Even his happiness is precarious, however, and must be guarded:

Why, some branch might fall; the colour might change; green turn blue; or a leaf shake; and that would be enough; yes; that would be enough to shiver, shatter, utterly destroy this amazing thing this miracle, this treasure which was his had been his was his must always be his . . .

The happiness of Woolf's character Mrs Dalloway is more straightforward, although just as precarious. 'What she liked was simply life.' The novel *Mrs Dalloway* captures the central irony of happiness; it is as much about death as about life, as much about regret as about joy.

Someone who has considered happiness deeply is Dr Tom Stevens, at, appropriately enough, California State University, Long ▶

❛ Happiness has many aspects and comes in more guises than we may readily recognize. ❜

The Truth *(continued)*

◄ Beach. His website (http://front.csulb.edu/success/) includes links to happiness articles and resources, as well as quizzes (not unlike the one Maggie takes) to test one's level of happiness and potential for joy. I completed an online questionnaire at a different site and learned that my five 'signature strengths' out of the twenty-four tested in the survey include love of learning, zest, gratitude, creativity and curiosity – all of which I hope to put to use in writing my second novel, *Nicolo Piccolo*, which is, as it happens, much like Stevens's website, about the getting and giving of advice.

While it doesn't yet seem to have been created, I would be interested in a site called www.indirecthappiness.com since I believe that happiness is a by-product of other goals and activities. Deeply happy people are noticers and thinkers. They are attentive. They are aware of and appreciate beauty and goodness and complexity. They find a way to do meaningful work or they have the knack of investing the work they do with meaning. They stay connected to the people they enjoy, creating and strengthening bonds that become themselves the source of joy. Happy people believe that the future will be good, and these expectations become self-fulfilling. For a happy man or woman, a setback is temporary, and even terrible events are instructive and can be put to use in the development of wisdom or humility or character or ways to avert similar events in the future.

Life is the crucible for sorrow and for happiness. We are all in the process of

❝ Deeply happy people are noticers and thinkers. They are attentive. They are aware of and appreciate beauty and goodness and complexity. ❞

learning, throughout our lives, how to create, notice, build, act and lead. We can believe, as happy people do, that the future holds good things, and these expectations will become self-fulfilling, not on their own, but through conscious application of all that we are to the world as a whole and, more manageably on the day-to-day level, in our workplaces and homes.

The best kind of happiness is the happiness one creates for oneself, quite incidentally, out of the everyday materials and commonplace beauty of the world immediately at hand. ∎

If You Loved This,
You Might Like ...

Unless
Carol Shields

Reta Winters is a writer and translator, married with three children and living in Toronto. Her life seems uncomplicated and without drama. But then her teenage daughter leaves her college place and room to sit on the street begging and sleep in a homeless hostel. She refuses to talk to her mother, and Reta's life is thrown into turmoil, her certain surefootedness undone.

Accidents in the Home
Tessa Hadley

Clare is a married mother of three, the glamour in her life dependent on what she finds to wear in the charity shop; her best friend Helly is a successful actress, her looks plastered over billboards. When Clare discovers that Helly is going out with a man she had sex with as a teenager, the odd coincidence starts to affect and unravel her life.

First Aid
Janet Davey

After Jo's husband leaves her, she must raise her three children alone. Living in a seaside town, surviving on the income from working in a junk shop, she hopes that a new love will lead to a new beginning. But when her lover hits her, she packs up the children and catches a train to London to be with the grandparents who raised her. However, shortly after they set off, her daughter jumps off the train and runs away. Taking place over one summer weekend, *First Aid* tackles the tangles of family life and the ever-present desire to start again.

August and *I'll Go to Bed at Noon*
Gerard Woodward

Two books charting the rise and demise of one family, the Joneses. *August* tells the family's story from 1955 to 1970, relating how their relationships with each other and with the place of presumed happiness, a campsite in Wales where they spend their annual holiday, change over the years. *I'll Go to Bed at Noon* continues their story, in the 1970s, as several members of the family succumb to alcoholism and the destruction it engenders.

Bel Canto
Ann Patchett

In a South American country, the guests at a vice-presidential mansion are taken hostage by a group of terrorists aiming to capture the president who, luckily for him but not them, has stayed home to watch his favourite soap opera. One of the hostages is a world-renowned soprano and her voice makes their ordeal palatable. As days stretch into months, and the inevitable denouement approaches, relationships develop between hostages and terrorists which will change their lives for ever. Winner of the Orange Prize for Fiction 2002.

Cat's Eye
Margaret Atwood

Elaine's return to Toronto brings back ▶

FIND OUT MORE

Vancouver
www.tourismvancouver.com
www.discovervancouver.com
www.vancouver-bc.com
Part of the landscape of *The Sad Truth About Happiness* is the city of Vancouver and these websites will help you discover it in all its glory.

Happiness
www.authentichappiness.com
A website dedicated to the work of Dr Martin Seligman, a psychologist whose work focuses on positive psychology. Try out some of his (18!) questionnaires to determine whether you are happy and what would make you so.

Breast Cancer
www.breastcancercare.org.uk
The UK's largest provider of information and resources on breast cancer. Also includes links to the Lavender Trust, specifically set up to help younger women affected by the disease.

If You Loved This . . . *(continued)*

◄ horrible memories of her childhood and of the girls who made it a misery. Cruel and aggressive, ringleader Cordelia destroys Elaine's self-esteem and haunts her for the rest of her life. Now an adult, Elaine must come to terms with her past. ■